Stella

Stella

HELEN EVE

St. Martin's Griffin ❧ New York

YA FIC Eve

STELLA. Copyright © 2014 by Helen Etty. All rights reserved. Printed in the United States of America. For information, address St. Martin's Press, 175 Fifth Avenue, New York, N.Y. 10010.

www.stmartins.com

Library of Congress Cataloging-in-Publication Data

Eve, Helen.
  Stella: a novel / Helen Eve.—First U.S. edition.
    p. cm.
  ISBN 978-1-250-04817-2 (hardcover)
  ISBN 978-1-4668-4109-3 (e-book)
1. Popularity—Fiction. 2. Boarding schools—Fiction. 3. Schools—Fiction.
4. Cliques (Sociology)—Fiction. 5. Americans—England—Fiction. 6.
England—Fiction. I. Title.
  PZ7.E9005Ste 2014
  [Fic]—dc23

2013046168

St. Martin's Griffin books may be purchased for educational, business, or promotional use. For information on bulk purchases, please contact Macmillan Corporate and Premium Sales Department at 1-800-221-7945, extension 5442, or write specialmarkets@macmillan.com.

First published in Great Britain by Macmillan Children's Books, a division of Macmillan Publishers Limited

First U.S. Edition: April 2014

10 9 8 7 6 5 4 3 2 1

To my parents

'Behind the furthest end of the brewery, was a rank garden with an old wall; not so high but that I could . . . see . . . that Estella was walking away from me even then. But she seemed to be everywhere . . . She had her back towards me, and held her pretty brown hair spread out in her two hands, and never looked round, and passed out of my view directly . . . I saw her pass among the extinguished fires, and ascend some light iron stairs, and go out by a gallery high overhead, as if she were going out into the sky.'

Charles Dickens, *Great Expectations*

Prologue

Everyone wants to hear a story about an underdog, don't they? A kid with a stammer getting a recording contract; an ex-con winning the lottery. The public's sympathy might always lie with the underdog rather than the deserving winner, but, even so, I won't try to deceive you. I'm not an underdog. Far from it.

Our English teacher, who preferred dreary Jane Eyre to the more interesting Holden Caulfield, told us that the best narrators are trustworthy and easy to empathize with. Luckily for you, reader, he and I never saw eye to eye on that concept. As a narrator, Jane Eyre I'm not. In fact, rather than trying to win you over, I'm immediately going to alienate you, and here's why.

I have everything. If this were fiction, I couldn't be the heroine, because with no obstacles for me to overcome there would be no plot. I'd be underused as a secondary character; the cheerleader who briefly makes life miserable for the rightful heroine. I wouldn't even get to die at the end. I'd instead become comically overweight, be (deservedly) cheated on by my footballer boyfriend or fail my exams. But my life, needless to say, isn't fiction.

The first thing you should know is that I'm seventeen. See, you're already alienated. You think I've got the best years of my life ahead of me; that none of my problems could possibly be worth reading about. You know what? You're probably right.

I'm blonde, of course. Blondes evoke less sympathy and have shorter shelf lives than brunettes. If you don't believe me, think about it. It was Jo March we cared about, not vain little Amy; Elizabeth Bennet, not sensible Jane; Laura Ingalls, not pious Mary. I have long hair, which I can straighten or leave to dry curly, and my eyes are blue and abnormally large. They are widely considered to be my best feature; in fact they leave such an impression that I have to go light on the mascara, and eyeliner wouldn't make me popular with other girls *at all*. I'm extremely petite – and I don't expect to grow any more – and effortlessly thin. My teeth are straight, without the train-track hell from which some kids my age have yet to emerge. I have a great dress sense, and everything suits me; so much so that shopping doesn't interest me. Well, not very much.

Have I lost you to a fit of envy? I imagine not. Looks are one thing, and brains are another entirely. People are usually forgiving of one or the other. But, aside from my physical attributes, you should know that I'm clever. Exceptionally so. This isn't ghostwritten, let's make that clear.

I'm also popular, partly because I'm good at sport. This is important: I'm not sure why, but I'm glad I struck lucky because PE is actually a form of organized bullying. At my school everyone has to take part in Sports Day every summer, even if they're fat, or unpopular, or uncoordinated. There isn't a corresponding event in Physics where you get booed if you can't do kinematic equations, but that's only

2

one reason why being a geek doesn't pay.

I attend boarding school, and home life seems some distance away from my existence at Temperley High. School is an ecosystem all of its own, where outside rules just aren't relevant. As a Sixth Former I have my own room, which is a relief as my girlfriends – there are six of us, and we're called the Stars, for obvious reasons – often bore me rigid. The dormitories the younger students share are supposed to help homesick people settle in: some kids cry about being away from home, which is a strange reaction. It may not be Malory Towers, but it's not a workhouse either. You can get away with murder if you know how to play it, and I do.

You won't be surprised to hear that boys love me, and as my school is mixed there are plenty of them around. Boys have noticed me for a while now, and continue to do so whether I invite their attention or not. And don't start thinking I could have any boy except the one I *really want* or anything lame like that, because there are no exceptions.

You've met someone like me before. If you're at school, I'm making your life hell. If you have a job, I've got the promotion you deserved. If you have a boyfriend, he's wishing you looked like me. You may hate me, but surely you know by now that life isn't fair. I can't help being perfect any more than you can help being, well, flawed.

Can you trust me? Maybe not. And can you empathize with me? I doubt it. But, even so, have I lost you to a story about an underprivileged child who becomes a concert pianist? Of course not. People love stories about the

3

underdog, and, despite everything I've said, you still think that's what I am. Poor little rich girl, you think, as if I'm hiding deep-rooted insecurities or the scars of a difficult childhood. Perhaps I'm about to tell a story of growth and redemption in which I lose my good looks and channel my inner beauty to become a better person. Every story needs a character arc, after all. Is mine going to be painful? That'll show me, you think.

Don't count on it.

Chapter One

Caitlin Clarke

By the time it was clear to me that, in high school at least, popularity and notoriety were one and the same, I was powerless to reverse the effects of either.

The cards and gifts by my bedside, the anxious visitors and my buzzing cell phone made it clear that I wouldn't be returning to anonymity any time soon. It was too late by then anyhow: on the night I should have beaten Stella Hamilton to become Head Girl of Temperley High, I was having jagged glass splinters removed from my face (they tell me I was under for that bit but I *swear* I felt it) and learning, as the blessed anaesthetic wore off, that not all my classmates had been as lucky as I had.

Lucky was such an overused word that I felt like screaming whenever I heard it. I was lucky to be alive. I was lucky to have fallen onto smoking rubble rather than the concrete paving seventy feet below. I was lucky I only had three broken bones. I was lucky I wouldn't be permanently scarred.

I wasn't ungrateful; of course I understood what I'd escaped. But sometimes, as I lay in that creaky, uncomfortable bed, having my blood taken three times a day and waiting for my leg to knit itself back together, being left behind didn't seem so lucky after all.

Not that I knew any of this when I started Temperley High halfway through Junior Year (or Lower Sixth, as they would call it). Back then I had no idea girls like Stella Hamilton even existed. Campion Hall, my prep school in Manhattan, was pretty normal – a school where we didn't wear a full face of make-up every day of the week; where we didn't select our classes based on the number of boys in the group; where we didn't choose the shortest skirt we could find for Gym (from Baby Gap, if necessary) and wear it doggedly throughout the year, even in the snow. And although my memories of Campion might be slightly idealized in the wake of events that followed, I'm sure we didn't backstab each other in the variety of ways I witnessed, and sometimes participated in, at Temperley High. We couldn't have, because Campion students tended to survive beyond graduation.

'Your mother and I have some news,' announced my dad one November evening. 'We're moving to England.'

'Who is?' I asked, looking around the dinner table. 'All of us?'

I already knew that he and my mom were having problems (the fights, which I usually tried to ignore, had reached fever pitch in recent months), but I wanted to hear him say it.

He looked wary. 'No. Your mother and Charlie will be staying here.'

'Are you getting a divorce?' I blurted out.

My little brother Charlie looked at me, startled, and I could have kicked myself, even though it wasn't my fault. I hadn't raised the subject in front of him, or caused the marriage to fail.

Dad nodded as he explained, in words that I understood but Charlie couldn't, that divorce was imminent, but they still loved *us* and respected *each other* a great deal. Mom was looking daggers at him and I wasn't convinced by the mutual respect part.

We were eating chicken – a soggy take-out that Mom always picked up on the housekeeper's night off – and I chewed a piece of meat until it was elastic, because the motion prevented me from crying. I gave Charlie a supportive smile that wobbled, patting his cheek before turning my attention back to my parents.

'Why do *I* have to move?' Dad was a litigator and was losing me in the finer points of their proposed separation. Not that I didn't care, but it made sense that I was most interested in my own fate. 'Why can't I stay here?'

He sighed. 'You're the reason I've decided to make this move, Caity. I'm not entirely happy with the education you're getting—'

'Why not?' I said, knowing I sounded defensive. 'I get straight As! I'm the class librarian! I make honour roll every week! How can you not be happy?'

'I know all that,' he said. 'And we're very proud of you. We just feel –' I looked at Mom for support, but she shrugged helplessly – 'that you're becoming introverted.'

My dad was English, so it stood to reason that he believed a British high school education was the best in the world. He went to some big private (except he called it *public*) school where the Prefects beat him and made him build fires for them and he was convinced it was all character-building and nurturing. But it was still hard to believe he wasn't satisfied when I had the highest GPA at one of the best schools in the county.

'What's wrong with me?' I persisted.

I hated sounding pathetic, but I could never figure out how to please him. Most fathers would have been happy with a daughter who got perfect grades, went to church and only socialized with boys he had pre-approved.

Mom finally stepped in. 'Nothing's wrong with you, Caity.'

She sounded upset, as if my dad had deviated from a prepared statement, and she broke off for a second to bite a stubby fingernail, as she always did when she was anxious.

'Your dad just feels – *we* feel – that Campion isn't giving you the edge that great Colleges like Yale will be looking for.'

I turned back to Dad. 'So where are you sending me? Your old school?'

He shook his head in horror. 'Good lord, no! That's no place for a girl. I've found a boarding school close to London that I think will suit you. There's a great emphasis on music, sport, drama, art – lots to get involved in.'

'Boarding school?' I whispered.

He nodded smoothly. Mind games, I decided: trying to make me think it wasn't a big deal. It was hopeless to argue with a lawyer and it made sense that Mom was always compliant. He was just too smart.

'You know I work long hours. This way you'll be around friends all the time rather than on your own with your head in a book.'

'But I'm no good at art or music or drama,' I said. 'And I never get picked for any sports teams. That's why I like school – because I can concentrate on studying.'

My artistic attempts were less accomplished than Charlie's and I couldn't imagine anything more terrifying than performing on stage. Even reading book reports in class brought me out in hives.

'I know you like studying,' he said patiently. 'And of course that's important. It's just that there's more to life. I don't want you to look back on your high school years and regret not going to a football game, or your prom, or doing a school play.'

It wasn't in my nature to argue back, and it would be pointless anyway. From listening in on his telephone calls (I had a phone in my room and sometimes there was nothing on cable but reruns), I knew he'd been discussing working abroad for some time. He'd made up his mind well before making me his excuse, whatever he wanted to pretend.

I excused myself and trudged upstairs. Our house in Carnegie Hill ran across three floors and my room even had its own walk-in closet and dressing room. I felt uneasy about these things, especially since our housekeeper Rosa had told me about her studio apartment in Woodside where her three little children shared a bed, but at least I knew how fortunate I was.

In my bathroom I carefully washed my face and stared into the mirror. I knew what he really thought: that I was boring. My school blouse was buttoned to the neck and my skirt ended below the knee. I wore thick tights and ballet flats. I only wore mascara on special occasions and my eyebrows were bushy. Hell, even my underwear was boring. I'd never had a boyfriend and my weekends were spent looking after Charlie or studying with classmates for extra credit. I'd never assessed my life so harshly before, but, although it embarrassed me, it was secure, predictable and governed by boundaries and rules that I understood. Was that so wrong?

Saying goodbye to my friends and the home I'd lived in all my life was bad enough, but everything paled in comparison with leaving Charlie. He was more than my baby brother; I flat-out adored him. Mom's research at Columbia kept her from home on evenings and weekends, and since we'd grown too old for babysitters I'd been the one to take him to school and put him to bed, arrange his play dates and organize his reading chart. I took as much pride in his development as if he were my own baby, and sometimes I liked to pretend that he was.

I loved his curly black hair and serious eyes; the gap where he'd lost a baby tooth falling off the jungle gym; the Band-Aids that peeled off his knees. How could I leave him to the kids who threw his lunch out of the bus window and made fun of his Spongebob socks? The thought of him growing up without me was agonizing even without worrying who would take my place. No one else knew our secret handshake; the cartoons we watched in bed; the prayer we said to keep the vampires away (at least I told him it was to keep them away). I cried for Charlie every day, and that was before I'd even seen Temperley High.

Mom figured less in my grief, perhaps because she was an easy scapegoat and being mad at her made my misery easier to bear. Besides, I saw even less of her than I did of Dad.

We left between Christmas and New Year, a dead time when Charlie had lost interest in his presents and was starting to whine about going back to school. Miserable to the core, I turned away from Mom at the departure gate. She looked tired and her dark hair was starting to go grey at the temples. Even though I hated myself for it, I wished she would try harder to look nice. Apart from her fuzzy hair, she was hardly ever out of a lab coat – or a lab, period. It wasn't surprising that Dad had stopped noticing her.

I clung to Charlie, kissing the top of his head and telling him not to forget me. He stared up at me, bewildered.

'Please, Caity,' Mom begged as I released him. 'Don't blame me for this.'

She held my hand tightly and I knew without looking that she was crying. I steeled myself against it, because losing my brother was bad enough without thinking about her too. I shrugged and picked up my hand luggage, wishing she'd stand up to Dad. Maybe then he wouldn't have spent the last seventeen years, and probably longer, having affairs with every woman he met. Despite a PhD and tenure at Columbia, she put up with him as if she deserved to be treated like crap. I was *not* going to end up the same.

'Charlie needs me,' I burst out, even though he could hear. 'Who's going to take care of him?'

Mom spoke quietly. 'Caity, I know you're devoted to him, but I think it will be good for you to be around kids your own age without so many responsibilities.'

'But you don't even know him. Do you know what he likes to eat after school, or his favourite Saturday morning movie? Do you know that he won't sleep without the Nemo toy I got him for his birthday?' I was crying now. 'Do you even notice anything that doesn't fit under a microscope?'

I bit my lip too late. Dad was already ushering me away, but not before Mom's face crumpled with hurt. The last thing I saw was Charlie struggling against her as he tried to run after me. I could still hear him wailing on the other side of Security, and, although it was wrong, I felt almost glad.

I resisted visiting my new school, ignoring Dad as he tried to read me quotes from the website. *I'm sure it's fine*, is all I remember saying before I resumed crying for the rest of that freezing English New Year in an echoing Belgravia house. I ran up an enormous phone bill to my friends back home, happy in the knowledge that Dad would be furious when he saw it, but despite the dutiful chorus of 'We miss you!' at the end of every call, I knew my departure had made little difference to the gang. After two years at Campion, I had to admit that Dad was right: exemplary grades didn't make a lasting impact, and soon no one would even remember me.

On the last day of my vacation I forced myself to take a cab to the King's Road and trail around in the rain, carrying a stack of British fashion magazines so I could at least try to fit in. Dad let me use his Amex for essentials and I brandished it defiantly, letting a personal shopper choose me smart, tailored clothes that *InStyle* promised would make me look like a *Sloane* (even if I wasn't entirely clear on what that meant).

Campion was almost one hundred years old, but Temperley High was on a different scale of ancient. The thick trees that surrounded the campus made it totally invisible from the outside world, and we drove down a long, dark drive which widened to show a stone-fronted mansion house with pillars at the door. There was a fountain in the courtyard decorated with hideous lions and fish, and everything was completely ordered and symmetrical. The trees, plants, paths – even the wisteria that grew around the school windows – nothing was a millimetre out of place. It was so immaculate that I thought we'd come to an English castle instead of a functioning school.

'Oh God,' I whispered in terror, gripping the car seat.

Dad seemed choked up with pride. 'Beautiful, isn't it?' he beamed. 'Do you think you can be happy here?'

Ignoring this incredibly stupid question I looked upwards, as if for a sign that I would be okay. A wooden clock tower topped the building, and my glance caught the slight figure of a girl leaning far out of its window and watching us. She had a cigarette in her hand, and her long blonde hair cascaded down, catching the wind and fluttering. The sunset made it flame, lighting up her face.

Suddenly she was gone, so quickly that I couldn't be sure I'd seen her at all.

'The clock's stopped,' Dad commented, following my gaze. 'Twenty to twelve. You'd think they'd fix it, with the amount of money that must go into the upkeep of this place.'

This sort of irrelevant remark was typical of him. I watched the window in case the girl reappeared, but

14

nothing of her lingered except a plume of smoke way up above and a faintly reverberating laugh.

Dad started making excuses as soon as he could, barely staying long enough to unload my cases before he raced off to enjoy his new freedom. He waved out of the window as he disappeared while I stood numbly, my hands clenched so tightly in my pockets that one of them tore through the silk lining.

My housemistress Mrs Denbigh met me inside the white-marbled entrance hall. She didn't seem very strict, and at least the room she showed me to in Woodlands, the Sixth Form girls' boarding house, wasn't as austere as I'd imagined. I unpacked my familiar belongings, hiding my favourite plush rabbit under a pillow and arranging my framed photograph of Charlie next to the narrow bed. I fought back the urge to cry as I kissed the glass.

'Goodnight, baby,' I whispered as bravely as I could.

Although I tried my best to sleep, alternately reciting the Periodic Table and emptying my mind, I lay awake until dawn, staring into the dark and wondering what was going to happen to me. If I'd known, I might have climbed out of the window and swum back to New York.

Chapter Two

Stella Hamilton

Welcome to my kingdom.

It's the first day of the spring term and I'm in the cafeteria at breakfast, working hard to ignore my best friend Katrina. We agree on most things, and her collection of Cartier watches is unparalleled, but right now she's in danger of boring me into a stupor. I'm half-aware that she's telling me about her Christmas holiday and half-hypnotized by the Minnie Mouse bow in her shiny brown hair.

'And Amber was being a *nightmare*.'

Amber is her stepmother. She's only five years older than Katrina, so you'd think they'd have lots in common, but friendship hasn't blossomed and the upshot of Katrina's story is that she cut off Amber's hair extensions during a misunderstanding over the remote control on Christmas afternoon.

'I mean, I left it a bit uneven, but I did her a favour – acrylic is *such* a fire hazard.'

Now her dad has banned her from the Great Missenden estate until she apologizes, forcing her to spend future holidays in Monte Carlo with her estranged biological mother.

I'm finding it hard to care. Her mother shares

many characteristics with mine, notably that she's never shown any signs of wanting children and treats Katrina as a costly encumbrance who must be intermittently tolerated. But Katrina feels the rejection more keenly than I do.

'Then I thought, I don't have to go to Monte Carlo, do I? I can come and stay with you.'

I snap back to attention. There's nothing I hate more than people depending on me, which is only one of the reasons why this is out of the question.

'Of course you can,' I say warmly. 'But is it a good idea to leave Amber with your dad all year round? Don't you want to keep an eye on her? See what's really going on with her anti-gravity yoga instructor?'

She scowls and I relax. Her father is at least sixty and I know how much she worries about her trust fund. I can't imagine her having to work – actually *work*, I mean, because hosting lunches for animal charities doesn't count – for her Manolos, and I doubt she can either.

I'm pleased to be part of (I might say *ruler of*) such an exclusive set of girls, because it prevents others getting close enough to hear what we're talking about. I've listened to enough male conversations to know that most boys are halfwits – even the popular ones. Especially the popular ones, actually. Huddled together, darting glances at the girls around them – I used to be intimidated by this until, by virtue of having a popular boyfriend, I was allowed to join one of their confabs and discovered that their principal conversation topics, which each lasted more than twenty minutes, were their favourite sandwich fillings (cheese and ham, the *timeless classic*, was the eventual victor) and the size of Steven Gerrard's football boots (it's a debate they can't settle). And these were the coolest boys in school.

Girls are different – more self-aware, more crippled by self-loathing – but even so, the Stars can be inane. Each of them contributes something crucial and unique, but sometimes I have to remind myself that as a unit we are very much more than the sum of our parts.

I inherited our cafeteria table from my older sister Siena, who coincidentally was leader of a six-strong clique called the Starlets. They carved a six-point star into the table along with each Starlet's initial, so all we had to do was update it with our own names. This ensures that no one sits with us in error and we avoid the stress of rushing to reserve the best spot. My point faces the window so I can see my reflection: that way, if the Stars are being unacceptably tiresome, I'm still guaranteed a pleasant dining companion.

'Happy New Year, girls!'

I groan inwardly as Ruby clacks over in new Jimmy Choos and a very tight Marchesa jumpsuit. On her breakfast tray is an apple – which she won't eat – and a black coffee. She's especially beloved amongst the younger students (it's prudent to cultivate across-the-board popularity) and it takes her a while to reach our table because she stops to greet each little girl who calls out to her. I push away my cereal and force a smile as she draws up a chair and starts talking breathlessly, complimenting Katrina on her cape-back minidress before turning her attention to me.

'Stella, can I borrow your *Hamlet* essay for some inspiration? You know I wouldn't ask, but Jamie is *so sweet* and I can't *possibly* tell him my excuse for not doing it. You can borrow the Zinnia in return.'

I roll my eyes at Katrina, who smirks. Sometimes I get sick of having to bail these people out, but Ruby got the new Zinnia bag for Christmas, and, as much as it pains me to say it, I didn't, so I dig around in my (mass-produced, last season) bag and hand her the essay. Such is school.

'What is your excuse, out of interest?' I ask, taking a liberal approach to the word *interest.*

Ruby flips her hair over her shoulder before replying. It's long and dark red – really beautiful – and the motion reveals the sparkly star earrings we all wear as a nod to our group identity. Sometimes I think this is a bit juvenile, but mostly I like wearing something that sets us apart. Not that other people couldn't wear stars if they wanted to – we've never trademarked it – but cheapening our symbol wouldn't be advisable.

She leans forward to build up the suspense and glances around to see who's listening. 'I was with Blake,' she hisses.

19

Blake is our PE teacher, although last term I found out that his real name is Glen. Even though we're Sixth Formers we have to take Games twice a week and Ruby is really reaping the benefits of the exercise.

Involvement with a hot teacher would usually garner respect from one's peers, but Blake isn't a real teacher: he's an exchange student from Australia and he's only nineteen. It's typical of Ruby to look for kudos in this way and get it so wrong. Blake's attractive, if you like the meathead look, but he's also easily led, and beneath his Speedos he's really not worth spending time with. He and Ruby go well together, come to think of it.

Katrina gives me a smile that Ruby doesn't notice. 'Which base?' she asks.

Ruby giggles. 'Only third. What do you take me for, Katrina?'

I don't comment on this information. She's had weeks to write that essay, so the twenty minutes she spent being groped by Blake behind a bin full of hockey sticks is entirely irrelevant. She's always looking for approval, but she should know by now that the cupboard holding the athletics equipment will never be the place to find it.

Katrina, having lost interest in Ruby's sex life, is checking her BlackBerry. 'You're trending, Ruby,' she says. 'Your bag is famous already.'

I look around the room to see several camera phones pointing our way. This is a commonplace occurrence,

20

especially after a holiday when everyone's outfits are newsworthy, but Ruby should never be the focal point.

'What else is trending?' I ask before she becomes intolerable.

My online presence is particularly crucial this year as I'll be competing in the Head Girl election in July. I'll certainly win, because no other student has more influence, power or sway, but in the interim it's important to keep abreast of Twitter gossip so I can judge whether someone close to me is feeding information or whether it's being fabricated in a cynical bid by less-popular students to gain followers. Although I'd never do anything as vulgar as post news about myself, it's notable that nobody trends as often as I do.

'The Asprey earrings you wore at Winterval,' says Katrina. 'Did they really cost a million pounds?'

Winterval, the Christmas dance, is one of our key events and always generates stories that last well into the New Year.

'Thereabouts,' I say, looking over her shoulder. 'What's that about you?'

Katrina scowls. 'People are still complaining about my punch, which is really unfair. I did explain that I'm very much a novice mixologist, but tagging it as *nativity anthrax* is totally libellous.'

'I know,' I say comfortingly. 'But maybe some people found the yard glasses a step too far.'

Edward and Quentin are throwing a football over everyone's heads. No one asks them to stop because it wouldn't be respectful: Edward is captain of the football team – the Stripes – and clever too, and everyone likes him. He's my ex-boyfriend (and his brother Jack dated my sister Siena), and although he no longer interests me that way I can still see the appeal of his messy black hair and impish, don't-blame-me expression. Although the Stars are exclusively female, Edward likes to think of himself as our seventh member and usually we're happy enough to have him around. In fact, it helps to have a male voice in the mix, because some girls can be bitchy when left to themselves.

He's laughing loudly and as he glances at me I see Ally, the Fifth Form rebound he settled for last term, trying to move into his eye line whilst scowling in my direction. I glare back half-heartedly. She should realize she was hardly a substitute for me, even in the short-term, and the comfort eating she's evidently been doing over the festive period hasn't helped her chances of rekindling anything.

Edward imitates my glare, crossing his arms and stamping his foot, and I laugh despite myself. We've known each other since we were little, the downside of which is that he's more like a brother than anything else. He used to imitate me in the same way when I was an eight-year-old hogging the swing, but sometimes his childishness is reassuring in its familiarity.

I look away from him as my phone rings. It's my baby sister Syrena, and I contemplate her face on the display – a blurry close-up she took of herself wearing tinsel and a Santa hat – until it stops. I remind myself to call her back later. She's at day school at home in London, as she won't be old enough to start Temperley High until September, so at least she's in safe hands.

We're joined at this point by the others – Lila, Penny and Mary-Ann – who have all been out riding. Lila and Penny are complaining loudly about the non-availability of Zinnia bags, which annoys me intensely. I hate Ruby to feel indispensable, because that's the last thing she is.

Mary-Ann is still wearing riding clothes, and she has straw in her hair and a streak of mud (or something worse) across her cheek. She often walks around with her blouse creased and labels sticking out, and even when I tell her she can hardly be bothered to correct it. It's lucky she has me to help her or she'd never know how much these things matter. And I'm happy to assist, because, as I sometimes remind Katrina, Mary-Ann's fierce intellect gives the Stars a gravitas with which even the most classic diamond timepiece can't compete.

I have a horse too, Pip (Siena named him), but I don't ride him because of the adverse effects of riding on the thighs. I used to ride every day, even though my mother Seraphina was forever telling me it would ruin my figure, but last year I witnessed keen horsewoman Priscilla Craven completely change shape as she trained for the inter-school gymkhana: she was like a weeble by the end. Now I bribe one of the stable boys to ride Pip and muck him out, and I groom him when time allows. I take a lot of Pilates and can only hope that no lasting damage has been done.

Katrina is terrified of horses, and she's embarrassed about the reason (I'd never tell anyone it's because of a really weird horror film she saw as a child), so Pip often provides a great excuse to get away from her. Now, though, I'm dying to bitch about Ruby, so I kick Katrina hard under the table and smile as she jumps in pain.

'Come on,' I say patiently as I wait for her to stop staring at Penny's toast. 'I need fresh air, and you know we don't eat complex carbs during months containing the letter *r*.

'Later,' I add as we leave, not making eye contact with anyone.

The Zinnia has unexpectedly elevated Ruby in the pecking order, rendering Katrina sufficiently insecure about her own place to waste no time in critiquing her.

'*I was with Blake,*' she mimics. 'God, she's so gullible. As if he cares about her!' Her voice is an indignant squeak.

I take a drag. We've been smoking since we were thirteen, when she smuggled a pack of Gauloises into school in her hot water bottle cover, together with a previous stepmother's Diazepam. It made for an interesting, indistinct term. As Sixth Formers we're allowed to smoke, although it's not encouraged. I wouldn't like any of the teachers to see me, but this space between two sheds, behind the cafeteria bins, seems safe enough.

'Did you see Edward staring at you?' Katrina continues. 'I suppose you heard that he kissed Penny at New Year. She won't stop going on about it.'

Edward's feelings for Katrina can most generously be categorized as tepid, but she's a romantic and calls him *a modern-day Heathcliff*. I might point out that she's unacquainted with the source material and seems to envisage Heathcliff as a sort of stand-offish Justin Bieber. Edward only shows romantic interest in her when he's drunk, but this makes her more determined. She might be quick to criticize Penny, but whenever he's single she thinks it's finally her turn.

She's still talking. 'It makes me wonder what you *do* to have all these boys falling at your feet when you aren't even nice to them. I wish you'd teach me.'

I tell her, as I always do, that it's simply a case of being the one who cares less. I don't know why she finds that so hard to grasp. We spray ourselves with Allure, and I borrow her breath freshener, and then we head to English.

Chapter Three

Caitlin

Stella and Katrina were absent when I was introduced to my class – they were probably outside smoking – but nothing could have prepared me for the heavily made-up faces of Ruby, Penny, Lila and Mary-Ann, who lounged across the back row as if they were being shot for *Vogue*. I'd arrived late, because every time I'd tried to get into the communal bathroom someone had cut in front of me. Finally I'd given up, raked a comb through my hair, pulled on the outfit my personal shopper had sworn would make me *blend right in with the Chelsea set*, and headed to my home room – *form room* – with the help of a shaky map Mrs Denbigh had drawn for me the night before.

I hovered at the door, awkwardly shifting my weight from one foot to the other, until Mrs Denbigh ushered me inside. There were almost one hundred Sixth Formers at Temperley High, split into five form groups which met for roll call and what Mrs Denbigh called *troubleshooting*. My group already comprised twelve girls (and six boys, but they mattered less). I was lucky number thirteen.

Awkward and pigeon-toed, I gripped my nerdy collection of box files and textbooks like a shield as Mrs

Denbigh happily told the class I was from Manhattan – *a real-life Gossip Girl*, she said as if that would help me.

My heart sank as the four girls in the back row smirked. Their clothes were expensive; their hair was glossy; their eyes were charcoaled; they radiated sheer, undiluted confidence. Sixth Formers didn't wear a uniform, but these girls had one that the prospectus hadn't alluded to and which was entirely at odds with my pathetic efforts: skinny jeans or tiny skirts, layered tank tops, oversized jewellery, messy bedhead curls (that took hours to perfect) and perilously high heels. Besides this were the silver stars that decorated not only their ears but their clothes and bags, giving them an otherwordly quality that was wholly calculated.

I *was* wearing Marc Jacobs – apparently – and was confident that these girls were sufficiently label-conscious to know, but I stuck out in my fitted suit and smart heels. Not to mention that I was already getting blisters. I realized too late that I was dressed for a job interview or a day at a polo match.

I breathed in hard and tried to collect myself before my new mascara started to run. *Of course they'll accept me. I'm from New York! I shop on Fifth Avenue!* In a movie, I'd be the star; as new girl it was my right to take centre stage. Besides, everyone envied American teenagers. Isn't that what all British kids aspired to be? And, apart from worse teeth (or so I'd heard), what did these kids have that I didn't?

I remained in my daze, a state that would soon come

to safeguard me from the sharper edges of boarding school life, as Mrs Denbigh read out a notice from Dr Tringle, the Headmistress, about the consequences of breaking curfew. After that, I was half-aware of a back row girl complaining that Matron's insistence on keeping the bathroom window open was making the surrounding area a *pervert's paradise* ('So stop posing there in your knickers!' shouted one of the guys), and another reminding the group that playing death metal on the Common Room jukebox was *a threat to modern civilization*.

Eventually Mrs Denbigh asked a girl named Lucy (who didn't sit in the back row) to take me to English Literature, whereupon she led me through packed hallways to a classroom on the second floor.

'How long have you been a student here?' I managed to ask as we fought our way up a narrow stairwell.

She nodded at a formation of little girls in straw hats and blazers who were running downstairs. 'Since I was a Shell. They're twelve.'

'A *Shell*?' English expressions made no sense to me and I immediately regretted asking.

She spoke rapidly. 'The youngest students are Shells, then Removes, Fourths and Fifths. The Sixth Form is split into Lower and Upper, and we don't wear a uniform, but you can tell what year the younger students are by the colour of the ribbon in their boaters.'

I lacked the energy to ask her what a boater was. In any case, it was at that moment that we entered the classroom, and then I forgot that Lucy was even beside me.

My first close-up of Stella was like a smack in the mouth. I wasn't tall, but she was tiny. Even in skyscraper-high Louboutins, which were hardly comfortable daywear, she was smaller than any of the other girls, and because she liked the back row she used to sit on a velvet cushion to see the whiteboard. Her size was a huge part of her appeal, simultaneously making girls feel elephantine while boys were desperate to (amongst other things) protect her. And the word *pretty* didn't get close to describing her face any more than it did her most striking and enviable feature: her waist-length blonde hair.

It was hair that made other girls study L'Oréal commercials like documentaries; steal her shampoo; trail her down hallways for a closer look. It was hair that boys involuntarily reached out for; hair that hypnotized them into adoring submission; hair that they would have climbed towers or fought dragons or smashed themselves against rocks for. And it was hair that she never, ever compromised or dyed or changed.

Those attributes aside, I tried endlessly in those early days to figure out exactly what people couldn't resist. *She's only human*, I thought repeatedly. *She must have good and bad features, just like everyone. And surely our imperfections – a cleft chin, a crooked nose – are what make us interesting. Perfection doesn't exist.*

Her enormous eyes slanted like a cat's and were

endlessly blue, darkening to violet when she was upset or disapproving or angry. Her eyelashes were so long that I thought them fake until Katrina told me she'd never seen her without them, even when she was sleeping or swimming. And her eyelids were heavy, so she blinked like a doll.

Her bottom lip was large – disproportionately so – and she had a habit of denting it with her teeth. Her nose, by comparison, was small. She had two dimples, one in her right cheek and the other below her mouth, but these were rarely seen because somehow, whether it was the arrangement of her features or something else, Stella always looked sad.

She was intensely creative and her most impressive work of art was herself. It was speculated that her clothes were vintage couture cut down to fit her, but every item was so heavily customized that its origins were never clear. Importantly – although I didn't realize then how much – she never followed trends. She didn't need to, because she appeared to be responsible for *setting* every single trend that existed at Temperley High.

Our English teacher, Mr Trevelyan, was tall with spiky dark hair and cute little glasses. He was in his late twenties, friendly and soft-spoken, and it was obvious from the way the girls shimmied past him that he was a popular member of the faculty.

Instead of listening to him tell me which books my classmates were studying, I stared at this girl in the back row who was so fascinating I could have watched her all day. She looked perfectly blank and uninterested and didn't flicker until Katrina (dressed in a fur gilet despite the central heating that rose unpleasantly from the floor) whispered something that made them both giggle. I looked away, my cheeks flaming, and prayed that I wouldn't be seated near them. I felt safer at the front of the room close to Lucy, even though the girl on my other side was so wide that I barely had space to fit my chair under the table.

Somehow I could feel Stella's eyes appraising me, assessing my outfit, my hair, the back of my neck. I hoped she couldn't see how red my ears were. Her brain must have been working overtime as she wondered whether to ignore me, victimize me, or whether I constituted a sufficient threat for it to be in her interests to befriend me. I could see even then that all her relationships worked like this.

Stella ruled Temperley High like the star of every teen movie I'd ever seen. As venomous as Heather, as influential as Regina, as fragile as Marissa, she was eighty-five pounds and five foot and half an inch of every nightmare that had ever woken me up screaming. She treated staff and students like pawns, and under her reign we were little more than this. I know how ridiculous it is that we were so affected by her, but I maintain that people who never met Stella can't understand. That's my excuse – and everyone else's, for that matter. By the end, it had to be.

Chapter Four

Stella

We aren't allowed to call our teachers by their first names, even though Temperley High is quite progressive, but because Mr Trevelyan is our youngest teacher we always call him Jamie, and usually he doesn't bother to correct us.

I took English because it doesn't involve Bunsen burners or fieldwork, but the other Stars only chose it because you can always see Jamie's nipples through his shirt in cold weather. The six of us sit together at the back, which I can only think is allowed so that Jamie can confine us to one section rather than risk us contaminating the whole class with unattainable life aspirations. He likes to pick on the others (usually Ruby) to check they're listening, but not me. I expect it undermines his teaching skills to see me get full marks irrespective of whether I turn up, fall asleep, listen to Katrina's iPod or spend the entire lesson flirting with Ravi and Christopher. I know for a fact that I'm Jamie's favourite because he puts a silver star on all my essays, something he never does for anyone else.

I lean across the aisle and nudge Penny. The exertion of her morning ride has fanned her soft flaxen hair around her shoulders like thistledown, giving her a misleadingly innocent demeanour.

'What?' she hisses, busily arranging her pink pencils into size order.

'You and Edward, hey?' I prompt.

She tilts her chin defiantly. 'It's too late for you to warn me off him. I know you don't want any of us to be with Edward, but we've already kissed, and who knows what's next?'

'I don't care if you're with Edward,' I say. 'We had an amicable, mutually respectful break-up. Has he called you since?'

There's a pause. 'No.'

'It's for the best, Pen,' I say. 'You wouldn't want to be his girlfriend. You'd be a nervous wreck like Ally, furious every time he speaks to another girl.'

'I don't think Ally minded when Edward spoke to other girls,' Katrina corrects. 'She only minded when he *kissed* other girls.'

Edward, across the room, looks up at the sound of his name. Penny looks hopeful, but he wolf-whistles at Katrina instead. 'Nice hair, Marchbank.'

I never know if Edward's being sarcastic, but Katrina flushes with pleasure and adjusts her bow. 'Thanks, Edward,' she says breathily.

We both turn away, but she gasps when some screwed-up paper hits her on the back of her head. 'Edward!' she moans. 'I know it was you!'

'You're so lucky, Kat.' Penny is plaintive. 'Edward never throws *anything* at me.'

Jamie is introducing a new girl, Caitlin something, to the class, and I can tell, because he and I have a connection, that he's wondering whether to trust me and Katrina to look after her. Deciding against it, he asks her to sit at the front with Hannah Wise glowering on one side and Lucy Ainsworth grinning inanely on the other. Both of them are a complete embarrassment, and I can't believe he thinks they're good ambassadors for the school. Lucy, for example, is wearing boot-cut jeans circa 2004 and a red jumper that looks like viscose. And she's presentable compared to Hannah, who takes up two desks on her own.

It's not fair that being fat makes you unpopular, but really there's no excuse. Hannah is forever banging on about an underactive thyroid, but she's always first in the queue at mealtimes and buying out the vending machines. She's never around during prep, which this year we're allowed to do in our rooms (although you never do unless you have no friends, because everyone knows prep time isn't about work), and I can imagine her in her lonely pink bedroom, stuffing herself with Walnut Whips. All the Stars are thin, but if we weren't, we'd starve until we were. There's no sense ruining your life over a simple matter of self-control.

The new girl is small like me, and pretty with long dark hair and what looks like a Marc Jacobs jacket. She looks unmanaged, like a yearbook picture on *Before They Were Famous*, but the raw materials are there. I wish Jamie had let her sit closer to us, but I make a mental note to speak to her later. After all, I don't want her getting in with the wrong crowd.

Yet another English lesson is taken up reading *Hamlet* out loud. I never used to volunteer to read parts in class – it's so geeky – but everyone else is so god-damned slow that unless I do we won't finish it before we sit our exams. Unfortunately, since I've started volunteering, Katrina has too. Sometimes Jamie and I look at each other when she stumbles over something particularly easy, and, although he's too professional to show it, I know he feels my pain. Perhaps his New Year's resolution is to be more assertive, because today he ignores her raised hand.

Edward plays the lead while Penny and Lila are Rosencrantz and Guildenstern, which is an inspired piece of casting, and when I raise my eyebrows at Jamie he smiles. They've always dressed like twins and it gets stupider the older they get. Today they're wearing identical tea dresses with shearling cardigans and Charlotte Olympia Kitty shoes. They'll claim it's a coincidence, but I know for a fact that they meet secretly outside our official wardrobe meetings to coordinate outfits. Penny is baby-blonde and soft, while Lila is sharper-featured with long dark curls, and they function oddly like points of balance for each other. Penny's father treats her like a china doll, which has left her unable to make decisions, so I suppose she's lucky to have a protector like Lila, who will belt anyone who looks at her the wrong way. Their closeness is ammunition against any potentially damaging accusations that the Stars' friendships are more strategic than heartfelt. This, and the pro bono expertise that Penny's father's PR firm has offered us for the duration of the election campaign, makes them indispensable party members.

We all hand in our holiday essays except Ruby, who cinches in her belt and promises to get hers to Jamie before the end of the day.

'The computer room printer was out of ink,' she simpers.

I consider pointing out that she has her own printer. The computer room is only used by scholarship students and I doubt Ruby even knows where it is. Jamie isn't listening, though, so I don't bother. Anyway, I have a free lesson next and I've arranged to meet my boyfriend Luke. Katrina whines for a bit and then Penny takes her off to watch QVC.

Luke and I have been together for six months, but I like to play it cool. He sometimes gets a bit tetchy, but if he won't wait for me there are plenty of people queuing to take his place. He spends a lot of time in the gym, which I suppose is a constructive way to cope with it. He's planning to apply to Oxford to read Medicine, and I hope he gets a place, because Medicine is very competitive for a pastime that requires its participants to dismember putrefying corpses. If he doesn't, he might expect me to visit him in some godforsaken halls of residence in the north. Tuberculosis and numerous other diseases are rife up there and I'd be wary about the dangers of airborne viruses if I had to travel further from civilization than, say, Cambridge.

He picks me up from the Common Room and we go to the cafeteria where he orders a fried breakfast. Nothing could be less appealing at this time of day than the aroma of cooking flesh, but Luke gets hungry after football practice and I've learned that I can tolerate it as long as I avert my eyes from the cholesterol and lard, and breathe only through my mouth. All relationships must involve similar fortitude.

If I were any less pretty, I might feel grateful to Luke for being with me and insecure about all the girls who try to hit on him. As I couldn't be *more* pretty (unless I'm wearing a halo, which I limit to special occasions), our relationship is fairly balanced. He's tall and broad, he's always tanned because his parents' divorce qualifies him for twice as many foreign holidays as other people and his fair hair is bleached from the sun. Aesthetically he's pretty perfect (pretty *and* perfect). He's quieter than Edward, but he's sweeter too.

He spent Christmas in Antigua with his dad, and he's brought me some duty-free Silk Cut (even though he's totally against smoking) and a huge teddy bear. Syrena's room at home is already bursting with stuffed animals he's given me, but I don't mind because lots of girls are watching us. Although I'm not insecure, you can't take any chances, and Ally, for one, is staring over her iced doughnut as if she's going to combust with jealousy.

I tell him about Ruby and Blake, and he reports an unconfirmed rumour that Blake was going at it with Delia Henderson in the changing room showers this morning. We laugh because Delia has a hooked nose which, though smaller since her recent rhinoplasty, still overshadows the rest of her face. Personally I think this is a good thing.

When Luke has finished, and I've had as much Diet Coke as I can stomach, we go back to the Common Room. Luke sits down while I tell Lila about Delia and Blake. I make her promise to keep it secret, ensuring she won't, and then I watch her call Caroline and say something that makes them both burst out laughing. Caroline isn't a Star, partly because there isn't a vacancy and partly because she has fat knees, but we keep her in the loop, at a distance. For one thing, she's almost surgically attached to her Twitter feed and is always happy to act as an unofficial spokesperson for rumours we don't want directly attributed to us.

The Common Room is a hub of activity that enables me to keep tabs on everyone. Like everywhere else, there's a hierarchy. The Stars and Stripes commandeer the Chesterfield sofas and armchairs beside the French windows. Other people can use them when we're not here, but even if the room is busy we always have first refusal. It's the natural order. The furniture gets cheaper on a sliding scale of status, leading down to the old chairs with the missing springs next to the teabag bins.

Covering the walls is a mural of the seven deadly sins. When it was new, everyone had a field day trying to photograph as many applicable representations as possible. It was amusing, I suppose, to see Hannah eating a Yorkie beneath *gluttony*, and Quentin dozing against *sloth*. These days everyone's wary of sitting too close to the walls for fear of what it might mean, but sometimes I position Luke next to *lust*, just because I can. I'm usually against public displays of affection – they're unnecessary if you're in a successful relationship – but I orchestrate one every so often to keep other couples on their toes. There must be worse ways to spend a free lesson.

I sometimes worry that Luke and I have been together too long to be interesting, but as he's the best-looking boy in school there's nowhere to upgrade. I also like having easy access to the Stripes. These are the boys with the sandwich filling conversation, but I still listen in on them to ensure I'm not missing out on any salient advice or gossip. Some of the things they say about other girls are a real eye-opener, and it's great to know I'm immune to that kind of scrutiny. Today they're discussing Caitlin, whom they all fancy (except Luke, who naturally keeps a respectful silence). As you'd expect, she's in the unpopular corner underneath a large depiction of *envy*, with girls who wouldn't know a ghd if it ripped out their split ends.

By lunchtime everyone knows about Blake and Delia, which might make Ruby think twice about broadcasting her stupid flings around school as if they mean something. Nor should it be good publicity for Delia, but she seems to have misunderstood her portrayal as she's looking smug. She can't possibly think hooking up with Blake is an achievement, so perhaps she's just relieved that no one's saying she's a lesbian anymore, which is the rumour Lila started when Delia wore the same Erdem dress as her (three sizes larger) to Winterval.

Chapter Five

Caitlin

Of all the students in the group, Hannah and Lucy looked most comfortingly like my friends from Campion. Hannah didn't speak to me, but I figured she was shy, so when class finished I turned and gave her the biggest smile I could muster.

'I'm Caitlin,' I said brightly.

She looked behind her to check I wasn't addressing someone else and then smiled back at me. As we gathered up our books, two boys muttered '*blubber*' at her quite audibly, and Katrina and Ruby smirked as they flounced out like teen models.

'Shall we take Caitlin to the Common Room, Hannah?' Lucy said in the clipped accent I was still getting used to.

As we got up, I noticed that the back of her hair was covered in spitballs. Just how old were these kids? All that money and privilege, and they behaved like kindergarteners.

Lucy blushed red when I reached over and pulled some out. 'It's okay,' she sighed. 'It happens all the time.'

'Was it one of the boys?' I asked.

She and Hannah exchanged glances. 'Bound to

be,' said Lucy unconvincingly.

I wondered whether it had been Katrina or Ruby.

When I'd bonded with Lucy by brushing her hair, and Hannah had accepted that I wasn't going to make fun of her, they took me to the Common Room where everyone hung out between lessons.

They talked about their vacation, which had mostly centred on something called *coursework*, and passed around a bag of candy. I joined in as well as I could (except for the British chocolate, which I couldn't get used to), but they seemed almost as nervous as I was, so I looked around for a diversion. My gaze stopped at the boys playing pool.

'Who are they?' I whispered during a lull in conversation.

They fell over themselves to tell me. Finally we'd hit on common ground.

'The boy with black hair is Edward Lawrence,' hissed a pretty red-haired girl opposite me who'd just introduced herself as Caroline. She crossed her legs as she leaned towards me, showcasing polka-dot tights. 'He's always in trouble about something. Like, once he flooded the Chemistry labs – it got us out of practical lessons for weeks. And last term he let out all the locusts in Biology.'

'Why did he do that?' I'd already noticed Edward because he'd spent English class flirting with the back row girls.

'Just because he's super-rich, I suppose,' Caroline

said, as if this explained everything. 'His father donated new locusts as well as the new science wing. He has the most amazing house parties in school holidays and he invited me once. It was the best day of my whole life.'

Edward dominated the room because he was loud, but after a while I looked over at his friend. This boy hadn't spoken much since we'd arrived and he was frowning as he lined up his shot. In hindsight it's easy to overdramatize, but back then I had no idea of the complications.

Of course I'd had crushes before – mostly older brothers of my Campion friends, and once, humiliatingly, a Jonas Brother – but I'd never seen a boy like this. This boy shone like sunlight, making all others fade and blur around him.

'Who's he?' My voice sounded strange.

'That's Luke Richings,' Caroline told me eagerly. 'He's Stella's boyfriend.'

'Who's Stella?'

Caroline hadn't volunteered a surname, suggesting that, like Beyoncé or Gandhi, Stella was famous enough to go by one name only.

'I wish I didn't know who Stella was.' Hannah sounded envious. 'Count yourself lucky.'

'She's in our English class, right?' I asked. 'She sits at the back?'

I asked on instinct, but I was now sure she was the girl from the clock tower. I also recalled nervously that the name *Stella* was emblazoned on the bedroom door next to mine in swirling letters on a giant silver star.

I tried to swallow my disappointment: in my mind I'd put her with Edward. Both were conspicuous and impossible to ignore. It figured that Luke was taken – I felt embarrassed for even wondering otherwise – but before my good sense had reasserted itself I'd imagined him kissing me in the library as he helped me with a Math problem, or holding my hand in a busy hallway as other students stepped aside for us. For some reason I'd allowed myself to imagine that Luke had the power to change my whole life.

'That's her,' said Lucy. 'Estella Havisham.'

Hannah giggled nervously. '*Stella Hamilton*, she means.'

Luke was winning the game against messy-haired Edward, who tried to seize back the advantage by laughing at Luke when he missed a shot. He took no notice of me and I didn't expect him to. Boys that confident didn't have time for someone like me.

Luke was quieter and seemed oblivious to the way girls looked at him. His athlete's build was offset by soft blond hair that curled around his ears, and serious brown eyes; eyes that I wanted to drown in, right from that moment.

'So what's Stella like?' I asked.

They looked at each other uncertainly.

'All her clothes are vintage *and* couture,' volunteered Caroline.

'Her mother was a model, and she's friends with

Iman,' said Hannah, as if reading from a press release. 'And Princess Caroline of Monaco.'

'Stella's done modelling too. She never eats,' added Caroline. 'It's *amazing*.'

'And when she's elected Head Girl she'll be even more powerful than she is now,' finished Lucy gloomily.

I guessed they'd had this conversation many times before.

'So why don't you guys like her?' I asked. 'Is she mean?'

They looked at each other again.

'It's hard to explain,' Hannah said reluctantly. '*She* doesn't do anything. Nothing that she'd let anyone see, at least. She makes other people do things.'

'She's like the moon,' Caroline suggested earnestly. 'You know how it controls the tides and makes people act weird? That's Stella. People can't help themselves around her. She's a force of nature.'

Lucy nodded. 'It's her friends who are mean. They call themselves the Stars – you know, because they're part of her constellation? They all wear identical earrings and they do this stupid chant called the *Star Salute*. It's pathetic, but everyone worships them.'

'They're best friends with the football team, and they're always dating them, breaking up and crying,' Caroline said. '*They're* called the Stripes. Get it?'

I was about to tell her I did when Hannah laughed. 'Of course Caitlin gets it! She's American.'

I wanted to ask more questions, but at that moment

Luke potted the black loudly (cue cursing from Edward), looked at the doorway and grinned.

Stella was always central to proceedings. Despite my earlier doubts, she and Luke together made sense. They were show-stopping, but while she was self-contained and reserved, he was open and puppyish, and, perhaps most importantly, he didn't compete. I could see that she'd deliberately placed herself so everyone had a good view as he enveloped her in his arms, but she didn't check if anyone was watching and she didn't need to. She giggled and pretended to struggle as he lifted her off the ground.

'Put me down, Luke,' she said in faux-annoyance.

He grinned and kissed her several times, ruffling up her hair on purpose.

'Stella, do you want coffee?' one of her friends called.

Stella shook her head. She didn't need to say a word for people to listen. Luke took her hand and pulled her away, and the room, along with everyone in it, seemed gloomier once they'd gone. Edward grinned after them ruefully, as though used to being the consolation prize, and I could see how that would suck. He started a new game with another boy, and I watched him set up the table. Then he looked up, catching me off-guard, and winked. I blushed and looked away, hearing him laugh.

Chapter Six

Stella

We have to check our emails every morning, which is bad luck today as I have a message from Jamie marked *Urgent*. I'd intended to do an internet calorie check, but now there isn't time, so I throw my apple out of the window to stop it corrupting me later.

I run out of Woodlands and across the quad to his classroom. When I arrive, my heart sinks to see Ruby already in there, biting her lip and clutching the Zinnia to her chest. I know what's coming, but try not to show it on my face as I look at our essays on his desk. Jamie stares at Ruby, and then at me.

'Jamie,' I begin, hoping to defuse the situation.

'*Sir*,' he splutters, eyes popping.

This is worse than I thought: anger really doesn't suit his style of good looks. He collects himself before he goes on.

'Anything to say?' he asks quietly.

'About what?' Ruby counters, her green eyes wide.

'About why your essays are so strikingly similar.' He raises his voice. '*Do you have anything to say?*'

I'm surprised he's making such a big deal of this when he's never said anything before. Ruby shrugs and I glare at her, but I don't expect her to own up;

I wouldn't. Besides, I know how the Stars will react when they hear this, and her lack of backbone should work in my favour.

Finally Jamie lets her go, but keeps me behind. What he says – that he's sick of the other girls handing in watered-down versions of my work, and that if I do it again he'll throw me off the course because my influence isn't fair on everyone else – makes me spit blood.

'Fine,' I snap. 'But if you think any of them has a hope of passing without me, you're wrong.'

I'm seething as I snatch up my essay and desperate to have it out with Ruby. I'll definitely be able to borrow the Zinnia now, but for some reason I no longer care that it's the exact cobalt blue of my brocade coat. Jamie's words gnaw at me despite my efforts to block them out, and I swear to myself that I'll never rescue these idiots again.

As I reach the door, I glance at the paper in my hand. I blink hard, in case it's a hallucination, but when I open my eyes it's mocking me in bright red pen.

'You gave me a B!' My voice sounds unsteady. 'Is this a joke?'

He taps his pen on the desk. 'You need to buck your ideas up. That attitude won't wash with me this term.'

'I got the highest GCSE mark in the *country*! You can't deny I'm the best writer in this school.'

'Maybe; maybe not.' His indifference infuriates me.

'You may have got through GCSEs easily enough, but A levels are different. I think – I *know* – that you can do better than this and, if you're serious about Oxford, you'd better start trying.'

'You're penalizing me for what Ruby did.' It's all I can think of.

'No; I've given you the grade you deserve. And I'd suggest you stop treating me as if I don't know what you're up to. I'm not quite as stupid as you little girls seem to think.'

I slam the door behind me in an ineffectual attempt to retain some dignity.

I have Art next, which is the only subject I'm enjoying at the moment, even though it involves spending a whole hour surrounded by non-finessed non-Stars in whom I have little interest.

Art attracts people who don't care about paint under their fingernails rather than those who possess adequate levels of self-respect. I'm also different to the other students because I'm unwilling to take what they call *creative risks*: I won't work with wire, for instance, or anything dead. Our teacher Mr Kidd sometimes suggests I be more experimental, at which point I might paint some haphazardly placed dots, or a serpent emerging from a skull, or, on one occasion, a goat with the face of Delia Henderson, but I refuse to get my (Rag & Bone) overalls messy in the process. It's unnecessary.

Our current assignment is *Inspiration*, and our projects are starting to take shape. Renata is sculpting a Buddha from wood. Karen is painting her great-uncle, who was killed in World War II. Miranda is sketching a scene at Aspen. Harry is doing a charcoal of his puggle. My self-portrait is so large that I have to stand on a stool to reach my face. Mr Kidd just laughed when I told him what inspires me most, but today he asks me to go into his office. I see Miranda and Sarah exchange glances, as if they're hoping I'll be told to paint something else. Paul lifts me down from the stool and Mr Kidd asks me to shut the door behind me. He's holding a roll of paper.

'Stella, I thought you might like to see what your sister painted for this project. I've kept it for the last few years, wondering if I should show you, and I think now is a good time.'

I know what it's going to be, but, before I can tell him I don't want to see it, it's too late.

Siena chose her family as her inspiration, but I see cracks that didn't exist when it was created; cracks that disappear as I blink.

She painted it from a photograph of us on a boat trip in Capri when I was ten. She and I are in matching bikinis while Syrena is grasping a hideous toy rabbit by the neck and dangling it over the edge; I remember hoping she'd lose her grip. We huddle around our mother like orbiting planets, Syrena and me on either side of her and Siena on the seat behind.

50

I'm unsure why Mr Kidd has shown me this. Perhaps he's hinting that Siena's attitude to the assignment was less self-absorbed than mine. Perhaps he imagines that I miss her and would like a reminder of her. I look at him for affirmation.

'I thought you might like to keep it,' he says.

I can't think of anything worse, but I nod. 'Thank you, Sir. I'll come and collect it at the end of the lesson.'

My stool seems higher than before. I begin to paint, but a familiar feeling comes over me and I can't shake it off. It must be vertigo, I tell myself, but it's like an out-of-body experience as I watch myself fall over and over in a cycle that I'm powerless to stop.

Then I'm lying on the floor. 'Not again,' I mutter.

'Stella? Stella?' Paul is fanning me with a wad of sugar paper. 'She's awake,' he calls.

'Shush, for Christ's sake.' I hit him feebly and struggle to sit up as Mr Kidd rushes over with a mug of water. It's his painting-water mug, though, so I set it down next to me. Renata and Jessica exchange meaningful glances.

'Sorry about that.' I get up with as much dignity as I can muster. 'I . . . lost my balance.'

'You fainted!' Paul gapes at me as if I've lost my mind. 'You were out cold. Shall I take you to the nurse?'

He's looking for a way to miss the rest of the lesson.

'I'm fine,' I insist. 'I think I'll work on the floor for a

while. That stool is a safety hazard.'

Mr Kidd keeps staring, but he doesn't force me to go to the nurse. Perhaps he's worried it's his fault. When the bell goes, I'm first out of the door and he doesn't try to make me take the painting with me.

Wednesday afternoons are dedicated to enrichment activities. I usually help at the primary school in the village, but today I hide out in my room. The painting has made it impossible not to wonder how Syrena is: twice I half-dial her number; twice I fail to complete it.

Katrina's enrichment activities are always changing. She came to the school with me for two weeks before deciding she wanted to work in Marnie's, the village designer boutique. When she discovered that Marnie's is less of a shop than a museum (it's so minimalist that selling even one item seriously depletes their stock) she gave that up too. By then there weren't many options left and she was faced with the choice of the hedgehog sanctuary or the school sanatorium. She's scared of fleas, so she chose the latter, but then discovered she's scared of ill people too. I hope next year she'll give her decision more thought, but her regular Wednesday afternoon detentions restrict her options anyway.

After she's released from this latest incarceration (awarded for posting a video online of the Shells' housemistress Miss Finch dressed as the Baroness at a sing-along *Sound of Music*) we meet in the cafeteria, where I announce to all the Stars but Ruby (who's in remedial Maths) that sharing my work is no longer an option.

Katrina looks as if she's going to cry, as well she might; she can't string a sentence together, or understand the simplest of plots, and the prospect of taking responsibility for her own work must be deeply upsetting. I've decided to cut Ruby off, not just because of her unauthorized relationship with Blake, and it looks as if I'll have plenty of support. Zinnia or not, she's going to make us a laughing stock if she carries on like this.

'What *was* that essay about anyway?' Penny asks. She and Lila have come straight from the street dancing class they run for the Removes and are hot and irritable. 'I got my lowest mark ever, and I was already in single figures.'

They stare at their notes, which in Penny's case are mostly doodles of long-legged girls wearing fancy riding clothes, and, in Lila's, the words *Lila Ambrose, Lila Ambrose-Rodriguez* and *Lila Rodriguez-Ambrose* in shaky calligraphy. I don't bother to point out that her boyfriend's surname is Armstrong because I don't think he knows how to read anyway.

'I loved your essay,' Lila reassures her. 'It was really *au courant* to compare Hamlet's family dynamics with the Kardashians'. Do you still have it?'

'I'm sure it's in here somewhere.' Penny tips out her bag, showering the table in lip glosses and sweatbands before finding the crumpled pages. 'Perhaps I misheard the question.'

'It was supposed to be *appearance versus reality*.' Mary-Ann examines her plate closely. 'Speaking of which, what do you think this is?'

'Shepherd's pie?' suggests Lila. 'Either that or a burger.'

Mary-Ann pokes it with her knife. 'Lasagne,' she confirms.

'Appearance versus reality,' muses Penny, shading in the rainbow Lila has drawn across her page. 'That does sound familiar.'

'We did it for *Much Ado*,' I say patiently. 'And *Othello*. And *The Merchant of Venice*.'

'So why were we doing it again?'

I stare at Penny, hoping to convey that the real topic at hand is Ruby and not her own ridiculous excuse for an essay. 'Because it underpins *everything*. Don't you see?'

'I can't believe Mr Trevelyan got so angry with you, Stella.' Lila crosses out Penny's *F* grade and replaces it with an *A* and a *Keep it up!* in lipstick scrawl. 'You're his favourite.'

I'm glad she's noticed this. Sometimes I think they forget what I look like.

'Is he cute when he's angry?' asks Penny dreamily.

I think of him shouting, red-faced and bug-eyed, and edit carefully. 'It was awful.' There's a catch in my voice. 'He was so cold, and he wouldn't look at me, and –' I pause – 'he told me to call him *Sir.*'

There's a collective gasp. This enforced formality takes away the joy of English lessons and fires them with renewed anger.

'How could Ruby do that?' Lila sounds furious as she puts a supportive arm around me. 'It's so disloyal.'

Lila likes to pretend she's Spanish and often showcases her Mediterranean temper. She does look a bit Spanish, especially now she's started dying her mousy hair black, but actually she's from Maida Vale and her real surname is Rogers, not Rodriguez. I gather her mediocre performance in Spanish lessons isn't fooling anyone, but it's nice that she has a hobby.

Out of the corner of my eye I see Ruby rushing over. 'Have you heard what happened?' she says excitedly. She's stuck silver stars all over the Zinnia in the shape of her name, and silver star ribbons are woven through her French plaits. It's no wonder she's failing Maths.

Katrina takes the lead, as she should. She's the one whose marks will be most affected and she hates people knowing how stupid she is.

'Of course we've heard.' She scowls and Ruby recoils. 'You've ruined everything – we'll have to start writing our essays ourselves!' She's hysterical; her need to please Jamie is making her ridiculous.

Lila leans forward. 'Why did you just copy it like that? Mr Trevelyan's not an idiot! And copying off Stella as well – did you think he was going to believe *you'd* written that?'

I'm dying to smile. Ruby has never accepted that she's less academically able than the fat-free yoghurt on her tray, so Lila is really sticking the knife in. We stare at her disgustedly, although my expression is tinged with the distress of the unjustly accused.

'*And* you let poor Stella take the blame,' says Penny. 'This is unforgivable, Ruby.'

Last year we suspended Penny from group activities when she kissed Tom, who Katrina was involved with. Haunted by her temporary exclusion, she has a strong desire for retribution, even though she and Ruby are very close. In fact, Ruby defended Penny for that transgression – a hazardous move resulting in a singed tie when Katrina's rate of reaction experiment went badly wrong the next day. Katrina swore it was an accident and I believed her: she never could work a Bunsen burner, which was the only reason Ruby lost her tie rather than her nose. Now Ruby can't believe she almost went up in flames helping Penny and this is her reward.

It's the last straw, judging by her tears, but Katrina is determined to finish the job.

'We don't want you sitting here anymore,' she says triumphantly.

This may sound trivial, but you shouldn't underestimate the implications. Our corner gives us security: not for us the panic of walking through a sea of tables, frantically scanning for a friendly face or an empty space. It means we can eat, or more accurately not eat, any time we please. Perhaps this is the same anywhere, but at boarding school the significance of every disagreement, every false move, every bad outfit choice, is magnified. You don't have any other friends. Your parents aren't available, and if they were they wouldn't care – otherwise they wouldn't have sent you away in the first place. And we sit at that table three times a day.

Ruby looks at each of us in turn. She's desperate; her eyes are beseeching. It's important that I'm not seen as the ringleader, but my barely perceptible shrug makes it clear that my hands are tied. Finally she puts down her lunch tray, raises her trembling hands and removes her earrings. Defeated, she breaks into a loud sob and runs away, watched by the whole room.

'Going to find Blake?' shouts Lila after her, which I think is going a bit far: I doubt Blake will ever speak to her again now she's spilled the beans on their unethical and possibly illegal relationship.

Katrina tentatively puts her hand into the centre of the table and we all follow suit.

'Stars aligned,' we say in unison.

For a second there's a gap where Ruby used to sit. Then Katrina shoves her discarded tray into the middle of the table and Penny starts eating her yoghurt. Mary-Ann puts her bag on the empty chair and we all move closer together. In short, we re-form like liquid. Parental absence forces one to be resilient.

Chapter Seven

Caitlin

Starting school midway through the year meant that friendships were already formed, and at first I struggled to find my way around, to understand an unfamiliar curriculum and to tolerate the vile weather. Even so, something unexpected was happening. Ordinary and undistinguished at Campion, I'd made an impression here. I had no idea how or why – perhaps it was being a novelty – but everyone wanted to talk to me. Boys offered to carry my books; Shells and Removes asked where I got my clothes. Teachers called on me and seemed proud when I answered right.

The attention made life interesting, but, despite the way they'd stared on my first day, the Stars had ignored me ever since. I hadn't been part of a clique at Campion, but I found myself feeling restless and ungrateful as I hung out with Lucy and Hannah, watching the Stars out of the corner of my eye as if I were staring through a shop window at a display I couldn't afford. Everything they did grabbed my attention: whether it was speaking out in class (usually incorrectly), walking the halls after curfew in babydoll nightdresses and fluffy socks, or even just sitting around their special cafeteria table, I studied them incessantly. Aside from anything else, they provided a welcome distraction from the ache I got in my throat whenever I worried about Charlie and how he was doing without me. And sometimes, when I was overwhelmed by the need to speak to my mom, the dismissive way I overheard them speak of their own families made it easier for me to ignore her calls.

The day after their row with Ruby I was curious to see their reaction, but it appeared to be business as usual. Penny screamed when Henry tried to put gum in her hair, and Lila dumped orange juice over his head before comparing Math homework with Mary-Ann. Stella moved artichoke hearts around her plate in concentric circles and didn't eat a bite. Katrina held up magazine spreads of new season slingbacks and forced them all to vote on whether she should get them in pink as well as purple.

Caroline put an arm around Ruby when she drifted into the cafeteria and sank down beside her. Even though Ruby didn't try to hide the fact that our table was her last resort, no one seemed annoyed, and, when Edward left the Stripes' table and joined us, I understood why. Caroline surreptitiously pinched her cheeks to make them pinker, and even the perpetually studious Hannah and Lucy looked animated at his proximity. Apparently Edward's undeniable appeal wasn't limited to the Stars.

'How are you bearing up, Sinclair?' Edward asked Ruby with mock-sympathy.

Ruby collapsed against him. 'I miss them,' she

wailed. 'I can't bear it any longer. Please talk to them for me, Edward.'

Edward kissed her on the head. 'This is just a phase. You lot are such drama queens. You'll be back over there by the end of the week.'

She'd started to look hopeful when he turned to me and winked. 'If they don't already plan to replace you with Caitlin, that is.'

My face burned, and Caroline cut in before Ruby grew hysterical. 'Leave her alone, Edward. You're so insensitive! It's no wonder that Stella dumped you for Luke.'

If Edward was upset by Caroline's bluntness, he didn't show it. 'Wrong,' he said as he stole some of her fries. 'If you remember, Stella and I *mutually* decided to date other people.'

Apparently Ruby wasn't so upset that she couldn't make digs at other people. 'Luke's so in touch with his emotions,' she cooed, backing Caroline up. 'And he's not at all *possessive*.'

Edward rolled his eyes. 'Don't turn on me, Sinclair, when you've been well and truly ditched by the whole cluster. What will you do with yourself now?'

Ruby stared around in defeat. 'You're right. I can't sit here for the next year. It's worse than being dead.'

Lucy stepped in. 'Ruby, you're deluded. What's so great about being a Star anyway? Naked quad runs? Detentions? You should be celebrating your freedom, not crying over them.'

Ruby looked affronted. 'I'm sorry the Stars aren't always nice to you, Lucy, but that's not my experience of them.'

Lucy stuck to her guns. 'Then you have a short memory. I don't expect you all to be nice to me, but you aren't even nice to each other! You have no loyalty whatsoever.'

I could see that Ruby was searching her memory for evidence to the contrary, but she didn't stop Lucy ploughing on. 'And the teachers aren't pleased with you either. What about the trouble you got into last summer for breaking curfew? You're on an academic warning!'

Ruby scowled. 'It's just a formality. Honestly, this school is like a prison camp.'

'It's not just a formality,' Caroline corrected her. 'If any of you breaks curfew again, you won't be allowed to stand in the election. That seems pretty real to me.'

'If any of us gets *caught* breaking curfew, you mean,' said Ruby, pleased to have found a loophole. 'It was an overreaction. We were just having a party; we weren't doing anything wrong.'

Lucy was annoyed. 'You did plenty of things wrong, starting with drinking a fish tank full of tequila. Don't tell me Penny doesn't regret what she did that night. Not to mention Lila!'

Ruby turned to me. 'Lucy's making it sound much worse than it was. Last summer we had a party down at the lake. It got a bit . . .'

'Debauched?' supplied Edward.

'*Flirtatious*,' said Ruby demurely. 'Penny got drunk and slept with Olly – well, she thinks she did, but her memory never fully came back. Afterwards she pretended to have the flu and went to the hospital wing. Katrina took her some sexual health leaflets, and I don't think that helped. She'd made them into a sort of bouquet. But Penny's always been a lightweight.'

Caroline raised an eyebrow. 'What about Lila? She had to have her stomach pumped!'

'She wasn't supposed to drink the whole tank!' Ruby said hotly. 'She should learn some restraint. Anyway, Caitlin, lakeside parties were banned after Lila's mum turned up and threatened to sue the school. She kept screaming, "*Am I supposed to look after her myself?*" and so Dr Tringle had to come down hard on us.'

'Ruby, can't you see that being a Star isn't everything?' Lucy asked. 'You're all completely dysfunctional. Penny and Lila are weirdly co-dependent. Katrina doesn't even know how to walk without Stella pulling her strings. Mary-Ann's got . . . issues. Exactly why can't you imagine life without them?'

'You can say what you like, Lucy. But every single one of you –' Ruby looked at each of us in turn – 'would give your right arm to be a Star. Because the bottom line is that nothing in the whole world is the same without Stella. *Nothing.*'

I smiled uncertainly at Ruby. She was pretty, even with her lips pressed petulantly together. She had incredibly green almond-shaped eyes and the waist-length hair that was a staple amongst the Stars. She wore her beautiful cashmere sweater carelessly and I noticed an ink stain on the sleeve. I still wasn't sure what made the Stars so different to the rest of us, but they had a fashion magazine sheen that I couldn't hope to emulate. Even separated from her natural habitat she didn't fit in amongst us, and I felt ashamed at how very ordinary and unpolished we all must look beside her.

As the Stars prepared to go, I saw the salute Lucy had told me about. Stella stuck her hand into the centre of the table and said 'One'. In rapid succession, the others called a number and piled their hands on top of each other. After Penny called 'Five', there was a brief, Ruby-less silence before they all shouted 'Six'. Then they raised their hands above their heads, chorusing 'Stars aligned!'

Ruby burst into tears and Caroline reached to comfort her again. 'They are so lame,' she muttered to me, though I wasn't convinced by her tone. 'They've been doing that since they were twelve years old.'

'Lame,' I murmured in assent.

Just then Stella looked directly at me and raised an eyebrow. I had no idea why it happened, especially as I felt bad for Ruby, but something occurred to me for the first time. *Number six is free.*

Chapter Eight

Stella

Replacing Ruby as the sixth Star is such a sought-after position that many civilians lose all dignity as they clamour to be considered for membership. I wait for the perfect moment to introduce myself to the Chosen One, but in the meantime I'm reluctant to dampen the sense of hope and possibility that the vacancy has inspired amongst the other girls. I suppose I could have told Caroline that no amount of Fabergé eggs can compensate for the poor condition of her lowlights, or Delia that the pink Fendi bag she gave me clashes with my winter colouration, but I see no harm in prolonging such joyful excitement at an otherwise bleak time of year.

In fact, I'm almost disappointed when, on my way to the Common Room, I see her alone in the quad.

It's snowing, which has caused much excitement amongst the boys. I hate snow, but the Stripes, many of whom are of below-average intelligence, got up early to build snow objects in the quad. I say *objects* because although there are a couple of snowmen, there's also a snow – well, I'd rather not say what it is, but I'm pretty sure Edward was responsible.

The reason I hate this weather is that whenever

you step outside you get pelted with snowballs. This is a strange kind of compliment, because if you aren't popular the boys don't waste ammunition (unless you're so unpopular that they actually want to kill you), but it's terrible when it happens. Even though going onto the front line involves considerable personal sacrifice, I push open the doors and head towards Caitlin.

Up close I see she's crying. Usually I'd avoid such an emotional display, but the time is right, as her closeness to Ruby is becoming a concern. She's wearing a beautiful white Prada coat that I saw in *Harper's*, and her impeccable style, much more sophisticated than the tedious boho craze the Stars won't grow out of, is wasted on high street sheep like Caroline.

She hasn't noticed the peril she's in, and the Stripes are taking aim by the time I stand firmly in front of her.

'Back off, Edward,' I say, and he lowers his throwing arm disappointedly before turning his attentions to Ally, who from behind is an unmissable target.

I'm in a dilemma about how to broach the situation when she meets my eye and laughs.

'Sorry,' she says, wiping tears from her cheeks and folding up a letter that I can see is from a child.

'Are you okay?' I ask.

I have a great line in sympathy when I'm in the right mood. Besides, boarding school is probably tough if you're on your own.

She's obviously delighted, but my congenial approach – non-Stars are always taken aback when directly addressed – makes her cry more. No one would want to meet me not looking their best; I expect it brings home all their insecurities.

'Shall we get coffee?' I ask.

She's nervous, as one would expect, so I lead her to the Common Room. If the other Stars behaved in such a familiar way with a newcomer I wouldn't be pleased, but as I trust my own judgement I send Caroline to fetch us our non-fat lattes while we sit on the usual sofa.

Caitlin takes the lead, which is refreshing: most of the girls here are so lacking in initiative and basic etiquette that finishing school can't come too soon for them.

'I'm really sorry about that,' she says again. She's more composed now, and she's got the type of skin – clear and slightly olive – that forgives crying. Penny, for example, is so pink and white that any blemish makes her embarrassingly blotchy, but Caitlin now has delicately flushed cheeks and bright blue eyes even though she's not wearing any make-up.

'No problem,' I say. 'I remember how hard it is being new.'

I don't, actually: Katrina and I were as thick as thieves from the outset. Being new was hard for the rest of our intake purely *because* of us, rendering us exempt from the stress of it.

Caitlin looks relieved and I'm proud of my empathetic skills.

'It's so different,' she says. 'Everyone stares at me because of my accent and I don't think I'll ever fit in.'

I make my decision, although I shouldn't reveal it before telling the Stars in the form of a democratic consultation where everyone's vote, even Penny's, is supposed to carry equal weight.

'Where are Lucy and Hannah?' I ask.

She can't bring herself to smile. 'They went to feed the rabbits, you know, at the farm?'

Her plight is grimmer than I thought. The farm is only frequented by Shells, and not many of *them* would be seen dead there. It's mainly for scholarship kids, because no one who can afford their own animals has the slightest interest in being near them. Despite their questionable taste, Hannah and Lucy are not on scholarships, so this is inexcusable.

'I didn't know we were even allowed to go there in Sixth Form!' I say.

Her voice shakes with trauma. 'I went with them yesterday and there was a whole bunch of kids there. It was *awful*. I got all kinds of crap on my shoes – and the *smell* —'

I've heard enough. 'You'll never have to go there again.'

She looks appropriately impressed.

*

By dinnertime I can't believe I've only known her for a few hours. She's exactly what we've been waiting for. Mary-Ann is bright, and the private tutor Lila thinks no one knows about is really improving her Maths and Chemistry, but otherwise we're not exactly an academic group. I haven't minded this in the past, because it's preferable to be a bimbo than a geek, but Luke doesn't have much time for them. Men are hypocrites, of course, because he fell in love with me the moment he laid eyes on me and it wasn't because he cared how good I am at analysing metaphysical poetry.

Nonetheless, his indifference (and that's putting it mildly) towards the Stars can make life awkward, especially as Edward gets on with them all so well. Mary-Ann is the only one Luke speaks to (they mainly argue about cognitive evolution, but both seem to enjoy it); Penny and Lila he ignores, and Ruby and Katrina he despises. My mind is working overtime as I consider what this means for Caitlin. Setting her up with a Stripe will mean female company for me *and* double dates, so less opportunity for me and Luke to be alone. Stars shouldn't date anyone outside the Stripes (although sometimes they don't adhere to this statute), but right now only Lila is in a serious relationship, and proximity to her Neanderthal boyfriend Quentin is a direct violation of my human rights. Overall, I'm very pleased with the success of the afternoon.

'Where have you been?' Katrina sounds hurt when the Stars catch up with me. 'You were supposed to mediate in today's debate. It was *This house believes that no Star should exceed second base with any male without the group's approval.* It was your proposal!'

'That's okay,' I reassure her. 'I'll still be able to decide who won.'

A well-aimed missile from Henry has wiped the make-up off the left side of her face and flattened her hair to her scalp. Melted snow has saturated her bouclé jacket and soaked right through to her underwear. She's miserable, but not sufficiently so to go and clean herself up and miss out on the row the rest of them are having.

Everyone is furious with Penny for not telling them about her secret fling with the new stable hand (he's actually been here for months, but as none of them muck out their horses very often their paths haven't crossed). Apparently Penny has been at the stables at all hours of the day and night recently, and, instead of selflessly providing round-the-clock care for her colicky horse, she's been flirting with this boy who they claim looks exactly like Orlando Bloom. We're astounded by her selfishness.

I smooth things over for Penny (not that she appreciates it) by suggesting that they all go to the stables later to take a look at Orlando and let him see for himself which of them he likes best. There's no sense in ousting more than one Star at a time, and

I don't want the anger directed at Ruby to wane too quickly.

Katrina agrees at once, demonstrating the effectiveness of an Orlando Bloom lookalike as a cure for equinophobia, and then I change the subject.

'I ran into that new girl, Caitlin. She was crying because – well, you know who's in charge of her.'

Lila giggles. 'The Ugly Sisters?'

Mary-Ann murmurs something about Hannah and Lucy having nice personalities, which the rest of us ignore.

'She's really miserable,' I continue. 'You won't believe what they've been making her do – visit the farm to look at the rabbits!'

By the time Caitlin arrives at the table, the Stars are united in compassion. Scant encouragement is needed for Penny to put our spare earrings on standby, or for Lila to offer up Ruby's erstwhile seat to our new arrival. Our silent vote is almost unanimous, but Katrina is harder to convince. She has some abandonment issues because her mother emigrated without warning when she was ten, leaving her with a senile father and a series of hard-partying au pairs and teenage stepmothers. I'd never abuse my position as the securest thing in her life, but I like to keep her on her toes by cultivating a variety of friends. That way she's always grateful for attention.

By the time a red-eyed Ruby trudges in (even the Zinnia looks dejected), we don't bother to comment.

Predictably she makes straight for Caroline, who puts a supportive arm around her. Caroline's table is a dumping ground for the formerly popular. She's so desperate to be a Star that she always thinks the outcast will put in a good word for her, but if the period of exile is temporary she finds herself discarded within seconds of our reconciliation. She never learns.

'I can't believe Caroline,' I say to Katrina. 'She was bitching out Ruby the other day and now look at her.'

Katrina's eyes bulge, and the silver stars she's threaded through her hair tremble in annoyance, because Ruby's best chance of being reconsidered for membership is to demonstrate contriteness through isolation and penance. Aligning herself with a sub-group doesn't help her case at all; in fact it causes Katrina to join the right side and vote for Caitlin just in time.

By the end of dinner I can see that Ruby's exclusion is likely to be permanent, which might act as a deterrent to any other Stars who consider veering off-brand. Don't cause embarrassment, don't attract the wrong kind of attention, and don't date someone who could be detrimental to the group. How hard is that to remember?

Chapter Nine

Caitlin

Stella's cafeteria table buzzed with an energy that radiated through the entire school. The second I sat down, I understood. Not only would we be lesser people without her, but it was questionable whether we'd even exist. I struggled to answer their questions as I tried to figure out why Lila had called me over to sit with them. Across the room, Lucy and Hannah conferred worriedly.

'Did you have a boyfriend in America?' Penny was asking me. She was even cuter close up, her kitten-like blue eyes and round pink cheeks incompatible with the skull-and-crossbones scarf and sheer top that Lila had picked out for them both. She and Lila liked to match, but because their styles were so different one of them always looked a little uncomfortable. 'I mean, were you *going steady?*'

'No,' I said. 'I was dating, but no one special.'

This wasn't exactly true, but it sounded better than saying *I once went bowling with a guy named Eric that I met at Bible study and who always smelled a bit like chicken.* The most I could do was deflect attention away from my previous existence and hope they wouldn't guess how lacklustre it had been. Perhaps then I wouldn't toss away my first chance of experiencing the *extroverted* life my dad wanted for me.

As my eyes fell on the Stripes' table, I felt myself flush scarlet. 'She likes someone!' Penny crowed, twisting her silver star necklace around her finger. 'Caitlin, who are you *crushing on*?'

Lila craned her neck to see who was in my line of vision. 'It's not *Edward*, is it?'

'No,' I managed to stammer, but I knew I was blushing. They all exchanged meaningful looks and I swallowed nervously. They had way too much shared history for me to catch up on, and I was glad when Lila changed the subject.

'So, Caitlin, what was your favourite club in New York?'

'The Viper Room?' Penny suggested excitedly.

'That's in LA.' Lila was disappointed by this faux pas. 'You should know that, Pen.'

'I didn't go to clubs,' I said. 'I wouldn't have gotten in! Is that what you guys do?'

Penny was nonchalant. 'Sometimes we go to a club, but otherwise we go to the bar.'

'There's a bar in *school*?' I hated myself for sounding so uptight. 'For kids under eighteen?'

'All Sixth Formers are allowed to buy two drinks each,' Penny explained. 'Although no one ever notices if we bring our own as well. What's your favourite drink?'

'I've never really – I mean, I've gone to a couple of college parties, but I've never liked alcohol much.'

'It's up to you,' Mary-Ann told me comfortingly.

She was the quietest, and she smiled at me as if she understood how nervous I was. 'There are lots of weekend activities that don't involve alcohol. Like bowling, or ice-skating, or the cinema.'

'All those things involve alcohol,' Penny corrected her.

Mary-Ann beamed. 'This weekend we should have a Stars' night in and get to know Caitlin properly. We could watch a film!'

'I don't think so,' Lila said. 'You know what happened to Penny after we watched *Orphan*. I can't sit through group therapy again.'

They all started talking at once, but went quiet when Katrina held up her hand for silence. 'Have you forgotten that the campaign kick-off is on Saturday?'

'The Head Girl campaign, that is,' Penny explained to me. 'It's the night where the Head Girl and Boy candidates first present their teams to the school.'

'What teams?' I asked confusedly.

'Candidates run in teams of four, because each Head Boy and Girl candidate has a campaign manager,' Lila said. 'So we have Stella and Edward, with Katrina and Luke as their managers.'

Katrina flicked her ponytail proudly at this fact, which evidently made her the second-most important person at the table.

'And who are the other teams?' I asked her.

There was a silence, during which the Stars looked a little shocked. 'What do you mean, *the other teams*?'

Katrina ventured finally. 'Why would there be other teams?'

'I thought . . .' I started to worry that I was causing offence, even though I couldn't figure out how. 'I mean, the election is a big deal, right? I assumed other people would want to try out.'

Lila sniffed. 'You're right that they might *want* to.'

'Kick-off is also a big party,' Penny said quickly. 'It'll be a great chance for you to discover what your favourite drink is.'

'I don't think I'm going to have one,' I said. 'I'll stick to water.'

Stella was watching me. She looked angelic in her white broderie anglaise dress but her voice was distant. 'Caitlin, you know you don't *have* to attend kick-off?'

I winced, suddenly very aware that I was sitting in a spot marked *Ruby*. 'I'm sure I'll find something I like,' I managed.

'Good,' she said, still watching me. 'Because we have something to show you.'

She and Katrina conferred for a moment and then, as Katrina gave a nod, Penny excitedly handed me a tiny jewellery box. 'Open it!'

Inside was a pair of silver earrings in the shape of stars, identical to theirs.

'My ears aren't pierced,' I admitted, pushing back my hair to prove it.

Lila's green eyes gleamed, and she dug through her handbag for a sewing kit. 'I'll do them,' she offered, checking the sharpness of her needle with her finger. 'I did Penny's tongue last year.'

'Penny got septicaemia,' Mary-Ann said. 'She had to go on a drip.'

'That wasn't my fault!' Lila contested hotly. 'She probably got that from Olly.'

'Well, thanks.' I covered my ears nervously. 'I'll think about it.'

'They're like a membership card, but better, because they're white gold.' Penny was proud. 'My dad had them designed for us at Boodles. It's lucky we got the spare set, hey?'

I was about to put the box in my bag when Stella took it back. 'We don't just hand these out. But you really *should* think about getting your ears pierced, Caitlin. You don't want to be left out if the opportunity arises, do you?'

By the look on her face, I could see that this really wasn't a question.

Chapter Ten

Stella

I suppose it was inevitable that sex – or lack thereof – would start to dominate my relationship with Luke at some point, but I'd hoped to avoid it until after Elevation, which will be a new era entirely. It's imperative that I remain focused on the campaign for the next few months, exactly as a sportsman might abstain in preparation for an important match. None of the Stripes appears to be familiar with this strategy, which is perhaps why they haven't won a single game this season.

My efforts to avoid being alone with Luke stall, however, when he asks me to get a permission letter from my mother to leave school for Valentine's night, pointing out before I can say no that I won't even have to give her an excuse. This is true; even if Seraphina cared enough to check, vodka-induced double vision would prevent her from seeing what she was signing.

Keen on getting a second opinion about how long one can reasonably delay sex with one's boyfriend, I try in French to explain my misgivings to Mary-Ann. We're watching a film called *Mon père, ce héros* which is tedious (and morally dubious), but at least it's dark.

Mary-Ann is becoming really pretty, I've noticed recently. She didn't become a Star on looks; more because she came from prep school in Paris with an abundant designer wardrobe. She's a great clothes horse, even though she never seems to have a clue who she's wearing and is as careless with Chloé crêpe de chine as she is with her Aertex PE kit.

When she was younger she was kind of funny-looking, coltish and awkward. She's got long straw-coloured hair and she's really skinny, and we used to tease her for being clumsy and having big feet. We've rejected girls for less, but the truth is that I trust her with things I'd never want the other Stars to know. She has a really strong moral core and sometimes our behaviour shocks her, because the conscience planted by her religious upbringing denies her a lot of fun. We ignore her when she tells us off, but I admire the way she tries to do the right thing, even if I'd never do it myself. And after Fourth Form you don't get picked on for being skinny.

Her sheltered background has ensured she'll never have sex before she gets married, and perhaps not then, and she has a panic attack every time a boy tries to undo her bra. I look around to check no one's listening, hoping she'll understand.

'Luke wants to take me to a hotel for Valentine's Day,' I whisper.

She looks confused and stops taking notes, twisting her hair into a messy topknot with her biro. 'What's the matter with that? You've been together for a while now.'

'I don't think I'm ready,' I say under my breath. 'I haven't slept with anyone before.'

'You've never done what with anyone before?' she says loudly.

'Shut up,' I hiss.

Lucy turns round to *shush* us and I flip her the bird. I draw six hangman spaces in my exercise book and finally Mary-Ann manages to spell out VIRGIN.

Now she's listening. 'You lied!'

Already I wish I'd kept my mouth shut. 'I didn't lie.'

Her eyes are as round as pennies. This is the annoying side of her strong moral core. 'You *did*. You encouraged Lila to sleep with Hugo, right before she found out he was cheating on her with the rhythmic gymnastics second team.'

'I don't remember that,' I say flatly.

Mary-Ann has the memory of an elephant, if not for *être* verbs, then for sex-related scandal. She drops her ace with triumph. 'You told her that sex was *mildly exhilarating*.'

I press on with some damage control. 'Okay, maybe I did. But it doesn't matter – she didn't do it, did she?'

She shudders. 'Only because of the naked Facebook pictures. Who knew Hugo was so pliable?'

I think she's going a bit far. I might have some influence, but, honestly, what about free will?

She's remembered something else. 'You and Penny had a pact that you'd both do it at the lakeside party last summer, the night you and Edward broke up. She only did it because you promised her you'd do it too!'

I attempt a romantic insight. 'Sex should be special. You can't do it according to a formula.'

'So why did you say the first time you do it is always terrible? You told her to do it with Olly so she'd be good at it by the time she met someone she liked.'

I remember now. Penny's first time *was* awful (and not only because she got grass stains all over her Balmain skirt and a tree root was digging into her back throughout), so I was right. She should have thanked me for my wisdom.

Mary-Ann is looking at me as if I've done something terrible and I'm not sure what she wants me to say. I thought this talk was going to be about me and my problem, which she can surely understand is more important than Penny popping her cherry with some bit-part Stripe she probably doesn't even remember.

'*And* both Ruby and Katrina followed your rubric,' she continues. 'It didn't end well for them either!'

'I was saving face,' I try before she cranks open this Pandora's box any wider. 'Edward and I were going to do it, but it didn't happen, and then we broke up. I was too embarrassed to tell anyone the truth, and I guess he was too.'

Apparently touched by this show of vulnerability, she places her hand on mine. 'Luke's crazy about you; he'll wait until you're ready.'

For a second I think I'm saved from her unnecessary sympathy by the ringing of my phone, but it's my little sister again. Mary-Ann, who knows Syrena's Lady Gaga ringtone, gives me an odd look. 'Everything okay?'

'Fine. I'll phone her back later; it's not important.'

'She's been sending you letters, hasn't she? I'm not *prying*,' she says before I can accuse her of it, 'but Mrs Denbigh told me to remind you to empty your pigeonhole.'

She reaches into her bag and hands me a sheaf of letters addressed to me in Syrena's round handwriting. I pretend to concentrate on the film until she changes the subject.

'Don't worry about Penny,' she says as if I'd given her alfresco deflowering a second thought. 'She's fine now she's met Ben.'

'Who's Ben?' I ask distractedly.

Mary-Ann's commendable hearsay retention is a useful filter for Star gossip that's just too tiresome for me to commit to memory. 'You know – he's the stable hand.'

My nose wrinkles involuntarily. 'She's *dating* that labouring boy? Publicly?'

She appears not to see the problem. 'He's just on a gap year, and why does it matter what his job is? Penny thinks it could be really serious between them.'

I lose my patience. 'Penny thinks she's in a serious

relationship with every boy who blinks in her direction. She should think more carefully about how this impacts on all of us.'

Mary-Ann looks confused. 'I don't think there's a Star Statute about having to like each other's boyfriends. Otherwise surely Lila wouldn't be allowed to date Quentin?'

'I think it's time to pass a new bill on that issue,' I mutter as we gather our books. 'Excess sovereignty can be very dangerous.'

Chapter Eleven

Caitlin

Katrina, as Stella's campaign manager, took charge as we gathered in her room Saturday evening. A pink tape measure was draped around her neck and she'd tied up her long hair in an offcut of sequinned silk. It was the first time I'd seen inside her room and I checked it out as surreptitiously as I could, getting ideas of how to transform my own bare white walls. Katrina's life as a Star was showcased in an explosion of photos showing her and Stella posing at parties and sports meets, while dozens of designer clothes and accessories burst from her closet onto the floor. Her ceiling was covered in neon stars that shone in the half-light of candles, and the focal point of the room, above her bed, was a gold star-shaped poster with *Team Stella* printed in the centre.

'What's tonight's theme, Kat?' Penny, wearing Victoria's Secret underwear and green legwarmers, hopped on one foot in excitement. 'You've been very secretive about this.'

'Black,' Katrina said. 'So you can't wear that awful pink boob tube that makes you look like a Power Ranger.'

She wheeled a rack of clothes into the centre of the

room with a flourish. 'All the outfits are here. We have to look unified, so no arguments.'

She handed a coat hanger to each Star, leaving me until last. 'I'm so sorry we don't have a set for you,' she said, looking me apologetically up and down. 'Don't worry; we'll think of something.'

'That's no problem,' I said, relieved that I wouldn't be facing the public in an ensemble that was smaller than my bathing suit. 'I'll just find my own clothes.'

The Stars snatched wisps of fabric from each other.

'You're so talented, Kat,' said Penny, admiring herself in Katrina's mirror, which ran almost the length of one wall. 'Did you really design this collection yourself?'

The collection comprised black Daisy Dukes with an embroidered star on each butt cheek and a tiny black tank top with *Team Stella* emblazoned in silver sequins.

Katrina nodded proudly. 'Yes, and I had them made to our exact measurements . . .'

I followed her gaze towards Stella, whose miniature Daisy Dukes were gaping front and back. 'Oh no!' she wailed. 'What happened?'

Stella placed her hands on her hips. 'You must have measured me wrong.'

'But I couldn't have . . .' Katrina's voice died away as she stared at Stella's waifish frame. 'I'm so sorry, Stella. What kind of campaign manager am I?'

Penny looked smug. 'Maybe you shouldn't have measured us up when your mind was elsewhere, Katrina: you couldn't stop checking your phone when you were doing me. It's no wonder you got Stella all wrong, is it?'

Stella raised an eyebrow at Katrina and she crumbled at once.

'Penny's right,' Katrina confessed. 'I got distracted because Edward texted to ask me to meet him at the lake.'

'And then he kissed me . . .' Penny reminisced as Katrina glared at her. 'I'm *so* sorry it didn't work out for you, Katrina.'

Stella ignored them both as she stepped out of her oversized shorts, and I backed out of the room before anyone tried to pass her outfit onto me. Spending an evening with the Stars was going to get me attention enough without being forced into Stella's rejected doll-sized costume too.

Stella came into my room a few minutes later wearing her robe, and stood behind me, looking at my reflection in the mirror. I'd picked out jeans and a high-necked tank top, which I hoped was sufficiently similar to the Stars' outfits to go unnoticed.

'Nice earrings,' she said. 'I'm glad you took my advice.'

That afternoon Lila, the first of the Stars to get her driver's licence, had driven me and Penny to the nearest jeweller's. We were allowed to leave school on Saturday afternoons in groups of three or more, but it was only as we wove through the trees in Lila's Prius that I realized this was the first time I'd left campus since arriving a month earlier.

'I've never seen you look so relaxed!' Penny said as she twisted around to look at me.

I laughed. 'I'd forgotten what freedom is like. It's weird to be out.'

I wound down the window as we set off down the country road, savouring the air that didn't smell like pencil shavings or hardwood floors.

'Don't I need parental permission for this?' I worried as Lila parked by a small shopping mall, even though I knew I sounded lame.

'Of course not!' Penny said as she pulled me out of the car. 'Why would your parents care what you do to your body?'

'Is it going to hurt?' I asked weakly as I sat in the jeweller's chair.

'Hardly at all,' said Lila. 'It hurts way less than getting your belly button pierced.'

'And your tongue.' Penny stuck hers out to show a silver stud.

'It's just like being shot,' she added comfortingly as I closed my eyes.

Now I put my hands protectively on the studs I was supposed to wear for four weeks as Stella produced Katrina's dressmakers' scissors.

'Your outfit is out of the question,' she said. Before I had time to react, she slashed my tank top asymmetrically to reveal my midriff.

'I – I can't!' I stammered, staring at the discarded piece of fabric.

'Don't you trust me?' she asked.

Unsure how to answer, I fell silent as she cut my jeans into short shorts and shook up a little can of spray paint.

'Almost done,' she said, concentrating hard as the words *Team Stella* appeared in silver letters across my chest. I shivered as the cold paint seeped through the fabric onto my skin.

Penny wolf-whistled when I finally stumbled into the hallway. 'You look amazing!'

'Thank you,' I said dazedly.

Stella had plucked my eyebrows and covered me in so much make-up that I barely recognized my own reflection. *At least I fit in*, I repeated like a mantra.

'Where's Stella?' asked Katrina, looking me anxiously up and down.

Stella appeared on cue, locking her door carefully behind her. Everyone in Woodlands bedroom-hopped constantly, but Stella's room was always closed and I'd never seen anyone else enter or leave it.

She was wearing a silk coral dress that complemented her petite figure. Her hair hung to her waist, so shiny and golden that the light reflected off it. Her eyes were enormous and more than persuasive; her lips were full and her cheeks were hectically pink. All at once I understood: she was the rock star and we were such loyal groupies that we didn't even resent our lowly status.

'What about unity?' Penny protested, gesturing at her own *Team Stella* slogan. Lila had gone a little overboard with the gold body shimmer and her bare legs were tinged yellow. 'You could have picked an outfit more similar to ours, couldn't you?'

'It's probably best if we don't *all* match, Pen,' Stella said. 'We're not twelve, and the whole idea was a bit juvenile.'

Katrina looked devastated at this second snub. 'Stella, this will never happen again.'

Stella let Lila and Penny lead her out of the door as we all followed. They were delighted to have her walk with them, and we crossed the quad to a birdsong of praise from the Shells and Removes, who hung out of their dormitory windows and called to her in chorusing echoes.

Stella, you're beautiful . . . Stella, you're our favourite star . . . Stella, we love your hair . . . your dress . . . your shoes . . .

'They soon got over Ruby,' said Mary-Ann wryly. 'She was their number one for years.'

'They have good taste,' Penny told her. 'And they always move *right* with the times.'

I expected Stella to ignore the little girls' compliments, but like a professional politician she thanked each of them by name, causing more rabid hysteria. She even took the notebooks they held out to her from the lower windows, signing her name in each one inside a giant star.

'She's such a pro,' sighed Penny as we waited for her to catch up.

Katrina, relegated to the back beside me, nodded miserably. 'Matching outfits were her idea,' she said under her breath.

My first taste of popularity was intoxicating. The entire school seemed to be crowded into the oak-panelled school hall, but the Stars acted as if they were the only people around as they pushed open the double doors and shoved their way through.

The largest table, the epicentre, was empty. I made to avoid it, guessing it was reserved for someone important, but the Stars occupied it like an army. *We* were the important people. The six-point star they'd carved into their cafeteria table was here again, a name on every tip.

'Move along,' murmured Penny as I sat down. 'That's Stella's place.'

I saw that the tip with her name on was pointing directly at me. I shuffled to the end, uncomfortable to be in Ruby's seat once again and not daring to point out that Stella had been sidetracked by Edward and wasn't even with us.

'Shall I go and get us some drinks?' I asked.

Penny laughed. 'Why would you do that?'

I didn't see where they came from, but, almost as soon as she'd spoken, the table was filled with bottles of beer, wine and champagne.

'The Stripes bring our drinks,' Penny explained. 'Never let it be said that they don't have their uses. The more we drink, the happier they are, so everyone benefits.'

She giggled as I reached for a can of Coke. 'You don't want that,' she said kindly. 'It's not alcoholic. It's not even Diet! They must have brought it as a joke.'

'But won't we get in trouble?' I whispered. 'This is way more than two drinks each!'

She looked airily around the room. 'I don't see who with – the teachers hate kick-off. Apparently they draw lots to decide who has to compère. If they say anything, you should tell them that Quentin tricked you into it. Lila likes to have him in detention as often as possible.'

Hannah, Lucy, Ruby and Caroline were in the corner, sharing a bag of chips and drinking lemonade. Katrina nudged me as we walked past on our way to the bathroom.

'Go easy on the crisps, girls,' she said. 'They're fattening *and* they give you spots.' Raising a reproving eyebrow, she shimmied away in a fog of sequins and Chanel Nº5.

'They're letting you sit with them at kick-off as well as dinner?'

Lucy stared incredulously at my midriff as she took this in, and, although I couldn't bring myself to look at

Ruby, I guessed she was equally shocked.

'I thought it might be fun . . . you know, to try something different? Not that it's not fun to hang out with you guys,' I said hastily. 'I just want to make sure I'm getting the whole Temperley High experience.'

Caroline looked sick with jealousy. 'Could you ask if I can come and sit with you?'

I was confused as to why she was asking permission. I knew the Stars could seem a little intimidating, but it was a big table. And it wasn't as if they took up a lot of space. 'Why don't you just come?'

She shook her head fearfully. 'I couldn't. But maybe if you asked?'

I left them to catch up with Katrina in the bathroom, but mentioned this to her as we returned to our seats.

She sniffed and gave Caroline a scornful once-over. 'No way; too desperate. Tell her to have some dignity. And why's her hair so *flat*?'

I let her go ahead while I stopped again beside Caroline, hating myself as I muttered an excuse about lack of space. She wasn't fooled, and to make matters worse I glanced involuntarily at Ruby, whose face was a mask of pure despair.

'Thanks for trying,' Caroline said, her sweet face flushed and humiliated.

'I'm sorry,' I mouthed to Lucy, who smiled ruefully as she patted Caroline's hand.

'Not your fault,' she mouthed back just before Katrina returned to pull me away.

'Stop talking to them,' she whispered anxiously. 'Ruby's with them and it undermines our authority if we don't uphold her punishment. You shouldn't let Stella see. She's not in the best mood with me tonight.'

The noise was suddenly deafening as everyone left their seats and surged to the stage. Katrina tried to pull me after her but I lost my balance and stumbled, expecting to wipe out on the wooden floor, before strong arms pulled me upright.

'Careful,' Luke cautioned, putting me back on my feet.

One of his hands remained on my back while he steadied me, and I held my breath as if that would prolong the moment. His face was close to mine and his brown eyes were liquid.

Then Stella was beside us. Despite being so tiny she had avoided the crush, or, more likely, it had simply parted for her.

Luke laughed and shook his head at her as he took in my outfit. 'So you're already leading Caitlin astray?'

Stella smiled witchily. 'I'm opening her up to new experiences.'

Reaching forward, she straightened out my tank top so the logo could be clearly seen. She was holding Luke's hand, but he turned back to me right before she led him away.

'She's a bad influence,' he told me. It wasn't clear whether he was joking.

I took a breath as I prepared to launch myself back into the mob, but Katrina suddenly reappeared to rescue me. She helped me into a prime position in front of the stage, putting an arm around me every time someone shoved against us.

I wasn't clear on the purpose of kick-off, and, from what I'd seen so far, there wasn't one. Campion had held plenty of pep events to showcase the popularity of the in-crowd, and apparently they weren't limited to the States. I'd never attended – in fact I'd always been pretty scornful of school spirit – but then I'd never realized how exciting it was to stand on the right side of the fence.

Everyone was still fighting to get closer to the stage, and even with Katrina's support I was knocked off-balance in my heels. Finally Lila, Penny and Mary-Ann shoved me in between them, creating a force field where no one could touch me. Although the students continued to push, they didn't come close enough to drive us out of the way.

There was a brief lull as Mr Trevelyan, obviously resenting the loss of his only free evening, came out to compère. No one listened to his speech, but the surge receded long enough for me to check out the hall. It was only used for special occasions so I hadn't seen it before, and, as I stared at the thick velvet curtains, the elaborately painted ceiling and the portraits covering the walls, I did a double-take at the large image hanging in pride of place above the stage.

'Why is there a portrait of Stella up there?' I asked Mary-Ann in confusion.

Mary-Ann flushed a deep red. 'That's not Stella,' she said awkwardly, as if it were hard for her to get the words out. 'It's her sister Siena.'

I was about to ask why there was a portrait of Stella's sister up there when Katrina cut in. 'Siena died. Just so you know.'

'Oh my God.' I was sure that I'd blushed the same colour as Mary-Ann. '*How?*'

Katrina looked uncomfortable. 'She had an accident on Elevation night five years ago, right after she won the election.'

I felt a shudder travel the length of my spine as the girl stared down on us. She wore a gold crown, and a gold sash over her white dress, and, although she looked exactly like Stella, she wore her hair as Stella never did, twisted and curled elaborately around her head. She also wore an expression that I'd never seen on Stella's face. She looked truly happy.

Before I could ask what had befallen Stella's sister, Mr Trevelyan gestured to a group of students beside him on the stage.

'As we begin the process of electing our new team, I'd like to express thanks to our current Head Girl and Boy, Lorna and Mark, and all our Prefects. I'm sure you'll agree that they've done a wonderful job this year.'

The Prefects nodded awkwardly at the muted applause. In fact, I'd hardly registered them, and even now only dimly recognized some of them as kids from the Upper Sixth. They each wore a long black scholar's gown, identical to the one gathering dust in my closet ready for exam season, and they looked a little like bats. Anything less like the glittering Stars was hard to picture.

'*They* are our current Head Girl and Boy?' I asked Katrina, staring at the two students in front. With their mousy hair and nervous expressions, they were an odd pair of victors. 'If the election's such a big deal, how come I've never seen them before?'

'Since Siena died, the election's been a bit . . . serious,' Katrina explained. 'We've had plenty of good candidates, but the winners have all been boring Student Council members. They don't have a symbol, or a cafeteria table, or good hair, or *anything*, and all they do is lead prayers in assembly and campaign for things like vegetable allotments and cheaper stationery. This year is a return to the glory days, like a rebirth. You can see how desperately we're needed.'

'Will we have to wear gowns when we're Prefects?' Penny leaned worriedly towards us. 'I don't think I can bear to.'

'No,' Katrina said staunchly. 'I've tried every way of customizing mine and it's still totally unflattering. The first bill we pass will be to ban them altogether.'

'Good idea!' Penny's eyes lit up. 'Maybe we can get them replaced with Miu Miu capes.'

Siena would have stood out anywhere, but the

portraits surrounding her were particularly dismal and drab. I could see the Stars rising through these ranks from the age of twelve, building their empire until they filled the school's collective consciousness, and waiting for this moment, by which time no one would dare contest them, to seize absolute power. Lorna and Mark were already surplus to requirements even though they would officially retain their positions until the summer.

As they vanished into the curtains at the back of the stage, Mr Trevelyan spoke again as if he were rushing through his duties as fast as he could. 'Let's meet the students who could lead you next year. Will the first team please join me?'

Everyone cheered as Edward and Luke climbed the stairs and Katrina ran up to stand beside them.

'Where's Stella?' asked Mary-Ann. 'She's supposed to be there too!'

I turned around, locating Stella some way behind us, doing tequila shots with a gang of Stripes. When Mr Trevelyan called for her, she held onto Tom's shoulder as he lifted her off the ground and carried her to the stage. The Stars chanted her name as Luke pulled her up next to him, but when Katrina tried to take her hand she shifted away.

'All hail the Queen of Sheba,' I heard someone say sarcastically, but when I twisted around to see a group of Fifth Formers behind us I couldn't tell which of them had spoken. One of them spoke again as I turned back, although I was sure I misheard her. *Do you think she likes mud masks?*

Standing right beneath the image of her sister, Stella took in the crowd that was chanting her name with an expression that was impossible to read.

'Isn't she making a speech or something?' Lila asked.

'She doesn't need to.' Mary-Ann's voice was almost reverent.

'She could at least *smile*,' Lila said.

'She doesn't need to,' Mary-Ann repeated.

Mr Trevelyan could be heard asking for the other teams to take their spots on stage, but no one did and I could see why. There was absolutely no point.

Edward grabbed Stella's hand and raised it above their heads, but, as soon as she could, she edged away from him to stand beside Luke.

'*Awkward*,' Lila said next to me. 'Edward hates being second best.'

'What do you mean, second best?' I asked. 'Edward's going to be Head Boy, right? Luke's just his campaign manager?'

'In theory,' Lila said. 'But all that matters is which boy is with Stella.'

Penny nodded vehemently. 'Stella was a genius to create a love triangle. It's *so* original.'

Apparently kick-off was over, and Luke looked relieved as he took Stella's hand. The cheers – sounding mostly female this time – grew louder as he leaned over and kissed her, and I watched Edward's expression flicker for a second.

His green eyes locked with mine as they had on the day I'd first seen him, except that then he'd smiled as if he accepted his also-ran position. This time he seemed a little ruffled that, Head Boy or not, he'd never be first-tier as long as Luke was by Stella's side.

Chapter Twelve

Stella

Kick-off is a success even by my own exacting standards, and as we vacate the stage I allow Katrina to high-five me.

'I'm really sorry about your outfit,' she says for the hundredth time.

'I know you are,' I tell her. 'But please concentrate on the election from now on. *Not* on Edward.'

She nods as she leaves in search of champagne, and I take the opportunity to approach Edward while Mark bores Luke about hospital work experience. Lorna, our other excuse for a monarch, is loitering nearby, but scuttles away before I even have to ask her to do so.

'You have an admirer,' I tell Edward. 'Did you notice?'

'I have multiple admirers,' he corrects me, grinning. 'Which one are you referring to?'

'I'm sure I don't have to spell it out,' I say. 'She blushes every time you look at her. It's very sweet.'

He considers this. 'If you mean Caitlin, she *is* very sweet. Very wholesome. And *very* unlike my usual type.'

I'm smiling now too. Edward has this effect on me.

'But I'm not sure you're ready to see me with someone else,' he teases. 'You sabotage my relationship with Katrina every time we think about closing the deal.'

'Speaking of which, you didn't tell me you'd invited her to the lake,' I say. This invitation only ever means one thing and it's surprising – to say the least – that Katrina failed to mention it to me. 'When's that happening?'

'I expect we'll do it sooner or later,' he says casually. 'If you ever butt out of my life. Did you know Ally is still afraid to go out alone on dark nights after your manhole stunt?'

'Human involvement in that incident was never proven,' I say smoothly. 'Mrs Denbigh agreed that the flowerbed could easily have subsided of its own accord, like a natural phenomenon.'

Before he can question Mrs Denbigh's impartiality, I turn the subject back. 'Katrina really isn't your type.'

'But I like her,' he says.

'So do all the other Stripes,' I say pointedly. 'Caitlin is better for your image, which is an important consideration right now. I can help you if you like.'

He rolls his eyes, but I can see he's flattered by the attention. And he should be, because I wouldn't let my newest recruit go out with just anybody.

'She's very *vanilla*,' he ponders. 'She lacks Katrina's edge.'

He's probably winding me up, but this makes me

competitive. 'Caitlin has plenty of edge,' I say. 'Just as much as Katrina. *And* she has hidden depths. You should give her a chance.'

'Maybe,' he agrees. 'Although it depends on the moves Katrina pulls out tonight.'

We follow Luke to the centre of the dance floor where we're immediately surrounded by the other Stars and Stripes. Caitlin, shoehorned between Henry and Tom, risks being trampled or groped, so I pull her to the innermost circle where no one else can touch her. She smiles gratefully and I tousle her too-neat hair so it falls more sexily over her shoulders. She still doesn't look very badass, but it's not fair to compare her to Katrina, whose unequalled *hips don't lie* interpretation always has all the Stripes fighting to stand behind her.

'Stop trying to pimp Caitlin out,' Edward says into my ear. 'You're so transparent.'

'I'm not,' I correct him. 'I'm helping her maximize her potential.'

Caitlin isn't a bad dancer, but she's timid, so when Quentin brings my next drink I hand it to her and shrug when she asks what it is. Soon she relaxes in accordance with Quentin's generous measures and stops resisting when I push her towards Edward.

'You were amazing tonight, Stella,' she tells me earnestly as the spirits take hold. 'Really incredible.'

I note that she's the first person to tell me this. Even though victory for the Stars means victory for us all, sometimes even my campaign manager is apt to take my political flair for granted.

'And you look *beautiful*,' she continues. 'It was a great idea to wear a different colour, so you stand out from all the other Stars.'

'You're right on all counts,' I tell her. 'Katrina likes us all to match, but . . .'

She shakes her head vehemently. 'This is your night, and the focus should all be on *you*. It was a blessing in disguise that your clothes didn't fit.'

I was right about her hidden depths.

We move out of the spotlight as we continue our conversation, because playing hard to get might be a better tactic for her. By the bar, Ally is looking daggers at me and no doubt remembering the regrettable night last term when a concealed crater was discovered outside her bedroom window. She's on the ground floor and was sneaking out for what was to be her first lakeside meeting with Edward when she found herself waist-deep in muddy water. The alarm was swiftly raised, but her housemistress took a dim view and gated her for a month without parole. As Edward's patience in these matters is limited, he'd moved on by the time she was liberated.

Just as I decide that such proximity to her is a bad idea, she shows me why.

'Hey, Stella,' she calls.

There's probably time to step out of the way, but I have no need to as Caitlin, between us, deflects Ally's pint glass. With a deft flick of her hand she sends it flying, covering Ally in the liquid she'd intended for me.

'I'm so sorry,' Caitlin stammers at Ally, who stares in disbelief as her friends try to clean her up. 'It was a reflex . . . Is everyone okay? Are you okay, Stella?'

Her horrified expression is well-judged.

'I'm fine, thanks to you,' I tell her as the Stars and Stripes cluster around us in concern. 'How did you react so quickly?'

'I'm not sure,' she frowns. 'It's as if I sensed what was going to happen.'

'I can't believe I wasn't here to protect you, Stella,' panics Katrina. 'You could have been seriously hurt.'

'Yes, Franz Ferdinand,' Edward says to me in mock-concern. 'How could anyone have left you in such peril?'

'Caitlin was more than capable of handling it,' I tell Katrina, noting that she's now let me down twice tonight in favour of Edward. 'She obviously has great instincts.'

Seeing that the glass Ally tried to throw held muddy water, I feel a flash of gratitude towards Caitlin. Even if I'd dodged, some of it might have splashed my dress. Or, in a scenario that doesn't bear thinking about, my hair.

'What happened?' Mary-Ann is easily distracted by irrelevant details. 'What provoked Ally?'

'She attacked us *un*provoked,' I say, smiling at Luke as he puts an arm around me. 'We've done nothing to her.'

Quentin, who dug the crevasse, is keen to remind me of Ally's likely motive, and I recall that he responds well to direct orders.

'*Quiet*,' I tell him before he can speak.

Katrina, who helped him collect the frogs, turns to Caitlin in gratitude. 'It's lucky you were here,' she says.

'Isn't it?' I agree. 'Edward, did you see how well Caitlin handled your vicious ex-girlfriend? You should thank her for getting rid of Ally once and for all.'

Ally is trying to get Edward's attention as her friends hustle her out of the room, and he winces in embarrassment as she sobs his name. Caitlin really has done him a big service.

Katrina smiles at him hopefully as a slow song comes on, and he hesitates for a second.

'Edward?' I press. 'Don't you agree it was very *edgy* of Caitlin?'

Edward looks away from Katrina. 'I agree,' he says.

I chink my glass against his. 'I had a feeling you would.'

Chapter Thirteen

Caitlin

Ally's assassination attempt made Stella more celebrated than ever, and somehow the adulation rubbed off on me. Shots were lined up for her as she stood at the bar, and I shone in reflected glory as the attraction of being with her intensified further. I thought that if you were wasted enough she probably looked like a higher power.

It wasn't long before Penny's lipstick was bleeding, Lila had lost her phone, and Katrina was crying incoherently about her design error, telling anyone who'd listen that Edward had gotten her confused between inches and centimetres. Meanwhile Stella took a bottle of champagne from Tom, popping the cork and spraying everyone around her. Putting her mouth to the bottle, she caught some and let the rest spill down her neck and chest as the austere faces of the previous Head Girls and Boys glared down from their gilt frames.

When my feet hurt I headed for a seat, not believing my luck when Luke joined me. 'Are you having fun?' he asked, leaning so close I could smell his aftershave

Stella was far enough away not to have seen us. I don't know why I thought that mattered, except that

Luke's cheek was so close to mine he was almost grazing me. As I put my hand to my face, his fair hair brushed against it, and I jumped.

He was suddenly serious. 'Be yourself. Don't try and be like them.'

He nodded at Penny and Lila, who were dancing together, legs and arms entwined and, as far as I could see, almost making out as a group of guys looked on.

'I'm not.' It was hard to speak; I couldn't get words out clearly. 'They're all so pretty . . .'

God, where did that come from? I cursed myself. *Don't be lame.*

'You're a beautiful girl, just as you are,' he said sincerely. 'Anyone would be lucky to be with you.'

Suddenly Stella was between us and the moment was lost. She sat on his knee, her legs pushing me away from him, and kissed him on the lips. I turned away awkwardly and pretended to check my phone.

Finally she spoke over the music. 'Luke, wouldn't Edward and Caitlin make a great couple?'

He winced as if she'd deafened him, making a big deal of holding his ear. She laughed, pulling his hand away and biting his ear lobe. His pupils dilated and I felt a bolt of something like pain in my stomach. I'd never known that jealousy could feel like this.

Focus. 'Didn't Penny make out with him?'

She waved dismissively, but then I remembered the argument earlier. 'And I thought he and Katrina were hooking up?'

'That's completely over,' she said. '*Irrevocably*. So if you're interested, you should come to his after-party.'

The Stars ran for the door as the track cut out and the lights came on. Katrina took my hand, but Edward steered me away so we could walk on our own. He was handsome in a white shirt that showed off his tan, and his easy confidence contrasted sharply with Luke's winsome sincerity.

'I thought you said you didn't drink?' he asked, putting his arm around me as I tripped on the uneven ground.

'I didn't,' I admitted. I'd asked Stella a couple of times what was in the yellow drinks she kept handing me, but she'd only shrugged, and refusing them seemed rude. Besides, being drunk wasn't the big deal I'd always imagined. I was always so overly cautious about trying new things that I'd decided to fall into line on this one. It had been a great night, even if I was less steady on my feet than usual.

Everyone removed their shoes as we walked up the stairs in Riverside, the boys' house, towards Edward's room.

'Are we going to get in trouble for this?' I whispered to him.

'Not if we don't get caught,' he said as we went inside.

Stella pulled me down next to her on Edward's bed. 'I'm glad you came with us.' Her hair smelled of peaches and it fell onto my shoulder, soft like feathers. 'It's time for your initiation.'

'My what?' I asked.

Luke gave me a glass of water, but, before I could sip it, Stella took it from my hands and replaced it with champagne. I was starting to overheat but I drank some anyway, even though it was warm and almost flat.

The other Stars were lounging unsteadily next to us on the bed, drinking straight-up vodka from a bottle. Quentin was trying to make out with Lila, but she kept her back to him as she talked intently with Penny. At the word *initiation*, everyone sat up and took notice.

'Surely someone told you?' Lila said. 'You can't just *join* the Stars, you know. It's called *earning your Stripes*.'

She pulled a tie out of Quentin's back pocket, and he looked thrilled at the attention.

'We blindfold you,' she explained nonchalantly. 'Then we spin you around and you kiss whichever Stripe you stop at.'

I shrank away, and Katrina giggled. 'We've all earned at least one, Caitlin. Some of us almost have the full spangled banner.'

Stella glanced at Edward. 'And some of us don't think that's very classy,' she said.

'What if –' I was at a loss. 'What if I don't want to?'

'Then you should know that being a Star isn't for everyone,' Lila said. 'Caroline didn't make it either. Maybe you could find another group that suits you better? Brass band or something.'

I thought of Caroline's eager face. She was so

desperate to be a Star that surely she'd have done a simple kissing task?

Katrina seemed to read my mind. 'Caroline *did* the task. She just didn't *pass* it.'

Penny nodded earnestly. 'Poor Henry thought he was getting the bends.'

Henry pulled a face at the memory. 'I hope you don't have a saliva problem, Caitlin,' he said as everyone laughed.

I swallowed hard. How did you know whether you could kiss or not? 'Isn't there another task I could do instead?'

Katrina squeezed my hand. 'I don't think you'd like any of them. The easiest is a quad run with at least twenty witnesses. In your underwear.'

Stella spoke into my ear. 'Don't worry. I'll make sure you land on Edward.'

I gave up, letting her tie my blindfold. At least Edward was cute, and hopefully enough of a gentleman to keep the details to himself.

The Stars spun me hard and I stumbled, clutching at air and hoping not to throw up. A shove sent me careering off-balance before someone tall steadied me.

'Luke, you do know you aren't playing?'

Stella sounded amused, and I pulled off the tie to see that he was holding me upright once again.

Lila pouted. 'How come Luke has to sit out when Quentin doesn't? He's my boyfriend, in case you hadn't noticed.'

'Because you don't like Quentin,' Stella reminded her. 'He's overweight and his IQ is unusually low.'

'That's not the point,' Lila sulked. 'Why does he get to kiss Caitlin?'

'I don't think Caitlin wants to do this,' Luke said as I pulled away from him, humiliated. What was I to them, a toy?

'No one's forcing her,' Stella said sweetly, drawing my gaze from Luke to her. 'She can leave right now if she wants.'

Still dizzy, I watched her angel's face merge with Caroline's and back again. I was ready to surrender when Katrina froze.

'Someone's outside,' she hissed in panic. 'We need to leave.'

Stella sounded impatient. 'There's no one there, Katrina.'

'There is,' Katrina insisted. 'We can't get another detention or we could get banned from the election.'

Stella only got as far as the hallway before she and Luke started making out, but the others disappeared in record time. Edward caught my arm as I made to follow and pulled me back inside his room.

'I know this isn't the best time to ask, but usually you're surrounded by a pack of girls,' he said hesitantly. 'I'd like to take you out, if you'll let me.'

I tried not to look over his shoulder towards Stella and Luke. Their make-out session wasn't helping my nausea, and I regretted drinking the champagne.

Luke is taken, I told myself firmly. *Edward is cute and kind and exactly the kind of boy you've always wanted to date. Don't blow it for a stupid crush on someone who's off-limits.*

'Sure,' I said. 'I'd like that.'

He leaned forward and kissed me gently on the lips, but I ruined the moment by dropping my phone, then scrambling after it.

'Goodnight,' he said, and laughed. 'Catch up with Stella and stay out of sight.'

But by the time I'd left his room, Stella had vanished.

The hallway light snapped off as I crept inside Woodlands and collided with the door frame. Katrina had explained earlier which stairs creaked and which doorways would help me remain undetected, but my head seemed to be full of bubbles. I gripped the oak banister as I roiled to one side and then the other, hoisting myself up as if the stairwell were a mountain range.

'Stella?' I whispered into the blackness.

I heard a giggle.

'Stella!' I repeated, louder this time. 'Could you please turn on the light?'

There was silence, and then I held my hand instinctively in front of my eyes as a flashlight – *torch* – shone in my face.

'Caitlin?' Mrs Denbigh hissed. 'What are you doing out here? And who else is with you? Did I hear you calling for Stella?'

I paused, wondering if she'd believe I'd been to the bathroom in my coat and shoes. I was not cut out for espionage.

'Kick-off finished an hour ago!' She sounded outraged. 'Where on earth have you been?'

My voice was trembling. 'I just went outside for some fresh air.'

I was pretty sure my dad would advise me to say nothing else without an attorney present, and after a minute of silence she sighed in defeat.

'Go to bed,' she said. 'Come and see me tomorrow morning for your punishment.'

I waited for her to head downstairs before I started walking again. Almost immediately, Stella appeared from the shadows.

'You should have told me you were there,' she said. 'I'd have shown you where to hide so you didn't get caught.'

Before I could reply, she vanished into her room.

I undressed by lamplight in front of my mirror, stopping short as I pulled off my top to see the silver *Team Stella* slogan branded in shimmering letters across my chest.

Chapter Fourteen

Stella

Caitlin is at the lunch table when I arrive and she's dying to talk to me.

'I've got something to tell you,' she gushes. 'Edward asked me out.' She's shaking, although I can't tell whether it's with excitement or in anticipation of a painful death at the hands of one of Edward's myriad female fans. 'I tried to tell you last night but you disappeared.'

She's very upbeat considering that she's just been punished *and* should have a killer hangover, and I register admiration at this resilience. 'What did you tell him?'

'I said yes, but I wanted to check with you, because Edward dated you first.'

She looks embarrassed and shreds a napkin. I'm unwilling to discuss the finer points of Edward's womanizing history over lunch, but relieved that his attentions have overshadowed her first experience of Dionysus's special gifts.

'I'm delighted for you to date Edward,' I tell her. 'He's very special, and I'm glad he's finally found someone else worthy of him.'

She nods in relief. 'That means a lot to me, Stella.'

'I'm sorry Mrs Denbigh caught you,' I say. 'I can't *imagine* what woke her up: normally she mainlines enough Valium before she goes to bed to fell an elephant. Have you got *le punishment* yet?'

She looks downcast. 'I have to do my prep with the Shells for a week, and, if I get in any more trouble, I get *gated*. Whatever that means.'

'Is that all?' I frown. 'I thought –'

She nods. 'She explained that you're all on a warning, but because I'm new she hasn't banned me from the election. Not that that matters, of course.'

'Does she know who else was there?' I ask cagily.

She looks horrified. 'I'm not a tattle tale. I said I was alone. I think she knew I was lying, but she couldn't prove anything.'

I'm satisfied with her response. A simple knock on Mrs Denbigh's door was necessary to ascertain that Caitlin's fear of authority wouldn't override her loyalty to her friends, and she's passed this test with flying colours.

'That punishment's not so bad,' Katrina says comfortingly as she joins us. 'The Shells are too little to make fun of you. The Fourths and Fifths would be much worse.'

'I've never had a punishment before,' Caitlin admits. 'But it's worth it, now I've passed my Star initiation.'

Katrina and I look at each other and shake our

heads. 'I'm afraid you haven't passed your initiation,' I say regretfully.

'What?' She turns red. 'Why not? I earned my Stripe! Edward kissed me!'

'What?' Katrina's lip trembles.

'Stella, you saw him kiss me!' Caitlin insists. 'It was in his room, right before you went to bed.'

'I didn't see anything,' I say.

Caitlin's voice falters. 'He did kiss me.'

Katrina lets out a sob and runs from the table, which is probably for the best; one crying Star at a time is quite enough.

Caitlin looks at me in shock. '*Did* Katrina want to hook up with Edward last night? You told me they were over!'

I don't want to hurt Katrina, but last night's events show how urgently her crush needs to be dealt with. She'll see as soon as she stops crying that she and Edward would never work, *and* that her loyalties shouldn't be confused right before the election campaign. As manager she needs to be on top of her game, and a tumultuous relationship – which would be inevitable with Edward involved – would be terribly distracting. I can't imagine him reciprocating her feelings in any real sense, but Caitlin is useful insurance.

'I knew if I told you Katrina liked Edward, you wouldn't go out with him,' I improvise. 'And that would be stupid, because Edward really likes you.'

I have no idea whether this is true, but I'm delighted that one well-aimed arrow has culled so many birds. I *love* it when things go to plan.

'What – what about my initiation?' asks Caitlin in a small voice, as if she's ashamed to be thinking about herself instead of Katrina. Her encouraging commitment to the cause suggests she's not quite as *vanilla* as Edward thinks; in fact, as long as she gets through her task, she could be a real asset in the coming months.

I smile at her. 'Just leave that to me.'

Chapter Fifteen

Caitlin

I felt myself blush as I unpacked my pencils and books at a too-small desk. When I tried to wedge my chair under the desk I hit my knee painfully on the wood, and the Shells all giggled. How could little girls of twelve be more clued in than I was? By the way they were pointing and whispering I could see I was the main attraction of that evening's prep, and I kept my eyes firmly downwards as Miss Finch called for silence. She even glared at me as if I were to blame for the disruption.

I slumped at the prospect of a whole week of this torture. Injustice burned through me as I started my Physics exercise, methodically scribbling notes in pencil and trying to drown out the noise.

'She is . . . she's not . . .' the Shells hissed around me. 'She's not!'

I figured out that they were disputing whether I was wearing star earrings. Embarrassed to be taking the punishment for the misdemeanours of a clique that hadn't even accepted me, I shook my hair forward and tried to focus on my work. That was why I was here, after all. Star or not, I could at least be a good student.

I jumped as the door banged, digging my pencil into

117

the page and snapping the lead.

'Late, Mr Lawrence.'

Miss Finch was trying to sound stern, but the Shells giggled as Edward winked at her before taking his seat behind me. They flirted, pretending to drop their pens so they could prance past him, and flipping folded-over notes onto his desk.

'What are you doing?' I whispered, holding my hand in front of my mouth. 'Have you come here to make fun of me?'

Edward sounded surprised. 'Of course not. I told Mrs Denbigh it was my fault you broke curfew. I thought she'd lift your punishment, but she just gave me the same one.'

'Oh.' I felt guilty for thinking the worst of him. 'Then thank you, I guess.'

'Caitlin! Quiet!' snapped Miss Finch.

I looked back at my notes and tried to ignore Edward as he hissed my name.

'What?' I spun round as he kicked the back of my seat.

'I just wondered if you knew that your bag was moving.'

'I don't get your sense of humour,' I said, exasperated. 'Is that slang for something?'

He nodded towards my book bag, which was slung over the back of my chair. It was impossible, and yet he was right.

Checking that Miss Finch wasn't looking, I gingerly

put the bag on my desk and looked inside. A pink nose and some whiskers peeped out.

I turned furiously back to Edward. 'Why is there a rat in my bag?'

He feigned surprise. 'A rat? In your bag?'

I was taking Biology so I was used to the lab rats we were studying; I even recognized this one. It was white, but its eyes were black rather than pink, and Lucy and I had named it van Gogh because it was missing half of one ear. I had no idea what game Edward was playing, but I wasn't going to be a part of it.

As the rat made a bid for freedom and leapt onto my desk, I grabbed at it instinctively. 'Ow!' I threw it back inside my bag as it bit me. Blood streamed down my finger.

Miss Finch looked at me in abject horror as the Shells' whispering reached a hysterical pitch. 'Caitlin, what is the meaning of this?'

I held up my bleeding hand. 'I've cut myself. May I be excused to go to the bathroom?'

She turned pale. 'Please go,' she said urgently.

The Shells closest to me were overcome with excitement. The last words I caught as I left were, 'Caitlin is the coolest Sixth Former *ever*. No one's brought a rat to prep before!'

In the lab, I emptied van Gogh into his tank and pressed a Kleenex to my finger as I watched him lumber around. *What am I doing here?* I muttered, blinking back tears. *Why did I think I could be someone?*

I usually shut out memories of home, but for a second I allowed myself to think of helping Charlie with his homework at the kitchen table with a plate of Double Oreos as our reward. I thought of my subway ride to school; of picking up my latte before first period; of eating Froot Loops and watching Leno with Dad when neither of us could sleep. I thought of visiting Grandma once a month for appointments with Yale alumni whom she was convinced would give me an *in* with the Dean; of eating frozen yoghurt with my friends at Forty Carrots; of spending every Memorial Day on Nantucket with my cousins.

And suddenly each and every one of these memories overwhelmed me with their stifling tedium. I might have gotten into trouble and been attacked by vermin, but, whatever life at Temperley High had been so far, boring was not one of them. And I'd endured more than enough to become a Star. I didn't have to be such a pushover.

As prep was nearly over, I headed for the Common Room. It was busy, so there were plenty of witnesses, but none of the Stripes were around. This seemed a good time.

I was calm as I opened the French windows and walked onto the patio. It was dark and freezing, but at least this way I'd have done everything I could.

'What's she up to?' I heard Lila ask as I pulled my jersey over my head.

'She's not...?' added Penny in a stage whisper.

'She is!' Katrina said delightedly as I kicked off my sneakers and pulled down my jeans. It was only the same as going swimming, I told myself. Except without water.

Although I didn't like public sporting events, I had stamina. I took off as fast as I could, focusing on the pounding of my bare feet rather than the whooping students who'd gathered to watch.

I couldn't see where I was going and I cursed as tree roots and little stones pierced my feet. 'Think of the earrings,' I muttered as I pushed myself on. Then I skidded and pitched lengthways into a patch of wet grass. Unsure whether to laugh or cry, I twisted around to see someone running towards me and calling my name.

'Come on! Get up before you catch pneumonia.'

I noticed as Katrina pulled me to my feet that her underwear was a lot prettier than mine. But then, maybe she did this more often.

The path was pitch black. 'This is gross,' I complained. 'I can't even see what I'm stepping in.'

Katrina giggled. 'Still think it's worth it?'

The adrenaline and her glittering earrings gave me confidence. 'Katrina, I'm so sorry about Edward! If I'd known you still liked him, I'd never...'

'It's fine.' Her voice shook, but perhaps because she was out of breath. 'You did me a favour – I've wasted enough time on him. Please don't think any more about it.'

'Thank you!' I couldn't believe how nice she was. 'You're a good friend.'

I slowed down as we looped back on ourselves, not wanting to face anyone when I was covered in mud, but then I saw more figures in the gloom.

'You could've waited!' hollered Penny. She and Lila, also stripped to their underwear, were running towards us. They wore identical high heels and gold anklets.

'You fakers!' shouted Katrina. 'You missed out the hard bit. You just want attention!'

'We do not!' Penny was outraged. 'We're late because we were trying to persuade Stella and Mary-Ann to come with us.'

'Penny's wearing a thong,' Lila said as they reached us. 'Right now, she has no secrets from *anyone*.'

Nearly crying with laughter, Katrina bent down and smeared her hands in mud. Before Penny could run away, she had smacked her hard on the butt cheeks. In retaliation, Penny threw a handful of dirt at her and pretty soon we were all filthy from head to foot. Finally we ran back to the Common Room, holding hands in a long line.

'Look who's here,' Penny said in a sing-song voice.

'Oh crap,' I said, trying to hide behind the others.

The Stripes were now standing right outside the doors, barring our way.

Edward was grinning broadly. 'Looking good,' he said, casting an appraising eye over me. 'Where've you been all my life, Clarke?'

I ignored him as I rifled through the discarded clothes, unable to see which were mine.

The Stripes had been on their way to football practice and were in full kit. Edward deftly pulled his shirt over his head and handed it to me. I was grateful that it reached almost to my knees.

'Can I wear yours, Luke?' Penny asked him flirtatiously.

Luke laughed as he gave it to her. 'You're shameless, Ambrose,' he said.

I did my best to avert my eyes from his bare chest.

'*I'm* shameless?' Penny said. 'Edward's girlfriend is responsible for this, not me. You know what they say about the quiet ones.'

Luke turned to me in surprise. '*You?*'

I tried to push past Edward, embarrassed at being referred to as his girlfriend before we'd even been on a date, but he caught my arm. 'Are you mad with me?'

'You put a rat in my book bag!' My voice came out in a squeak. 'Of course I'm mad!'

He pulled me aside and lowered his voice. 'Can't you see why? I was helping you!'

I shook my head in disbelief. 'I want to go inside, Edward. I'm cold.'

'It was your initiation,' he explained patiently. 'I've seen you handle the lab rats, so I know they don't bother you, but the Stars thought it would be really scary.'

I stared at him. 'I'd already passed my initiation? I didn't need to do this?'

He seemed to be holding back laughter, which made me even angrier.

'Hazing is a crime in forty-four states!' I snapped.

He pulled me towards him. 'Then it's a good thing we don't have states in this country. Yes, I'm pretty sure you've passed initiation. But let's call this insurance.'

He rubbed my nose with his and then kissed me. 'You are *really* hot,' he whispered.

The whole student body seemed to be watching as I went back inside. I couldn't bear to look at Ruby, who was frozen by the French windows, her eyes wide in disbelief. Lucy, Hannah and Caroline looked shell-shocked and I suddenly lost my nerve, wanting only the safety of my bedroom. As I hurried to the door, someone said my name, and I turned reluctantly.

Stella was curled up on the couch with Mary-Ann, and she put down her textbook as I walked slowly back towards them.

'Don't you want your earrings?' she asked, pushing the box at me. 'I mean, that *is* what that little episode was all about?'

'Of course it was,' I said. 'So . . . does this mean . . . ?'

Stella smiled as the other Stars gathered around us. 'Welcome home.'

'I'm so glad you're here, Caitlin,' said Penny excitedly. 'We haven't had a chance to do a quad run in weeks. It really keeps me in shape.'

Katrina gently removed my studs, replacing them

with the silver stars. We formed a circle and Stella put her hand inside. It was tiny and delicate, her pink fingernails like pearls.

'One,' she said.

The others followed. After Penny called 'Five', they looked at me, and I put my hand on top of theirs. I hoped no one could see how ragged my cuticles were.

'Six!'

'Stars aligned!' we said as we raised our hands above our heads, our fists triumphantly punching the air.

From behind us came the distinctive click of a camera phone. And for the first time in my life, I felt like I mattered.

Chapter Sixteen

Stella

My permission letter is provided by Paula, who doesn't officially have a role in my life these days, but is more reliable than any of my blood relatives. She joined the family before Siena was born: employed firstly as Seraphina's *lady who does*, she graduated to the role of full-time nanny. Seraphina claimed to have post-natal depression, and maybe she did. She was only seventeen and it sounds a bit hellish – Siena was a difficult baby by all accounts and my father was never around even before he left for good – so even if there was plenty of money, it's fair to say she didn't have it easy.

It upset me that Paula's own flat was so different from our Hampstead house, and that her children were at a state school in Hounslow. Seraphina said we gave Paula a great opportunity in employing her, but for me it was the other way round, because without her I'd never have been taken to the park, or the swimming pool, or the zoo. I'd never have learnt to bake fairy cakes, or speak Spanish, or tie my shoelaces. And if Paula had worked weekends, I'm sure we'd never have attended the dinner parties Seraphina used to throw on Saturday evenings.

She would dress Siena as a miniature blonde novelty in Junior Chanel, propped up by cushions and eating asparagus and carrot sticks served on a platter. When I was very young I loved being carried out in my nightdress to say goodnight, because everyone gave me money and told me I would break hearts.

Siena attended the parties for years, but I was only invited once, when I was twelve, to the very last one. After that the dinner parties were an entirely separate reality, and yet I never forgot the way Siena worked the room and flicked her hair and looked at men through her eyelashes; the way her obscene, almost indecent beauty filled the room like scent.

Sometimes I don't think about how pretty I am, and sometimes it can be a downright nuisance, especially when I'm on public transport. I wonder what everyone's staring at, but the times I catch sight of my reflection without warning are the moments I crave; the moments I see Siena most vividly. On odd occasions beauty can be advantageous, but more often I try not to wonder why I look like this when Lucy Ainsworth looks like Stimpy; not to wonder if there's a hideous portrait of me rotting in an attic somewhere while my own beauty intensifies. It's just the luck – or otherwise – of the draw, after all.

Luke has booked me a taxi and the driver takes me to the Arden, a hotel and country club a few miles outside Reading. He's been smart enough to avoid anywhere the teachers might be able to afford, but the distance from school also scuppers any chance of friends joining us. This is the final blow, following swiftly from my failure to make the evening a double date.

'Luke won't mind if you and Caitlin come along,' I told Edward in the tone he never refuses.

He frowned in confusion. 'Stella, have you *met* Luke?'

'He's very easygoing,' I reassured him. 'Just don't tell him beforehand.'

'Do you think I want to spend my Valentine's Day watching you two undress each other?' he asked.

'That can't happen,' I said. 'Not as long as you and Caitlin are there.'

'Do you *really* think this is a good time to double date?' He didn't give me time to reply. 'And do you *really* see Luke agreeing to it?'

'It won't be weird,' I said defensively, but he was already walking away.

'This *conversation* is weird,' he threw over his shoulder. 'I thought you wanted me to make a go of things with Caitlin?'

I cursed myself for not approaching Caitlin instead. She'd have agreed like a shot to a slumber party, and then Luke and I could have stayed safely in different bedrooms.

Luke is waiting for me in the lobby, wearing his best suit and a silk tie. He's carrying a huge bouquet of roses, which is a relief because once he bought me lilies, which I hate.

'You look beautiful,' he says.

Because I look beautiful all the time, people don't mention it as often as they might, but Luke's really good at giving me compliments. I guess that's one of the reasons we get on so well.

'Thank you,' I say modestly. 'So do you.'

Luke really *is* beautiful; so much so that I notice it every time I look at him, so I don't feel funny about saying this.

He asks the concierge to take my bag upstairs while I wander into the Ladies' and stare hard into the giant mirror, wondering if I'll look different in a few hours' time. I spray Rescue Remedy in my mouth and then go back outside.

Luke's face lights up, as if he were worried I'd escaped through the window. He takes me to the restaurant and the maître d' shows us to our table. If I wanted this night to happen, I'd acknowledge that he couldn't have planned our first time better; if I have to surrender to the inevitable, I suppose it shows that good things come to those who wait.

And boy, has Luke had to wait.

We need Dutch courage, I decide. Luke looks surprised when I down a glass of champagne in one, but after that I relax.

Cosmo's advice was to avoid foods that bloat, so I ignore the bread basket and order a salad. Luke looks disappointed when I refuse to taste his steak, so I agree to share some tiramisu, because sharing dessert is mostly about the spectacle. I move cream around the plate, occasionally lifting a forkful and putting it back down, and he eats most of it without noticing before leaning across the table to kiss me.

'You're perfect,' he says.

I'm struck by how cheesy this is, but there's no point being coy because Valentine's Day is expensive and crowded and loud, and anyone who's not a complete show-off would just stay at home. It's safe to say I don't fall into that category.

When he's finished the tiramisu and I've finished the champagne, we look at each other. It's funny that our relationship has become so stilted and awkward, because it never used to be that way. When we were first together there was never enough time to say all the things we needed to. Any moments without him were spent clock-watching until I could see him again, and remembering how it felt to twist his hair around my little finger until he shivered; to trace my fingernails up and down his stomach as his breathing got shorter and faster and louder. Kissing Luke used to make my heart hammer and my legs buckle and my skin prickle like heat rash.

And as we stand silently in the lift, two feet apart, I wonder how it came to this. If I'd loved Edward, or had even been able to pretend, I'd have stayed away from Luke and never discovered how it felt to be near him.

If I'd been stronger, I'd have seen that surrendering to Luke could only lead here; to this hotel or another just like it; to a night that was never supposed to happen.

The room is covered in roses, and there are petals all over the bed. Luke is even playing the sappy Beach Boys song I always complain about but secretly don't quite hate. It's clichéd, but there's a reason for clichés, and it's truly the nicest thing anyone's ever done for me. And yet I wish we could stop here, because once it's done you can't go back. Everything will have a different meaning, and I'm not ready for that change, but I can't let him down when he's gone to all this trouble.

Whenever I think about sex, it's more abstract than this. The concept suddenly seems very literal, in a way I've never dwelled on, and I try to remember how I reassured Katrina before her own first time with Henry. Or perhaps it was Tom. *It's like falling off a log.*

At some point he pulls back. 'Your hair looks beautiful like that.'

My hair is tangled around my head, so I shake it out.

'Why don't you ever wear it up?' he asks, and, before I can brace myself against it, I'm falling.

I tell myself I'm being ridiculous, but however much I try to fight it I can't, and I suddenly know beyond all doubt that I can't go through with this. Ironically, Luke himself has brought this home to me by reminding me of the person I'm failing to live up to.

I push him away.

'What's wrong?' he says, alarmed.

I look at the ceiling and try in vain to think of some excuse.

He falters. 'I wanted to make our first time special. I thought we both wanted this.'

My hand clenches involuntarily, and he looks at me sharply. 'Are you leading me on?'

I try to answer, but still no sound comes out.

'Edward was right, wasn't he?' he says finally. 'Everything's just a game to you.'

I feel the gossamer-thin thread that has held us together snag and start to fray. The night is over, and I've got what I wanted and yet didn't want at all. I wonder what Edward has told him, but simultaneously can't stand to hear the answer.

'Forget it, then,' he says. His voice is tired.

I get up and shut myself in the bathroom. I feel sober now, so I get my vodka out of my handbag. This is a habit I should break, but sometimes I don't want to feel anything except the way it burns the back of my throat.

When I get into bed, Luke turns away. His back is rigid and even with my eyes closed I'm very aware of his presence. The thought of losing him sends fear surging through my body, paralysing me in a way I once knew to guard against.

Chapter Seventeen

Caitlin

I invited Lucy to hang out while I got ready for my date with Edward. I hadn't seen her much recently, because being a Star was so all-consuming, but luckily she hadn't held it against me. If anything, she seemed grateful that I still wanted to be her friend. The thought made me a little uncomfortable.

It was only a few weeks since my initiation, but my previous life was already a different dimension. I still wanted to pinch myself whenever I sat in my place – my *engraved* place – at the Star table and they competed to fill me in on important news. I still couldn't believe it when Stella's name flashed up on my phone and I heard her voice say *my name*. And when she smiled at me across a classroom, or sat close enough to lean her head on my shoulder, or whispered something to me that no one else could hear, I wanted to be near her forever. Being a Star was so incredible that, although I'd never admit it out loud, I felt almost grateful to my dad for helping me be part of Stella's incredible life.

'Your clothes are beautiful,' Lucy said enviously as she held one of my dresses against herself in the mirror.

She hadn't told me much about her background, but I knew that money was tight at home. It must have been hard to be surrounded by such conspicuous wealth; where it was commonplace for girls to have their clothes shipped straight from the designer, and Birkin bags carried textbooks and gym kits.

'You can borrow anything you like,' I said, hoping the offer wasn't insulting.

She flushed with pleasure. 'Really? You can borrow anything of mine too. If you want.'

Her voice faded as she looked down at her grey cords and plain tee.

'Do you want to hear some gossip?' she asked quickly, as if the knowledge was a better trade than the contents of her closet. 'You probably know all the Stars' secrets now, but . . .'

'Go on,' I said, looking at her reflection.

'Stella's a virgin,' Lucy whispered. 'I heard her telling Mary-Ann in French.'

I was confused. How could she be –

'A *virgin*?' I blurted out. 'But didn't she sleep with Edward?'

Lucy giggled. 'I was surprised too. But it seems not. Of course Edward would never damage his reputation by admitting the truth.'

I tried to process this. The Stars had spent all week discussing the fact that tonight would be Stella's first time with Luke, but not one of them seemed to know that it was her first time *overall*.

'So who's taking you out tonight?' Lucy asked, jolting me out of my daydream.

'Edward.' I smiled, ashamed that I'd been caught thinking about Luke. 'Can you believe he likes me?'

Lucy averted her eyes from mine and fiddled with the dress.

'Lucy?' I asked. 'Is something wrong?'

She looked mortified, as if she had to force out the words. 'Please be careful around Edward. You don't know Stella as I do.'

'What do you mean? She set me and Edward up.'

'You haven't been here long enough to understand,' she said. 'In this school, everything is about Stella. If she wants you to be with him then I'm sure she has her reasons.'

I sighed. 'Lucy, you're starting to sound paranoid. I don't see why it matters to you who I date. And why do you care what Stella does?'

She shrugged. 'I'm just tired of her. The Stars own everything in this school, including the election. I always hoped I might be able to stand, but the way everyone worshipped her at kick-off just shows what a stupid idea that was.'

'You should run if you want to,' I said. 'How can they stop you?'

'Easily,' she said. 'The Stars will do anything to make sure Stella wins, and they'll tread on anyone who gets in their way. Plus, she's a dead cert after what happened to her sister. Who would compete against her now?'

I opened my mouth to ask Lucy exactly what had happened to Siena, then shut it again. Gossiping about it made me feel disloyal to Stella, and I'd started to worry that she'd somehow know we were talking about her. I searched desperately for a new subject.

'Is this smart enough?' I asked finally.

I had the feeling that Edward would be taking me somewhere pretty expensive so I'd chosen the outfit my personal shopper had selected as *formal*: a beautiful green shift dress.

She nodded, trying to smile. 'Edward will love it. He and Stella always used to row about how short her skirts were.'

When she'd gone, I swapped the dress for a shorter one.

After our dinner at le Rive, we took a cab back to school and Edward walked me across campus.

'Caitlin!' I turned around as I heard my name and saw a group of Shells leaning out of their dormitory window. 'You look *gorgeous*!'

'So do you, Edward!' yelled another. 'You're our favourite Valentine's couple!'

After a moment's hesitation I blew them a kiss. They were sweet, and it was nice to be around kids again, not to mention to be called their favourite. None of them had spoken to Ruby since she'd ceased to be a Star, so perhaps they were in need of a replacement.

'Will you come in?' I asked as we reached Woodlands. 'We're still ahead of curfew.'

The little den on the first floor was empty: as it was

supposed to be girls only, no one ever used it.

'I like that dress,' Edward said as we sat down. 'Although I don't think anything can top the way you looked covered in mud.'

I blushed, unsure how to react whenever anyone mentioned my quad run. It was still hard to believe that I'd done something so completely out of character, but, as days had passed and I'd received so many compliments about it, my embarrassment had mixed with pride.

Edward pretended to flick dust off his jeans and then put his arm around the back of the couch. 'I'm glad you agreed to go out with me.'

'Me too,' I smiled. 'It was fun. And what a great restaurant!'

Actually, le Rive had been stressful. I'd never had a Valentine's Day date before and the other couples had been incredibly competitive, constantly leaning across their tables to kiss and show off their jewellery.

'I really like spending time with you,' he said. 'You're different to the other girls here.'

This wasn't welcome news.

'In a good way,' he clarified, seeing my expression. 'You're clever, and beautiful, and you eat actual food! That's quite a novelty in this place.'

I started to worry about the steak and fries I'd ordered, not to mention the crème brûlée. Was I supposed to pick at salad, or pretend I couldn't manage a whole dessert?

Before I could reply, he'd picked up my hand and was looking at it closely. 'Is this one of those American rings? Stella said it's called a purity ring or something.'

I'd wondered whether to leave my ring behind when I moved to England: they might be commonplace at Campion but I hadn't wanted anyone making fun of me here. I'd decided against it, because I didn't see why I should have to change my beliefs for a bunch of kids I hadn't even met. New start or not, I was pretty sure that the fun my dad wanted me to have didn't involve the removal of the ring (or anything else).

But whatever the truth about Edward and Stella's relationship, living with any number of Edward's exes didn't make me feel good. The Fifth and Sixth Form girls were so uninhibited that I was Laura Ingalls by comparison.

'Is it a problem?' I felt wrong-footed to discover that he'd discussed it behind my back, especially since Stella had never mentioned the ring to me. 'I know some boys have expectations and I don't want you to think I'm leading you on.'

He lifted my chin gently and looked right into my eyes. 'You don't need to worry.'

The champagne we'd had with dinner – infinitely better than the bottle I'd drunk after kick-off – made me unguarded. 'I did feel a little better when I found out that you and Stella hadn't slept together.'

He looked taken aback. 'Did she tell you that?'

'I found out that she's never slept with *anyone*,' I

138

said, biting my lip too late. 'Maybe she should wear a purity ring too.'

He stared at me for a moment and then laughed. 'I'm sure that's about to change. I don't think Luke's booked them into a hotel so they can talk all night, do you?'

'No.' I fell silent as I considered how many people Stella had misled. Despite his efforts to pretend otherwise, I could tell Edward was surprised to hear that she and Luke hadn't slept together yet. Luke, who probably believed that she'd already slept with Edward, would be making a big effort tonight to compete. And the Stars, misinformed on both counts, had run headlong into their first carnal experiences based only on a desperate need to fit in.

I refocused my attention on Edward as he leaned closer. 'We've got plenty of time; you just have to let me know what's okay,' he said. 'Like, is this allowed?'

He kissed the back of my hand.

I laughed. 'Of course.'

He pushed my hair behind my ear and kissed my temple. 'This?'

I nodded, feeling his breath on my neck. Then he kissed me on the lips and moulded his body around mine, our legs tangling. I pushed my tongue against his and heard him moan softly in the back of his throat. For the first time I wondered whether my rigid beliefs were such a good idea. Playing with the rules was way more fun than I'd imagined. Especially now I knew Stella hadn't gotten there before me.

Chapter Eighteen

Stella

A garden of pink roses runs underneath the clock tower, creating a tunnel of rose bushes with a clearing in the centre. When I was a Shell, I used to crawl inside when I needed peace and autonomy. The clearing was safe because access to it was awkward, not to mention thorny: I had to edge along the tunnel on my hands and knees, and I was the smallest student in school. I'd never imagined that anyone else would contemplate trying, but one day I was interrupted by an avalanche of rustling.

'What are you doing here?' I asked as Luke pushed and shoved his way into the tiny space beside me.

His hair was full of twigs and burrs, and there was a scratch on his cheek. We'd never spoken before, but sometimes I'd caught him watching me. It made me nervous, for reasons I couldn't explain.

'I thought you might want company,' he said. 'I heard you crying.'

'I never cry,' I said.

He shrugged easily. 'Were you thinking about your sister?'

Before I could tell him I didn't know what he meant, he looked above my head where the corner of Siena's gold memorial plaque was visible through the leaves. *Beloved sister, daughter and friend.* The rose garden was hers, but it only felt that way when I sat right inside at the heart no one else could pierce. No one seemed to know why the clock had stopped at the exact time of her death, but placing my hands flat at a particular point on the ground never frightened me; in fact it provided a lulling relief from the dizzying images that haunted the rest of my hours.

'Losing her must have been very hard,' he said finally.

I mentally flipped through my repertoire of stock responses, but none of them fitted the situation as easily as they did when teachers asked me how my mother was coping, or if I wanted to talk, and I was able to tell them *extremely proactively* or *no, thank you,* in a tone that prevented them from ever asking twice.

Perhaps I was tired, or perhaps it was because, in the limited space between branches, we couldn't see each other's faces, but I said something entirely unexpected.

'Yes,' I said.

Luke told me about his parents' divorce – coming home from prep school to find that his father now lived in Edinburgh with a woman he'd met at a conference – and how it felt to see him only twice a year.

'But at least I do get to see him,' he added.

I told him that sometimes I felt I'd lost my mother

too, because she no longer noticed anything that wasn't shaped like a bottle of vodka. And he didn't say anything back, but what should have scared me – admitting something so monumental out loud – became almost manageable.

Reaching forward, he combed his fingers through my hair. 'This is how I found you.'

As he pulled a leaf from the tangles, I was transported from the rose garden back to that family holiday in Capri.

Caught in a riptide, I had kicked and fought against thrashing waves that blinded and deafened and consumed me. But, gradually, as I forgot what oxygen felt like and which way was up, it was easier to stop struggling and let the water fold over me like peace. I was almost annoyed when Siena caught me up with a force greater than the swell and towed me back to shore; when she laid me on hot sand and slapped my face and shook me harder than the tide had done. Breathing was more painful than the alternative, but, as warmth flowed back into my skin and I blinked into the light, her face reminded me why I was alive.

'How did you find me?' I had asked her as she picked up yards of my wet hair and twisted it tightly around her hand.

'As long as I don't let go of this, I'll always find you.'

*

Amongst the roses Luke reached between thorns and ivy sprigs for my hand, and I let him take it. Light broke through the leaves above us and I looked up as if I felt something warmer than mere sunlight.

He and I were equals for that second, because we both knew secrets about each other, but as the moment lengthened I snatched my hand away and waited for him to leave. His touch had flooded life back into my leaden limbs as painfully as Siena had, but this time I didn't want the cure. Because without Siena I didn't need to know which way was up.

Luke and I didn't speak again for a long time, but whenever I crawled into the tunnel there was something waiting for me. Love hearts, or a necklace with my name on, or, once, a tightly folded piece of paper that just said *I'll wait*. At first I liked it, but then I started to visit only because of what he might have left for me. So I wrote a note telling him not to go there again, and I started going out with Edward a full month earlier than scheduled.

After that I didn't like to remember the way Luke had held my hand and whispered *You'll be okay* as if I were a skittish stray cat. It meant I also had to forget the relief of transcending pain with someone who could share it, but that was necessary because surrendering to it would have weakened us both.

Today Luke goes straight to the shower before it's even light outside, leaving me in bed. We've never really woken up together before, except on a school trip when he had to sneak out of the tent before anyone noticed, and I never once imagined that it would be like this. I lie facing the wall, hugging my knees to my chest, until he gently shakes my shoulder.

In the lift, he touches my chin so I have to meet his eyes. 'Are you okay?'

'I'm fine,' I say. The other things I want to tell him stick in my throat.

Back at school I cling to him for a moment, but he kisses me on the forehead and lets me go. My legs are unsteady and I wonder how you regain control once it's slipped away.

Katrina runs over when I come into the Common Room and the others follow.

'Don't make such a fuss,' I hiss.

I feel irritable because I'm hungover on top of everything else, and I just want to go to bed and read *Ballet Shoes* (don't tell anyone I said that).

'Come on, don't be mean,' sulks Katrina. 'Tell us the details! Is Luke everything we thought he'd be?'

I talk about the roses, and the dinner, and Luke telling me I'm perfect, and the Stars' tearful reactions cheer me up. I'm confident now that I can act as if everything's fine, and that acting it will make it so, but, as I get up to leave, Caitlin corners me.

'You slept with Luke?' she says.

'Of course.' I shrug. 'It was Valentine's Day.'

Caitlin is every bit as idealistic as Katrina so I'm

expecting her to ask for more romantic details, but she stops me in my tracks. 'But it was your first time, wasn't it?'

'It was my first time with Luke,' I say.

'No,' she insists. 'I mean, it was your *first time*. That's a big deal, and I just wanted to check that you were okay.'

I weigh up my options as I wonder how she knows. Mary-Ann would never blow a secret of this magnitude, and the idea of Edward voluntarily admitting virgin status is even less plausible. I consider asking her, but can't risk letting her see that it matters.

I stay calm. Caitlin and I might have spent a lot of time together recently, but that doesn't mean she can behave in such an over-familiar way. 'I didn't lie.' I sound so forceful that my own voice takes me by surprise.

She swallows nervously and edges away. 'You know I'm not trying to cause trouble, Stella. I only wanted to help.'

Responding will make this worse, so I walk away, leaving her staring as I toss back my hair in the most nonchalant way I can manage.

Chapter Nineteen

Caitlin

'Have you noticed that the Shells have started carrying pet rats in their bags?' Penny announced sternly over lunch. 'It's very unhygienic.'

Katrina rolled her eyes. 'The Shells are completely indiscriminate – they'll copy anyone. No offence, Caitlin,' she added as she caught my eye. 'But I wish they hadn't chosen this incident to recreate. A Black Death association can't be good for us.'

'I don't suppose it matters,' put in Lila. 'Caitlin's done us a favour by getting the Shells back onside now we've lost Ruby. We need to think of every student as a vote, and fighting with Ally has made Stella unpopular with the Fifths. The last thing we need is for them to offer support to another student so that we end up with two candidates. And before you tell me that won't happen, guess what I found out this morning?'

Stella was missing, but no one had asked why. She'd started skipping meals lately, as well as lessons and sports meets, but the Stars rarely questioned anything she did. This meant they didn't speak about Luke either, even though I was sure he was avoiding her. I tried my best not to think about him, but sometimes I found myself wishing that they'd just break up already.

'What's up with her and Ally?' I asked. I still didn't understand what had happened at kick-off, but now Ally hated me too. I'd apologized to her more than once, but her furious glares made me gladder than ever to have the protection of the other Stars.

'Stella hates anyone who dates Edward,' Penny said.

I must have looked as stunned as I felt, because Penny's eyes widened in shock as she tried to explain herself. 'Not you, Caitlin. I mean, she totally created your relationship with him. It's fully endorsed.'

'Created it?' I asked, confused, as Katrina winced.

'You look nice today, Caitlin,' Mary-Ann cut in hastily.

I looked down at myself, trying to forget Penny's comment. 'Thank you.'

Edward and I had gone shopping together in a free afternoon and I'd taken full advantage of my dad's latest guilt gift. Mom hadn't been happy when he'd set me up such a big expense account, especially because he signed off the bills without even looking at them. That made it easy to pretend I was buying school supplies rather than clothes, but he didn't seem to care anyway. A new wardrobe was way overdue: my blouses and twill skirts, so appropriate for British aristocracy, looked Victorian in this bohemian, supposedly free-thinking school. This time I'd shopped with Stella and Katrina in mind, buying miniskirts and skinny jeans, layered tank tops and gilets.

Edward had been surprisingly helpful for a straight guy, recommending the Stars' favourite shops and the clothes they'd have chosen themselves. He'd also been totally sympathetic when I'd told him how much I was missing Charlie, as if he understood how I felt, and had picked out a bunch of toys that Charlie had loved. That my mom was less pleased with the offerings, especially the whirring remote control car (that he'd crashed into her leg during a conference call to the Sorbonne) and the wind-up parrot (which Edward had confessed to reprogramming so it cursed endlessly in Swedish), was an unexpected bonus.

Lila craned her neck as Lucy walked past. 'Caitlin, is Lucy wearing your dress?'

'Yes, she borrowed it,' I said. 'She doesn't have a lot of clothes and I have way more than I need.'

I'd been so eager to cheer Lucy up after our talk on Valentine's Day that I'd donated her half my closet.

Penny wrinkled her nose and brushed a speck of dust off her leather pants. 'Well, donate to an *unrelated* charity next time. She might tell someone it was yours, and that would reflect very badly on us.'

I was about to ask why, but when I looked at Lucy more closely I wondered if the dress did look kind of funny on her. She stooped a little, so her posture was weird, and as a result the fabric hung unevenly on her thin shoulders. I felt bad thinking it, but perhaps it *was* better that people didn't connect it with me.

Catching my eye, Lucy waved and grinned. Her retainers were very visible. I was about to wave back, but, when Katrina shot me a warning look, I pretended to flex my hand instead.

'Speaking of Lucy, will you please let me finish?' Lila reverted to her previous conversation topic. 'This is big news. She's standing in the election!'

I was pleased for Lucy, but the other Stars gasped.

Despite the fact that someone seemed to mention the election every few minutes, I still failed to see why it mattered quite so much. At Campion I'd loathed the afternoons in the dark auditorium listening to preppy girls mumbling about representing the student body in an effort to get into the Ivy of their choice. Here, of course, student politics was a lot more glamorous, but now the excitement of kick-off was over it was hard to feel invested in it.

'I don't get it,' I interjected. 'I know we want Stella to win, but can't Lucy try out if she wants to? It's not as if she'll take a year group's support away from us.'

'Caitlin's new, remember?' Lila told the others, who looked aghast at my question. 'The Head Girl position is Stella's birth right. No one should mess with her family line.'

'But what if she wins?' I asked. 'What do the Head Girl and Boy actually *do*?'

'The school pays their fees,' said Mary-Ann. 'And they sit on the stage in assembly . . . make decisions on school rules . . . go to Oxford . . .'

'You take the fun out of everything, Mary-Ann,' Penny complained.

Lila nodded. 'That's the boring bit. The election

result is announced at Elevation, the summer ball, and the Head Girl gets a gold crown. There was a matching sash too, but it went missing a few years ago. It's on the fourth of July, so you should save the date. It *should* be the biggest moment of the entire year, except that the most boring candidates keep winning and ruining it for everyone. Last year –' she shuddered – 'I heard that Lorna's dress was from *Debenhams*.'

'I'm sure that was just a rumour,' reassured Mary-Ann.

'That's Independence Day,' I said happily. 'I wondered if I'd get to have a celebration this year.'

Lila continued as if I hadn't spoken. 'Plus, the Head Girl and Boy each choose five Prefects, so it's really important for us that Stella wins. The Prefects can rule the school, but you haven't seen the potential because our current team is such a damp squib. The runners-up were *so* much more desirable. Minka, who totally deserved to win, spends every June in Cannes and never sits a single exam. You probably haven't seen her around because she's shooting an art house film in Romania. She'd have been the perfect Head Girl.'

Penny interrupted. 'Even being a Prefect isn't the best bit. Most exciting are the dresses the Head Girl candidates wear to Elevation. It's like *Next Top Model* – better, even, if you can imagine that. Lots of people – mainly girls, and the boys from the *Les Mis* society – don't cast their votes until they've seen the outfits.'

'Isn't that a bit shallow?' I asked. 'Should a Head Girl be elected based on a dress?'

'Of course she should.' Penny sounded puzzled. 'What other criteria are there? Other than hair, of course, and no one can compete with Stella on that score.'

Lila nodded. 'You wouldn't trust a leader with bad fashion sense, would you? And if you need any proof that everyone's priorities have got really warped since . . .' She tailed off and started again. 'Then look at our current leaders. Would you trust them with *anything*?'

Lorna and Mark were hard to spot. They hung out with lots of different people, and, instead of having their own table, they sat wherever there was space as if they were regular students. Right now they were talking animatedly over a big dusty book as a group of Removes flicked chips at each other.

'But if people vote for the glamorous – *deserving* – candidates and their dresses, why don't they win?' I asked.

The Stars exchanged glances. 'We think there's a staff conspiracy,' whispered Penny. 'Allegedly there was a lot of corruption in Siena's year, and now they manipulate the votes to get the winner they want. There's no other explanation for the success of such *grey undesirables*.'

Now I understood why they only wanted one candidate. 'So that's why Lucy could be a threat?

Because the teachers might choose her even if the students don't?'

Even though they'd just admitted as much, the Stars looked affronted.

'There's only one reason the teachers wouldn't want Stella to win, and that's because it could bring back bad memories for her,' Lila clarified. 'But there's no chance of that, because Stella's totally come to terms with her tragic past. She's very Zen.'

'Another Star could stand in her place,' I suggested. 'If the teachers are worried about Stella in particular.'

'Stella is our candidate,' Penny said. 'She always has been, and Lucy is just a mild inconvenience barely worth discussing. Even if the teachers want her to win, they can't ignore the public frenzy. You saw the reaction to Stella at kick-off: it would take someone pretty high-profile to compete with that. And she has Edward too. Their level of support is unbeatable.'

Lila nodded. 'However many girls stand, there'll only be one candidate, and the teachers will have to accept it. It just saves time and humiliation if no one else bothers.'

Penny looked around, apparently only just noticing. 'Where *is* Stella?'

I spoke without thinking. 'She's in the clock tower.'

The image of Stella high up in the tower like a princess waiting to be freed had fascinated me since my first day. I'd learned that the heavy wooden door in a corner of the courtyard led up to it via a spiral stairwell, but it was always locked, and the school rules – a heavy, leather-bound book kept in each student's room – stated that it was permanently out of bounds and punishable by expulsion.

I looked up every time I walked past, but although I sometimes saw smoke I'd never glimpsed Stella at the window again. Several times after dark I thought I'd seen flickering lights inside, but they were never clear enough for me to be sure.

I'd tried the door a few times, fiddling with the iron bolt and invariably breaking a nail, but earlier that day I'd seen Stella darting towards the door. I'd called out to her, hoping she'd invite me up to her secret place, and she'd turned briefly but then disappeared. By the time I reached the door there was no one there, and it was shut as tightly as ever.

The Stars were staring like I'd lost my mind.

'The clock tower?' Lila said. 'What are you talking about? I mean, aside from the fact that Stella gets a nosebleed on the vaulting horse . . .'

Katrina laid a hand on my arm. 'Hasn't anyone told you what happened to Stella's sister?'

'No,' I said. 'Only that she died in an accident.'

'It happened in the clock tower,' Katrina explained. 'She fell.'

'Oh my God,' I stammered. 'I had no idea . . . Stella never talks about it.'

'Well, would you?' Lila said. 'If your sister had . . .'

Her voice faded.

'She didn't . . . ?' I tried in vain to think of a tactful way to phrase it.

'No one knows what happened,' Katrina said quickly. 'Back then, all the Sixth Formers used the clock tower as their place for, you know. So it wasn't weird for her to be up there.'

'But it *was* weird for her to be standing out on the window ledge,' Lila said. 'No one's ever been able to explain that.'

Penny looked pale and shaky. 'What if Caitlin really did see someone up there? What if it was a ghost, or . . . ?'

'No, Pen,' Lila said firmly. 'There are no ghosts. And the tower has been locked for five years. No one can get up there and no one would try. Least of all Stella.'

'If there are no ghosts, how come the clock stopped at the exact moment Siena died?' Penny persisted.

'Remember what you learned on your enlightenment retreat,' Lila said. 'There's a rational explanation about the clock, and Caitlin made a mistake.'

Mary-Ann valiantly tried to shift the conversation on as I tried to remember exactly what I'd seen. The light had been dim, after all. Maybe it hadn't been Stella, and, if it had been, perhaps she'd disappeared in a different direction. Surely she was too careful to jeopardize her election chances by getting in trouble.

Lila turned to me as she and Penny got up to leave. 'Whatever you imagine you saw, don't *ever* mention it to Stella.'

154

Chapter Twenty

Stella

'Stop asking me,' I tell Edward for what feels like the hundredth time. 'I'm not wearing that thing.'

We're in the art room, and I sit carefully on the floor before the conversation can take an unsteadying turn.

He won't give up. 'Stella, no way are you *allergic* to fancy dress. Tell me the truth: what do you have against rabbits?'

'I hate rabbits,' I tell him flatly. 'Go and find us different costumes, and maybe I'll consider it.'

Edward mumbles under his breath a theory about rabbits being inoffensive creatures, as well as the one true Christian symbol of Easter.

'I'm starting to wonder if you're taking this campaign seriously,' he says more audibly. 'Are you going to be obstructive every step of the way?'

'Katrina's my manager,' I say. 'Go and speak to her.'

He laughs. 'Do you think Katrina would advise her candidate to turn down *any* opportunity for publicity?'

'Fine,' I say, losing my patience. 'Get someone else to do it with you. Your faces won't be visible anyway.'

He looks at me in exasperation and leaves.

*

It was hoped that Siena would outgrow her rabbit fixation before our garden was overrun with them, and that her ambition of creating a myxomatosis vaccine would remain unrealized. It's no surprise that rabbits featured prominently in her election campaign, but it strikes me as ironic that her chosen symbol of new life should have featured equally prominently at an event that was anything but. Although, now I think about it, people did insist on calling her funeral a *celebration of life*, which was as absurd as it sounds.

I spent the nights following Siena's death sitting on Syrena's windowsill, training myself to be apart from her as if I could stretch and warp the thread that bound us. In moments of weakness I climbed into Syrena's bed and placed my hand on the sheet to feel the miraculous rise and fall of her baby chest; closed my eyes and imagined a breathing, living sister on each side of me. Syrena's hair streamed across the pillow, and, remembering what Siena had told me on the beach, I wove it into my own so tightly that I couldn't see where she ended and I began; so that I felt every movement she made as if it were my own; so that we were entwined as one sister in a perennial golden braid.

During daylight hours, Syrena behaved as if nothing had happened. She picked daisies; she sang tunelessly to herself; she baked inedible cookies with Paula. The only concession she made to Siena's memory was to resurrect the stuffed white rabbit with enormous teeth that Siena had made for her as a school project.

Siena was supposed to be good at Textiles, but I think she'd miscalculated the pattern, as the rabbit's neck was disproportionately long. Syrena had compounded this deformity by winding it around the handlebars of her bike and sometimes tying it in a knot. Part of Siena's brief had been to equip the rabbit with red LEDs for eyes, a feature that made it look demonic, especially when it was pressed unexpectedly against one's face in the middle of the night. It was also, for reasons that were never clear, missing its left hind foot. The very sight of it made me shudder and I'd been relieved when, after years of dragging it across a variety of terrains, twisting its neck grotesquely around the swing cord and augmenting its features with lipstick and bronzer, Syrena had finally taken up with a Skipper doll instead. Now it was back with a vengeance.

Seraphina hadn't wanted Syrena to attend the funeral, but for once she was overruled by Paula, who forced Syrena's resisting elbows and knees into black velveteen and gave her a handbag that held nothing but tissues. Syrena swung it around her head and hit the cat, which swiped at her idly, and when Paula had brushed her hair she tipped her head upside down to mess it up before zooming around the room and scuffing her patent shoes on the skirting board.

'She needs closure,' Paula told me after watching

an *Oprah* bereavement special. I looked at her with trepidation.

The church was full of people I'd never seen before, but I looked only at the floor as I held my breath to avoid the overpowering scent of lilies and led Syrena into our pew. Seraphina stared straight ahead and I edged away from her unnaturally sweet smell towards Syrena's baby softness. I kept my eyes averted from the coffin, but I didn't need to, because, even though I don't remember crying, something made me blind.

Syrena stayed motionless during the service, impassive and impeccably behaved even as the eulogy spoke of our *overwhelming and unimaginable loss*, but as the coffin disappeared from view she climbed onto her seat and started to scream. I reached out for her, but everything was distorted. The coffin zoomed into painful close-up and I looked at the ceiling, only to duck at the sight of the stone angels in the eaves that seemed to swoop towards me. I clutched at my wooden seat to remind myself that I sat on something solid, but it shifted away. Then, as if in slow motion, I saw a girl falling from above, and I lost my balance.

As the stone floor rose to meet me I was aware of two things: the sigh with which Seraphina said *What did I tell you?* and the rabbit's expensively painted face.

'Stella,' comes a voice from somewhere, and I realize that my eyes are closed. It's Luke.

'What are you doing?' he asks as I realize how

strange I must look hunched on the floor with my head on my knees.

'Pilates,' I tell him, pretending to stretch.

'We should talk,' he blurts out. I nod stoically as he takes a deep breath and begins at high speed.

'You haven't spoken to me since Valentine's Day and I have to know what's going on. Was it – was it my fault?'

'Of course not!' I push rabbit images to the back of my mind because I hate to see him in this kind of distress. 'Please don't think that.'

He shakes his head. 'I wish none of it had ever happened. I thought it was what we both wanted, and I can't understand how I got it so wrong.'

We talk about the way we felt that night, and the way sex takes on a life of its own and makes everyone feel abnormal if they're not doing it, and abnormal if they are. I'm surprised by his understanding, and the idea that maybe boys and girls aren't so different after all, but it doesn't change anything. Luke and I can only be together for as long as we can skirt around this issue, and the most I can hope for is that we can do this until the election is over.

'So what now?' I ask.

'We have to stick together,' he says softly. 'The next few months aren't going to be easy, and we can't let anything get between us. Don't shut me out.'

He pauses as we leave the art block and head back to the main school. 'I wish I'd talked to you sooner.

159

But I didn't know how to, and Caitlin said I should give you space, so . . .'

'What?' I interrupt. 'You talked to *Caitlin* about this?'

He looks alarmed. 'Well, only because we were in the library together . . . no, not really.'

What's her game? I suddenly wonder as I remember our conversation after Valentine's night.

He reaches for my hand. 'What do you feel like doing? Making popcorn and watching a film with the others?'

Last term, when the election seemed a long way hence, it seemed acceptable to while away time with the Stars and Stripes and believe it would always be possible to have Luke near me with no regard for the future; to ignore nagging memories of a night when a falling girl had changed the course of my life in unfathomable ways. But as Elevation night approaches at speed and nothing is as it should be, his suggestion seems out of place.

Without replying, I steer him into the Common Room.

And there is Caitlin. She and Edward are on my sofa, and, although it seems petty to say so, she must *know* it's mine. She's the life and soul of the party rather than the little mouse she was, and Luke's comment has made me doubt the wisdom of making her a full-blown Star so quickly. She looks different too; she's changed her wardrobe so she looks more like me, and it makes her a bit too pretty. I'm not used to playing second fiddle, and the worst thing is not being able to find it in myself to retaliate.

The Stripes discuss which of them has the best chance with the new Spanish assistant (Henry, because she winked at him when he mastered *el subjunctivo*), who got caught looking through the girls' changing room window (not Luke, thankfully), and who's having the most luck with the Fifth Formers (all of them). I hardly listen, because it's impossible to forget that Caitlin's there. Why did I think *my* Stars needed another girl? I might as well have introduced Ebola.

Finally I get up, shake my head when Luke asks if he should come with me, and barely look at him as he kisses me goodnight. So much for not shutting him out.

In my room I'm trapped with the time of day I dread; when there's no one to distract me. I undress in the dark and pull my hair tightly out of my eyes, winding it around my hand.

I'm floating in limbo, facing an uncertain future as my days here ebb away. Everything – friends, enemies, academic work – is spiralling away from me. The thought of not winning the election never crossed my mind until recently, but, now everyone's watching and assessing their own chances, I have to acknowledge that victory is no longer guaranteed. Then again, perhaps it never was.

Chapter Twenty-one

Caitlin

In the bathroom, I tugged at my hair with my harshest comb. I hadn't seen Stella and Luke together in so long that I'd started to imagine it was only a matter of time before Luke forgot her and started to look elsewhere. At me, specifically. Yet tonight he'd appeared with his arm around her as if she'd never broken his heart. Now we were in parallel cliques we spent plenty of time together, but as soon as Stella stepped back into the room it was as if no one else existed.

Eventually I knocked on Lucy's door, hoping she'd be able to distract me from my thoughts. At least she knew how it felt when Stella monopolized everyone's attention.

Music was playing, and when I walked in I saw she was having a mini-party with Hannah and Caroline. Ruby was there too, smoking melancholically out of the window. These days I hardly ever saw her in the Common Room or cafeteria, and tonight she appeared more miserable than ever. She was very thin, her shoulder blades sharp against the straps of her black nightdress and her green eyes dark in her pale face. She looked haunted, as if she were literally pining for her friends.

'Hey, Caitlin,' Lucy said excitedly. 'Come in!'

I waved at everyone, giving Ruby a sheepish smile as I perched on the bed, and worrying as I always did about how she'd react to me stealing her spot in the Stars. So far she'd done nothing worse than stare at me, so probably Ally had made me paranoid.

Then I did a double-take when I noticed a bulge in the curtain and some brown legs and studded heels sticking out underneath it. Ruby twitched it, smiling for the first time, and Katrina appeared.

'Were you hiding from me?' I asked her in confusion.

'Not exactly,' she admitted. 'You can't be too careful . . . you know Ruby's not exactly flavour of the month. No one would ever think of looking for us in *Lucy's* room, of all places.'

Her tone was superior, even though Lucy was helping them out.

'So you're hiding from Stella?' I asked.

A terrible silence filled the room and Katrina looked quickly around as though Stella could see through walls.

'Did you hear the news?' Lucy finally asked. I noticed that, as well as wearing my dress, she'd curled her hair in the same way I'd started wearing mine.

'It was such a great idea to convince Lucy to compete in the election, Caitlin,' said Hannah. 'We've been trying to persuade her for ages. Imagine if she won!'

'I didn't convince her,' I said quickly. 'I mean . . . this was totally Lucy's decision. Not mine. I just think everyone should be able to do what they want.'

'And now they can,' Lucy said happily. 'I'm so glad I met you, Caitlin.'

Katrina sat next to me; she appeared to be listening hard. 'Everyone should be able to do what they want,' she repeated quietly.

I was silent as they all chattered about the campaign; who would be Lucy's manager and what colour posters they'd have. It had seemed so natural to encourage her to stand up for herself, but now I felt stupid for not considering the implications. What if Stella found out?

After a few minutes I made an excuse about having homework to finish, but, as I was leaving, Ruby jumped up and hugged me. 'I feel so much better,' she said. 'You've made impossible things seem possible.'

'I didn't do anything, really,' I stammered, torn between relief at Ruby's good nature and panic at having unwittingly caused this degree of independent thinking in her.

I backed awkwardly out of the door, almost colliding with Stella as she left the bathroom opposite.

She baulked at my dorky polka-dot pyjamas. 'Comparing fashion notes with Lucy?'

I hoped she couldn't hear the voices in Lucy's room. I edged forward, tugging the door shut behind me. My heart was pounding.

Stella was looking at me hard. 'No one should forget whose team they're on, *or* who picked them for it. Do you agree?'

I nodded mutely, but right then Lucy's door

swung open to reveal Ruby.

'Caitlin, you forgot your comb . . .' she began before her voice died away. She hurriedly shut the door behind her as Katrina's distinctive giggle rang out, and stood protectively in front of me.

'Caitlin didn't know I was in there, Stella,' she said steadily. 'She wasn't breaking any statutes.'

She squeezed my arm imperceptibly as she walked past us both. Once she'd gone, Stella turned back to me and I realized she was still waiting on an answer to her question.

I thought of the fun I'd had horseback riding with Lila and Penny the day before. I thought of the upcoming mixer with a nearby school that none of the Stars could stop talking about. I thought of the way my life would be without Stella to spend every possible moment with, even if we were just lounging in someone's bedroom or doing homework.

And I thought of Lucy's sadness as she talked about the Stars; of Ruby, tear-streaked and shaking as she tried, and failed, to navigate life without them, like a broken bird pushed from its nest. It would be suicide to put myself in the same vulnerable position.

'I definitely agree,' I said.

Stella looked – did I imagine this? – relieved. 'Good. Because I'd hate to think what would happen if you didn't.'

She walked into her room, slamming the door so hard that I felt the vibration in my feet.

165

Chapter Twenty-two

Stella

I force myself to go to breakfast and pick up an apple. Katrina and Caitlin are missing, but the other Stars are in their places when I arrive.

'You won't believe what I saw last night,' I begin, sawing into my fifty-three calories with a plastic knife.

Before I can share the news about Caitlin's worrying – not to mention ungrateful and disrespectful – conflict of loyalties, she and Katrina enter the cafeteria. They're heading for our table when Edward calls them over and pulls Caitlin onto his lap. As he wraps his arms tightly around her, Katrina takes the seat next to Luke and starts drinking his coffee. Before I can even take this in, Ruby has joined them. It's the first time in weeks I've seen her in here, and, although she still looks scared, I sense that something – or someone – has given her the confidence to do this.

'What's going on over there?' I ask in outrage.

Mary-Ann, rubbing pencil dust off her cream trousers as she abandons a giant Venn diagram, doesn't seem surprised. 'I don't know, exactly. But don't let your pride get the better of you.'

'Why do you say that?'

'Caitlin's been getting quite friendly with Luke

recently, and you don't want him confiding in her instead of you. I know things aren't great between you two right now.'

'What are they talking about?' I ask, trying to see what Luke and Caitlin are staring at.

Lila cuts in, taking a break from the essay she's drafting for Penny. 'It's totally boring, Stella. You'd hate it!'

Mary-Ann looks impatient. 'It's Luke's TB research project. He's just won a grant to join a team at Columbia over the summer. He's really excited about it.'

Lila wrinkles her nose. 'Stella, you're lucky that Luke hasn't bored you with it. If only he had the same respect for us. How have you managed to avoid it?'

I dredge from my memory a conversation Luke and I had last week. *I know you hate science, so I'll explain it fast,* he said. *Twenty seconds, and then you can finish telling me why your new shampoo has revolutionary properties.*

Why didn't I listen to him? If I had, maybe he wouldn't have talked to Caitlin instead. I glare at her as something even worse occurs to me. What if she's not faking interest because she has a crush on Luke; what if she's showing *actual* interest? Of course he'd prefer someone to listen voluntarily than force information into them. I'm practically giving him to her.

'Columbia's in New York,' I say suddenly. 'Does Caitlin have something to do with this?'

Mary-Ann is looking at me as if I'm mentally defective. 'Sometimes I wonder what your head is filled with,' she says. 'Caitlin's mum is head of this project. Caitlin told Luke about the grant and helped him apply.'

I'm not equipped to deal with bad news. I'm using up all my energy pretending to eat my side dish of Cheerios whilst willing them to dissolve magically into the milk. I stir it furiously, slopping some over the side, and then push it away, frustrated and disgusted.

'Edward and Caitlin are a really cute couple,' Lila muses. Penny puts an arm around her as she starts to check over the essay, and, with their heads close enough to mingle Penny's blonde and Lila's dark curls, they look like negatives of each other. 'He's so mature and romantic with her. Who'd have thought *she'd* be the girl to help him get over you?'

I try to interrupt, but she cuts me off. 'Yes, I know it was a mutual break-up. Whatever. Are you ever going to tell us what really happened? We all thought you'd be together forever.'

'Edward and I had a conflict of interests,' I tell her as I think back to that lakeside party where we broke up.

'Here?' I'd asked him, looking dubiously at the picnic blanket he'd laid in a patch of undergrowth. I could still hear the chants of the other Stripes as they encouraged Quentin to set his trousers on fire, and I was worried about stinging nettles.

He was trying to open a bottle of beer with his teeth. 'What's wrong with here, Hamilton? I thought this was going to be the night I finally stopped begging you.'

I nodded as he pulled an impatient face. 'I promised you, didn't I?'

He spat out the bottle cap and took a swig before kissing me. 'So are you going to tell me why it had to be tonight?'

'I wanted to wait until the end of GCSEs, as Siena did,' I explained.

'Stella, Stella.' Edward sighed as if I were ten years old. 'Is that seriously the reason we've been waiting? I could have told you ages ago that Siena and Jack didn't do anything else from the Fourth Form onwards. Why do you think their song was "The Bad Touch"?'

He launched into his favourite verse from the song.

'It wasn't!' I protested. 'Siena told me it was "Flying Without Wings".'

He convulsed with laughter as I stared at the hole in the threadbare blanket and began to reconsider.

I thought of that moment months later when Luke told me that our song was the conceptually conflicting 'God Only Knows'. And I wondered if, despite my best efforts to conform, Siena and I were insurmountably different.

'What's Ruby doing for Easter?' Penny asks. 'I presume she's not staying here?'

'I don't know,' Lila says without much interest. 'Although I hear Coventry's nice this time of year.'

Our Easter holiday is so short that most Sixth Formers don't bother going home. It's actually considered unwise to leave because hierarchies can change so much during one's absence. You might leave a major player and return an unknown, and it's not worth the risk, especially during an election campaign.

Penny is staring so hard at the Stripes' table that she's smeared Nutella on her nose without noticing. The very fact that she's eating chocolate suggests severe disturbance to her mental state.

'Aren't you going to do something about Ruby?' she asks in outrage. 'You haven't given us the go-ahead to speak to her, have you? Why are Katrina and Caitlin allowed to be friends with her *and* us? What happened to loyalty?'

I'm glad when Mary-Ann cuts in. 'You can't expect Ruby to sit on her own until we speak to her again!'

Penny turns her attention from this ethical dilemma to Caroline, Hannah and Lucy, who have also crowded around the Stripes' table.

'Look at them all! Stealing *our* Stripes! I don't like it, Stella, and I want to know what you plan to do about it.'

I stare past her to the window, but for once my reflection is exactly no help. In fact, I look even more bewildered than I feel.

I'd planned to cut English, but decide in the circumstances to attend. By the time I arrive, Caitlin is in my seat.

'Excuse me,' I say, slamming my books down.

She looks shocked, but doesn't move. 'We just chose our partners for the vacation project,' she explains. 'You weren't here, so Katrina asked me to work with her.'

'I'm here now,' I snap, resisting the temptation to tell her that the correct word is *holiday*.

'We've already started,' she says timidly, gesturing at the books they've spread across the desk.

Jamie looks up. I smile in relief as he walks to the front row and pulls out Caitlin's usual seat between Hannah and Lucy. 'Into your seat now, Stella, and stop gossiping.'

'But Sir,' I say, wondering if he actually expects me to sit there, 'I'm going to—'

'*Seat*, Stella,' he says, lifting the chair and letting it fall.

Penny and Lila stare in indignation, but several nearby civilians smirk. To ensure they know how unwise this is, I swing my bag so that Caitlin's pencil tin smashes to the floor. She looks humiliated as she leaves her seat and bends down to collect her pens, but Edward bounds across the room to help, ignoring Jamie's annoyance and even kissing the tip of her nose.

171

He glares at me when he straightens up. 'Do you have to be so horrible?' he mutters.

I ignore him and sit down firmly next to Katrina. Caitlin looks at me for a moment in disbelief before walking slowly to the front of the room. Lucy grabs her hand under the table as she sits down, while Jamie shakes his head at me.

'Why don't you want us to sit together?' I hiss at Katrina when she's gone.

She shrugs. 'You heard Caitlin – you weren't here. *Again.*'

Jamie shoots us a warning glance and I continue by writing on my notepad. *What are you thinking, being friends with* <u>Ruby</u>? *That's not what we agreed!*

She looks at me loftily and then speaks out loud as everyone turns to stare. 'I'm capable of choosing my own friends, especially as you've barely spoken to me since kick-off. You don't need to do it for me anymore.'

I try to leave English without speaking to anyone, but Edward catches my arm and leads me to a window seat in the corridor.

'I don't want a lecture,' I tell him.

'This isn't going to be one,' he says, his voice uncharacteristically soft. I start to feel panic: this tone always means bad news, and I mentally run through the possibilities. But when he speaks, it's something I've never considered.

'We can't run in the election together,' he says.

I sit completely still, waiting to hear that he's joking.

'Stella, did you hear me?' he says gently. 'It just isn't working.'

I place my hand on the wall. 'Is this because of what I did to Caitlin? Because I can tell her I'm sorry if I have to. I'll even buy her a new pencil case.'

He sighs. 'No, although it proves that we can't work together anymore. We have to move on.'

'You *promised*,' I say. 'When we broke up, you promised me we'd still run together.'

'And once you promised me that we'd never break up,' he says wryly. 'Things change.'

'This has been planned for years,' I say. 'It's been planned since . . .' I try to say the word *Siena*, but as usual it sticks in my throat.

'People are supporting us as a team,' I argue instead. 'They won't buy into us separately.'

'We're already separate,' he says. 'You and I can't be a team with Luke standing between us.'

'But you know why I have to win,' I whisper. 'You know what this means to me.'

'But Stella, it means a lot to me too.'

I worry that I'm going to cry, and I distract myself by playing with my hair, repeatedly braiding it and combing it out.

'Is there anything I can do to change your mind?' I ask finally.

He lowers his voice as a group of Removes walks

past. 'You could break up with Luke.'

I let go of my hair.

'You barely speak to him anyway,' he says. 'And a break-up would be a good campaign tactic to keep everyone guessing. Penny's favourite celebrities do this stuff all the time.'

'Luke isn't a campaign tactic,' I say flatly. 'He doesn't even want to be in this election. I don't want to break up with him, Edward. Not even for this.'

'And I don't want to be a third wheel,' he says. 'It's demeaning. I know Luke doesn't want to compete, but he'll step up to replace me if he has to.'

I stare at him furiously. 'You asked him to replace you before you told me?'

'Of course.' He sounds surprised. 'I wasn't sure he'd agree, and I didn't want you to be left on your own.'

'Who else have you told?' My voice is raised in annoyance and he puts a finger on my lips.

'No one else yet. And I won't announce it until our new teams are official.'

I consider who his replacement running partner will be and allow myself a brief moment of relief that there are no other girls in our year popular enough to compete with me. The relief quickly subsides, because the thought of him running alongside anyone else, no matter how poorly dressed they are, feels like a violation.

'Why can't we carry on as things are?' I ask.

'You know why. And you and Luke aren't the only problem.'

'Caitlin?' I ask bitterly.

'She's a consideration,' he concedes. 'If I feel awkward about our three-way, I'm sure she does too. But there's also Katrina. Have you stopped to wonder whose side she's on these days?'

'There's no issue with Katrina,' I say, sounding defensive because I'm not at all sure of my ground. 'She's on my side and she always will be.'

He half-smiles. 'A few months ago, that's what I'd have said about you.'

'Don't do this,' I say, trying not to sound desperate. 'This isn't how it's supposed to be. How can I run without you?'

I reach out, but he snatches away his hand before I can touch him. '*No,*' he tells himself as if he's an alcoholic wavering before a glass of wine.

Staring fixedly at the curtains behind me, he starts to tell me that I should learn to accept change and that it's not good for me always to get what I want. I can't listen, so I climb unsteadily down from the window seat and walk away.

Chapter Twenty-three

Caitlin

On the last day of the semester, I woke in the dark with the realization that someone was sitting on my bed. Before I could scream, something soft was pressed over my mouth.

'Keep quiet!' they hissed.

I shot out my hand and switched on my lamp. As I blinked furiously, the figure came into focus and I sat upright in horror.

'What are you doing in here?' I stared, wondering if I were dreaming. 'Do you have any idea how much trouble you could get us into?'

Edward leaned forward and kissed me. 'Why do you think I was trying to keep you quiet? Nice outfit, by the way. You must have been expecting me.'

I crossed my arms, trying to hide my babydoll nightdress. 'Never mind me. What the hell are *you* wearing?'

Edward stood up and spun around, his arms outstretched. He was dressed in a rabbit costume, complete with fluffy tail, long floppy ears and a plastic nose with whiskers sticking out. His hands, that he'd tried to gag me with, were furry paws.

'I'm the Easter bunny. Do you like it?'

'You've broken into my room at –' I grabbed my alarm clock and waved it at him – 'five a.m. dressed as the Easter bunny, when you know we're allowed to sleep late today. What am I supposed to say?'

He pulled me out of bed and held an identical costume against me. 'You don't have to say anything. You just have to put this on and follow me.'

'And if I don't?'

'If you don't, I'll have to tell Mrs Denbigh that you ordered me for the night in my professional capacity as a bunny strip-o-gram. And I don't think she'll be very pleased with you.'

'Fine.' I grabbed the costume from him and pulled it on over my nightdress. 'But I think you're crazy. And I really don't want any more punishments this semester.'

'You won't,' he said. 'There's no rule against being a bunny – I've checked.'

'That doesn't fill me with confidence,' I said grimly. 'You couldn't see any rule against dyeing the swimming pool red as part of your Plagues of Egypt re-enactments either.'

He put his arm around me as I stumbled down the stairs. 'You don't want to deny me my one good deed of the year, do you?'

As he led me outside, I immediately tripped over something lying on the path and looked down to see a huge sack. 'What is this?'

'Surely you know what an Easter egg hunt is,' he

said. 'Or are you New Yorkers too sophisticated for such things?'

'Of course not!' In fact, I made Charlie an Easter egg hunt every year, even though I always ended up eating more candy than he did. 'It's just hard to take you seriously right now.'

'You don't find bunnies sexy?' He wiggled his tail. 'I think you make a sexy bunny.'

'No comment.' I ran ahead as he hefted the sack over his shoulder, leaving him to follow me on his fake fluffy feet.

When we'd finished, the entire quad was covered in chocolate eggs and my mood had improved.

'The Shells are going to love it,' I said, proud of our handiwork. I pulled off my bunny hood and nose, and then reached over to work on Edward's. 'But why didn't you ask me about this earlier? Was this costume meant for someone else?'

He gave me a look that I knew only too well. 'Do you have to ask?'

I glanced down at my ridiculous outfit. 'You seriously thought that Stella would agree to dress as a bunny?'

He nodded. 'Yes, of course. As did our siblings before us. But Stella has a strange aversion to rabbits, so I was left to continue the tradition solo. You've been an excellent replacement.'

'I'm glad I could be of service,' I snapped.

I shouldn't have been surprised, but it was still galling to have been drafted in to fulfil a task Stella considered beneath her. She'd barely spoken to me since the incident in English class and I got a horrible feeling in the pit of my stomach every time I thought of her being mad with me.

He ignored me, reaching into the pocket of his costume for a card. 'This is the very first invitation to my Easter party. You aren't *really* going back to New York today, are you?'

I had a calendar next to my bed that Charlie had made me. It was a countdown to the vacation so I could cross off the days until I'd see him again. He'd even pasted a little picture of himself next to the last day and written *Welcome home, Caity!* in his square print letters. I had a heap of presents that Edward had helped me choose for him and I'd already planned the stuff we'd do together.

'I'm all packed,' I reminded him. 'You said you'd drive me to the airport this morning. You know how much I want to see Charlie.'

Edward was looking upwards, and I followed his gaze to the windows in Meadows. Grinning, he put his fingers in his mouth and emitted a loud whistle.

'What are you doing?' I said in panic. 'No one can see me like this!'

He whistled again as the windows started to open. 'Good morning, children!' he yelled to the tousle-haired Shells and Removes staring out at us from their dormitories.

They pointed in confusion for a moment. 'It's Edward

and Caitlin!' someone shouted, jumping up and down in excitement.

'Now what?' I said uneasily as they disappeared from the window.

Edward counted down under his breath. 'Five . . . four . . . three . . .'

The door swung open and a swarm of kids surged into the quad. They pushed and shoved as they picked up Easter eggs, the littlest girls sometimes breaking ranks to hug us.

'We love you, Caitlin,' they said sincerely, exactly as I'd watched them say to Stella at kick-off. 'You're our favourite Star!'

'Why are they so excited?' I murmured, watching the hysteria. 'Have they never seen candy before?'

Edward smiled. 'Did I forget to tell you about the jackpot?'

His voice was drowned out by a red-haired girl crawling out from the rosebushes. Her slippers fell off as she jumped up and down in delight. 'I've got the golden egg!'

'What's she got?' I craned to see her crack open the plastic egg to reveal bank notes. My mouth fell open in shock. 'How much did this cost you?'

Edward sounded casual. 'It's just a little incentive.'

Just then Miss Finch appeared and started to herd the students back inside. 'I thought we agreed there would be no cash,' she snapped.

Edward smiled ruefully, as if it were beyond his

control. Miss Finch tried to keep the students away from us, but it seemed that every single one stopped to hug me.

'I assume I can count on your vote next term?' Edward said over and over again as he shook each of them by the hand.

When they'd gone, he turned back to me. 'So you'll stay here? My party is today.'

I thought again of Charlie, who usually had a ton of play dates and school activities scheduled for the vacation; of my mom, who was giving a paper at Duke instead of meeting me at JFK. And I thought of the Shells, who might have found a new favourite Star by the time I returned.

'Are the other Stars going to your party?' I asked.

He looked at me as if I'd said something really stupid. 'Everyone's going.'

He held my hand. 'I'll walk you back to Woodlands and you can tell your mum you've changed your mind.'

Chapter Twenty-four

Stella

Luke is planning to drive me to Edward's party, which lasts an entire day and night and is the highlight of most people's Easter break, but as I head outside to wait for him I see another familiar car.

'What are you doing here?' I ask Paula as I open the passenger door of her battered Corsa. 'Is something wrong with Syrena?'

She looks resigned to managing the timetable of a family who are unable to communicate directly. 'Your mother told me that, as you won't pick up your phone, she sent your invitation in the post.'

I think of the overflowing pigeonhole that Mary-Ann empties for me every week. 'What invitation?'

'It's Syrena's birthday,' she reminds me. 'You're all going out for lunch.'

I look at my watch. Luke might possess saint-like patience but he must have a limit somewhere. I half-dial his number and then cancel the call, unable to face letting him down yet again. I'll deal with him later. And at least Caitlin will be safely trapped in New York.

Although Seraphina isn't keen on birthdays, I'm only half-surprised about this invitation. She isn't good with children, so a day celebrating with Syrena – or worse, Syrena's friends – must be a terrifying prospect.

They are sitting out on the restaurant terrace when I arrive, which is less about waiting to greet me than giving Seraphina quality time with her Gauloises. She looks the same as ever – icy, blonde and sort of metallic in her white Chanel suit and stilettos. She stands and air-kisses me four times before looking me carefully up and down for signs of body fat. The restaurant, which is French haute cuisine, may not have been Syrena's choice.

I'm braced for Syrena to launch herself at me as she always does, a tangle of gazelle limbs and yellow hair, but she remains in her chair with her legs decorously crossed, stirring a glass of elderflower. For a second I think I see her take a drag of the lit cigarette Seraphina has balanced in the ashtray, but, as she bats the smoke away, that seems absurd.

'Happy birthday,' I say, kissing her on the head before she can stand up and show that we're the same height.

Syrena's childish grin has evolved into something harder to define, but she kisses me back, smudging her lip gloss. It's only four months since I last saw her, but she's changed tangibly. The last of her baby fat has been subsumed into her growth spurt, and her cheeks, once soft and roundly pink, have hollowed out. I feel an unexpected pang for the child who set off fireworks in the summer house so she could enjoy them at close range, who mistook wallpaper paste for porridge and spent a week in intensive care, and who amused herself one rainy afternoon by industriously shaving her guinea pig.

Seraphina leads the way inside. 'Hamilton,' she announces to the maître d'.

'Mrs Hamilton,' he murmurs as he searches his pad for her booking.

Beside me, Syrena winces.

'*Miss* Hamilton.' Seraphina's voice is glacial.

The maître d' looks as though he might collapse under the weight of his error as Seraphina follows him through the crowded space towards our table. I listen to the hypnotic click of her heels on marble before registering that they echo not only in symphony with my own, but with someone behind me. Turning, I look at Syrena's feet for the first time.

'Are those my shoes?' I ask in surprise as I take in her studded Louboutins.

She nods. 'Although, if I keep growing, your shoes won't fit me anymore and I'll have to switch to Siena's.'

'You're supposed to grow,' I tell her. 'You're twelve years old, and you're lucky that you're going to be tall.'

'I want to be little like you,' she says.

I remember standing on tiptoes each birthday as Siena measured me against the kitchen door frame.

I want to be tall like you, I'd tell her enviously as each year showed me further and further behind her at the same age.

You're lucky to be petite, I hear her reply. I wish I could tell her that I'm still a good six inches off that final, seventeen-year-old mark.

Syrena is a dancer who skips and twirls barefoot, and even in shoes has always been unfettered and unself-conscious. Sometimes she moves instead of speaking, as if it's easier for her to communicate that way.

Now my shoes hobble her like clamps, rooting her to the floor.

'Take them off,' I suggest as she struggles to keep pace with me. 'They're bad for your posture.'

Seraphina turns and stares as if I'm mad. 'Are you suggesting she goes barefoot?'

'She should always be barefoot,' I say.

I hang back at the table so that Syrena takes the place beside Seraphina and leaves me to sit opposite them. Sometimes I want to reach out for Syrena so badly that I have to sit on my hands to stop myself. I have an idea that, once I yield, I won't ever know how to let her go.

'Is that my dress too?' I ask her as the maître d' takes her coat.

She's wearing the red silk Dior that I wore to Winterval last year. It hasn't needed much altering, and the effect unnerves me.

'You're wearing Siena's dress,' she correctly observes.

Seraphina looks impatient as she takes in these facts. 'You both own the entire Moschino spring–summer collection, yet you persist in wearing hand-me-downs?'

The champagne arrives immediately and a waiter stumblingly tries to address the atmosphere by telling Seraphina it will be free.

'*Mrs Hamilton*,' Seraphina mutters in disbelief as he staggers away with her alimony-funded mink. She stares at her sapphire engagement ring. 'As if I kept anything of that man's.'

When I slide Syrena's champagne glass away from her, Seraphina glares as if I'm ruining her party. 'It's Syrena's birthday,' she snaps.

'Syrena's *twelfth* birthday,' I point out, 'shouldn't be the first time she gets drunk.'

'It won't be,' Syrena reassures me as she takes it back.

I pick up my own flute, drinking at speed with some idea of keeping alcohol away from her. This doesn't work, and Seraphina, having kept pace with me, looks disappointed as she finishes the bottle to discover that no waiters are in range.

Sitting back in her chair, she allows Syrena to rest her head against her shoulder as she absentmindedly combs her fingers through Syrena's hair. As usual it tumbles to her waist but Seraphina brings it under control, pulling curling strands away from her face. This level of attention is unprecedented: I haven't seen her so occupied with one of us for years. Something about Syrena today has reanimated her and restored her to the present.

'That reminds me,' Seraphina says as she reaches for her tote with her free hand. 'Your gift, Syrena.'

Syrena produces a present from her own matching Balenciaga bag. 'Can I open this one first?' she asks me.

Although she'll thank me in September, Syrena is currently underwhelmed by the Temperley High inventory I've ordered for her. I'm momentarily relieved that I appear to have bought her something else, and I lean over to see what it is.

'Where did you find that?' I ask, staring at the red tissue paper with her name printed on it in my handwriting.

'It was in your room,' she says. 'It's addressed to me!'

'It is for you,' I say slowly as she rips it open. 'I'd forgotten all about it.'

She uncovers the battered copy of *Ballet Shoes* that Siena gave me on my own twelfth birthday with instructions to impart. At some point I rewrapped and addressed it ready for Syrena, and then managed to put it out of my mind.

Now I see Siena's familiar, forgotten inscription inside the cover.

'*If you ever wonder which of the Hamilton sisters you'd choose to be . . .*' Syrena reads.

'*One day you'll see,*' we say in unison. We look at each other, but we're thinking of someone else.

Seraphina hands Syrena a silver package that I know Paula has wrapped for her. Childish for a second, she rips it open and gasps at the sight of the sharp-toothed, sapphire-embellished comb that glints under the lights.

'Is it mine?' she asks incredulously.

Seraphina twists her fingers into Syrena's hair until it's an aureate rope. She picks up the comb, pushing its teeth deep and fixing yards of spun gold into an elegant chignon. Syrena takes a mirror from her own handbag and studies herself, restraining the pleasure I know she feels at this attention. She moves her head back and forth, examining her hair, her face and her slender, elegant neck.

'Well?' she asks. 'Am I pretty?'

Seraphina inclines her head away from me and kisses Syrena's cheek before whispering into her ear. Syrena sits up straight and looks past me with an expression I recognize. As she lowers her head and looks upwards through her long eyelashes, I notice that she's wearing mascara.

She smiles, and moments later an ice bucket is in front of us.

'Who ordered that?' I ask the waiter, who blushes and gestures awkwardly behind me. Turning, I see a middle-aged man sitting directly in Syrena's eye line. He smiles, and I glare at him until he lowers his gaze.

'Don't think you're having any,' I warn Syrena as the waiter pops the cork.

'It's Dom.' She sounds disdainful. 'I prefer Cristal.'

As Seraphina laughs delightedly I reach for my handbag, walking the length of the restaurant to the balcony doors. Seraphina follows me, but I stand with my back to her, leaning over the balcony to stare at Notting Hill in the springtime. Then I draw back as the height makes my palms sweat.

Chapter Twenty-five

Caitlin

I drummed my fingernails on the window ledge as I waited for Mom to pick up the phone. I hadn't spoken to her in weeks and was half-hoping I could leave my news via answerphone, but she answered just as I was about to hang up.

'You should be glad I'm making new friends!' I said before she could argue with me. 'Isn't that why you forced me to come here?'

'I thought you wanted to come home for your vacation,' she said. 'You were so excited to see Charlie. Please don't punish him because you're angry with me.'

'I'll see him for the summer,' I argued. 'And you'll only be working.'

She sighed. 'I've taken time off, actually. I thought the three of us could go to Nantucket for a few days.'

My resentment swelled. Why did she get to make me feel guilty? She'd pushed me out of my own home without a second thought, and now she needed a babysitter she wanted me to come back. Even though I should be happy that she was spending time with Charlie, it felt even worse to know that she'd only started to make an effort once I was in a different country. She'd been content for days to pass without seeing me when we lived in the same house.

'Say hello to him, at least,' she begged. 'He's been so looking forward to this. His teacher says you're all he talks about in school.'

Charlie's last letter, composed in purple crayon, had told me he'd *growed* a quarter of an inch and lost another tooth. He had twelve new words and wanted me to take him to the movies because Mom wouldn't let him spray cheese on popcorn.

I heard his high, babyish voice as she passed him the receiver. 'Caity? Caity? Hello?'

Suddenly I missed him so much I felt like the walls were closing in. A lump in my throat made it hard to speak, and I didn't want to try. The more contact we had, the harder it was to be apart. How could I spend the vacation with him, knowing I had to leave again?

I hung up and sat on the floor, trying to stop myself from crying. It didn't work.

'Caitlin?'

I was mortified when Luke put his head around the door, and suddenly very conscious that my cheeks were streaked with tears.

He had the decency not to comment. 'Have you seen Stella?' he asked. 'We're supposed to drive to Edward's together, but I can't find her anywhere.'

I nodded. 'I saw her leaving in a car this morning. I didn't see who with.'

'Leaving?' He scratched his head, looking baffled.

I searched for words to make him feel better, but what

could I say? 'Do you want to come in?' I managed finally.

'Aren't you flying home this morning?' he asked. 'I don't want to make you late.'

'Edward persuaded me to stay after all,' I admitted. 'I've got plenty of time if you want to talk.'

I expected him to say no, but he sank down beside me on the floor, picking up and stroking my plush rabbit. I wondered if it was acceptable to hug him.

He looked exhausted. 'Why does she do this? Why doesn't she tell me anything?'

I was still trying to figure out what to say when my phone rang. Luke looked at the display as I answered.

'Hey, Edward,' he said loudly.

'Luke?' Edward said. 'Have you kidnapped my girlfriend?'

'Luke's having a bad day,' I said, putting Edward on speaker.

'I'm about to leave,' Edward told Luke. 'Come with us. I've got a house full of beer and girls, and I'm pretty sure that none of them will be called Hamilton.'

Luke and I smiled at each other. 'Can we make a pit stop?' Luke asked Edward. 'If Caitlin's not going home to her family, she can at least drop in to see her dad.

'If that's okay with you,' he added quickly as I hung up the phone. 'You look a little unhappy and I thought that might help.'

I leaned over to kiss him on the cheek, and we both blushed. 'Stella's crazy if she can't see how perfect you are,' I said.

192

On my mall trip with Lila and Penny, I'd been so desperate for freedom that I'd wanted to open the window and gulp fresh air like a dog. New surroundings had made me giddy, like I was being released from a cage. This time was entirely different. I stared back as the majestic buildings vanished from view, thinking not of what lay ahead but only of what I might miss. I was suddenly grateful to Edward for persuading me not to leave the country.

'Is anyone at home?' Luke asked when Edward pulled up outside my house. The neighbourhood was as deserted as ever, and the memory of staying there with only my dad for company made me shudder with loneliness.

'I wanted to surprise him,' I said. 'He'll be around somewhere.'

My dad hadn't answered the phone when I'd called earlier, but I'd figured I could just show up. He sometimes visited the gym on Saturday mornings, but more often he stayed home to read the papers and catch up on his sports on TiVo.

The house had never seemed like a home, but it seemed more unfamiliar than ever when I stepped into the massive hallway.

'I didn't know your dad had a girlfriend,' Edward said conversationally.

I gritted my teeth at the huge selection of expensive-looking women's coats on the rack and the neat stack of high heels that had appeared beside the front door. 'Neither did I.'

Edward grabbed my hand as I stalked into the kitchen. Evidence of female inhabitation was everywhere, and this was a woman I'd never encountered before. My mom would never have shopped at Cath Kidston. She'd never have baked oatmeal cookies, let alone bothered to ice them with Easter chicks. She'd never have arranged a vase of spring flowers on the table. Our home in New York was more likely to be covered in research papers and books, and, if Rosa wasn't around, my dad was lucky if he got a grilled cheese sandwich before midnight. I'd once been so proud of my mom's academic accomplishments, but now I just wished she'd tried harder to keep my dad happy.

'I want to go,' I said. 'Right now.'

'Don't read into it,' Luke said quietly. 'You don't know how serious it is.'

I shook my head. 'He doesn't know I'm coming. If I go now, I can still make my flight.'

I marched back down the hallway, where I kicked the front door, hoping it would leave a mark, and outside. I sank down on the step and burst into tears, talking incoherently.

'He didn't even tell me he was dating someone. He totally has his own life now. And he pretended he was moving here for me when he was probably seeing this – this *woman* – the whole time.'

Luke sat next to me and offered me a piece of candy. 'For the shock,' he said earnestly.

At least I could smile at this. 'I thought he and my mom would get back together,' I admitted.

He nodded in sympathy. 'I thought that about my parents too. I know it hurts, Caitlin, but now I see that they're happier apart.'

'Thanks, Mrs Doubtfire,' Edward deadpanned as he sat down on my other side.

I laughed as he put his arm around me and wiped away my tears with his sleeve. 'Parents suck,' he said. 'I only see my dad about once a year, and even then he spends the whole time checking his BlackBerry. That's exactly why we need a huge blowout to take your mind off it. Don't go home!'

I leaned against him as he kissed my cheek.

'Did I tell you exactly how big this party was going to be?' he asked.

'You might have mentioned it,' I said. 'Once or twice.'

Luke sighed as he checked his phone. 'Still no message from Stella.'

'*Quelle surprise*,' Edward said drily. '*Please* forget her so we can go and have the fun we deserve.'

As we took off in Edward's car, he turned up the radio loud so we could all sing along. It was my dad's idea that I be more sociable, after all. What could be more sociable than this?

Chapter Twenty-six

Stella

There was a time when I liked to be close to my mother. Perhaps because I so rarely saw her, she fascinated me, and her lengthy dinner party preparations were an unrivalled opportunity to indulge this interest. For years I watched the dinners unfold from outside the glass dining room doors as she and Siena sat equidistant from each other and their chosen dates; as they controlled every man in the room with a gravitational pull. At neat increments across the mahogany table, they were geometric in studied indifference.

Of all the dinner parties, I remember the final one most clearly. I wouldn't start Temperley High for another few months, but Siena was expected home after her Elevation ceremony to share all the details of her inevitable victory and I was to be allowed to attend a special celebratory meal.

Siena was Seraphina's most treasured possession. For as long as I could remember she had kept her close, whispering secrets and decorating her with extravagant jewellery as if she were a trophy to be competed for and exhibited.

'Why does everyone watch you and Siena?' I asked

that afternoon as Seraphina spread a rhapsody of beauty products across her dressing table. 'Why not me?'

At twelve I knew that she never sugar-coated her comments, but I still hoped to hear that I was just as beautiful, and that my time would come.

Turning from her mirror, she surveyed me like a teacher assessing a new student. 'You're too old to look like this.'

My hair hung hazily to my waist. I'd always worn it like that, untied and unadorned, not taking account of the elaborate updos that my mother and Siena always wore, weaved and teased and threaded with gold flowers and jewels and leaves.

Seraphina started to brush my hair, winding it into a long skein and pulling loose strands away from my face. She looked so pleased that I swelled with pride. Siena was far and away her favourite, but now my face seemed to absorb her as if she were seeing it for the first time.

'Can I wear make-up?' I asked, eyeing the cosmetic feast before me.

She batted my hand away as I reached for her lipstick, swivelling me towards her. I'd watched her enough times to know to pout when lipstick was applied, to suck in my cheeks for blusher, and look upwards for mascara. She worked serenely, never smiling but occasionally nodding as she adorned me with a diamond necklace or crystal-studded tiara that she thought suited me particularly well.

'Why do you think everyone watches Siena?' she asked as she handed me a tissue.

I blotted my red lips carefully. 'I don't know,' I admitted. '*She* never looks at *them*.'

She studied me from different angles as if I were an exhibit, and then took from her jewellery box the sapphire-embellished comb that I had long coveted but never touched.

I stared at the comb and then at Seraphina. 'That's Siena's!'

She twisted my newly tethered hair around my head before securing it in the comb's sharp teeth. I moved my head back and forth to see different angles, finally jutting out my chin and elongating my neck as I'd watched Siena do so many times.

'Exactly so,' Seraphina murmured, kissing my cheek.

'How does she know they're watching if she never looks at them?' I persisted.

She turned me back to the mirror and gestured at my face. 'That's how she knows.'

Without my long hair, my face looked different. Not taking my eyes off myself, I reached for Seraphina's glass of apple juice. It tasted bitter, but, as she never made a face when she drank, I maintained an expression of perfect composure as the liquid burnt my throat.

Evening wear wasn't available in my size, but I

stood barefoot on a stool while Seraphina ripped and sliced and shaped one of Siena's beautiful cocktail gowns to fit me as well as it had fitted her.

'Don't be so pleased to see Edward,' she warned me later as I hopped impatiently on one patent shoe, anxious for him to arrive. Although his mother was resting in Geneva, he and his father would be joining us for the evening. 'You must learn to create a little distance.'

'Edward's my friend,' I objected. 'Why can't I be pleased to see him?'

She put down her hairbrush and, for the second time in a day, gave me her full attention.

'Because that won't break his heart.'

'You and Siena argued that night,' I remind Seraphina now. Instead of turning around, I watch a blackbird fly back and forth from its nest in the roof collecting straw in its beak.

'Siena was territorial,' she says after a momentary silence. 'She was protective of what was hers; I notice that you are less so.'

'The comb was hers,' I say. 'She was angry that I was wearing it. That's why you fought.'

Seraphina is guarded. 'I don't know why you think we'd argue about a comb.'

As the balcony door slams behind us, I hear our own front door on that night.

*

The table was filled with Seraphina's usual guests, many of them friends of my father. To my knowledge he'd never contacted any of us since his departure seven years earlier, hefty monthly transfers excepting, but Seraphina allowed the guests to feed her details of his whereabouts like nourishment. They competed to share information, bathing in her full attention as their reward. The candlelight made her fragile and brittle, as though she might tear under pressure like a paper doll. Her cheekbones stood out starkly and I put my hand to my own soft and rounded face for comparison.

Edward was subdued by the suit he'd been forced into and the way in which, with one eye on Seraphina's silent instructions, I sat opposite him rather than close enough for him to whisper to me and share his dessert. He ruffled his black hair and looked bemusedly at the orchids, candles and white silk streamers that formed our sterile celebration. As he fidgeted, balancing peas on his knife and making shapes with the butter, I reached for the nearest bottle of wine and filled up my glass. Not wanting to be outdone by a girl who drank Montrachet as carelessly as cordial, he poured his dad's scotch into his lemonade. Then he turned away to hide his watering eyes.

I watched the clock as eight, eight-thirty passed, and finally I knew Siena would be on her way following the nine o'clock announcement.

'She's here!' I said excitedly as the front door slammed.

I was about to jump up when Seraphina placed a warning hand on my wrist, and I kept still. *We don't chase*, she had told me. I copied her pose, reclining slightly and crossing my legs, tossing my head so that my earrings caught the light and sparked like flame.

On cue, Paula wheeled in the cake. It glittered silver across four tiers of royal icing and pearly stars, and was topped with sugar figurines of Siena and Jack dressed in their Elevation outfits. It was an exact replica of Seraphina's wedding cake.

Across the table, Edward's gaze on me was penetrating, and from that moment on I never had to check if he, or anyone else, was watching me.

Siena was laughing as she crossed the hall towards us and waited for me to run and launch myself into her arms. I wanted nothing more than to mould and mesh myself into her, but Seraphina tightened her grip on my wrist, and I sat still.

Her Elevation dress wasn't new, which had seemed to me a wasted opportunity, but rather Seraphina's own wedding dress, which she had altered for the occasion. For months I'd watched Siena stand on a stool as the dress took shape around her. Once I'd demonstrated that I could be trusted not to rub fingerprints on the fine silk, I had held handfuls of pins, passing them dutifully to Seraphina whenever she snapped her fingers, and I had sometimes helped to sew gold-plated roses to the tulle and porcelain leaves to the organza. Syrena, whose hands were always sticky, spent much of the time sleeping, dormouse-like, in gauzy nests of discarded chiffon.

That night, watching Siena in her sash and crown, iridescent in the candlelight, I understood that Seraphina's plans were coming to fruition as her eldest daughter emerged from the wings to be the most coveted prize in the room.

Jack stood at Siena's side as if she were responsible for every breath he took. But Siena was watching me.

'What have you done to Stella?' she asked Seraphina.

Seraphina crossed the room and kissed her on the cheek. 'Aren't you going to share your news with our guests?'

Siena looked from me to Jack, who watched her with his usual mix of adoration and agony. 'You should leave now,' she said.

'Okay,' he said faintly. 'When will I see you? Tomorrow?'

She didn't relent. 'We can't be together anymore, Jack.'

He was bewildered. 'But Siena, I love you.'

'I know you do,' she said. 'And that's why I can't speak to you again.'

Jack was like Edward, spiky and animated, and he held Siena's hand as he begged her to reconsider. He seemed unaware of the other guests murmuring excuses and melting away around them. At twelve I could piece together the heartbreak from my memories of Seraphina's own erstwhile shrieks: *Don't leave me,* she'd begged as my father shut the door and drove away from us. Now, freed from the receiving end, she watched Siena and Jack as impassively as if she were directing them in a play.

'You have free choice,' Siena said. 'Without me, you have everything. Don't you see?'

Her expression crumpled as she looked at my sapphire comb. 'How could you?' she asked Seraphina.

Mr Lawrence hauled Jack out of the house as Edward ran after them. I remained in front of the cake, watching the candles burn down.

The connection that Siena shared with my mother was notable for its invisibility. They never demonstrated closeness as Syrena and I did, with fingers and hair and speech so interwoven that we behaved as a single entity. They rarely touched, but their bond was nonetheless evident to me in the way they watched and circled each other as if observing a pull that allowed only so much distance between them.

I'd never seen Siena angry with our mother, and nor had I seen our mother unnerved by Siena; so while I may not have understood this moment, I sensed its magnitude.

'You released him,' Seraphina said, wary of behaviour that she had neither orchestrated nor approved. 'Why?'

Siena's voice was tight. 'You don't understand why?'

'No,' Seraphina said. 'He doesn't want to be free!'

'I released him because of what I've become. Because I finally understand what you've made me.'

'Why are you speaking to me like this?' Seraphina sounded taken aback.

'I'm speaking the way you taught me,' Siena told her. 'You like me to be cold.'

'I don't like you to be cold to *me*!'

'But you trained me so well that I can't discriminate,' Siena said. 'You trained me to break Jack's heart, and you succeeded. You can't blame me now if I break yours too.'

'I wanted to protect you from the pain I suffered,' Seraphina argued.

'But you made me heartless.' Siena held her head high, but her voice shook. 'You made me a weapon to carry out your revenge. Can't you see that I'd rather suffer pain than inflict it on others?'

'I wanted to make you strong.' Seraphina reached for Siena's hand. 'You can't deny that I succeeded.'

Siena stepped away from her. 'I'm alone,' she said as a tear shone on her eyelashes and fell. 'I'm unable to feel love; unable to form attachments. Do you really think me a success?'

'It's better this way,' Seraphina said. 'You're better off like me, even if you can't see it yet.'

There was a silence, and when Siena spoke again

her voice was soft. 'I still have time to change. I have my own mind, and I will never be like you.'

'You're already like me,' said Seraphina. 'And not only you. Stella is my daughter too.'

Siena's face flooded pale. 'Stella is my sister,' she whispered. 'Please don't ruin her.'

'It isn't me that Stella copies,' Seraphina told her. 'It's you.'

Although I'm adept at evading it, there are moments when missing Siena is unavoidable. Following dreams in which she carries her school cases through the door and spins me until I can't stand, or in assemblies when I sit beneath a giant portrait that exists like a memorial to my shortcomings, or when I believe for an exquisite, crippling second that the reflection I see in a window is her, I drown as if I'm still in that riptide. Now I stumble, laying my forehead on the cold metal balcony as pain like venom, as giddying as a fairground ride, shoots through me. And I know that I'm losing Syrena as Siena lost me.

When I straighten up, I take the cigarette Seraphina hands me. My forehead is sweating. 'It was my fault,' I whisper numbly. 'Siena left that night because of me.'

I grind out my cigarette with my foot. The balcony door slams behind me and people turn to stare as I walk at speed towards the exit, the hypnotic ring of my heels all I can hear until the sound of my name makes me turn on an instinct that I can't ignore.

Syrena stands so quickly that the champagne bucket crashes to the floor.

'Stella, come back,' she shouts. 'Don't leave me.'

I see once more the newborn who cries for the father she'll never meet; the grasping toddler who trails after me with a dummy and a toy rabbit; the seven-year-old whose very existence keeps me alive on nights when I want to reject every breath I take. Syrena is still no more than that little girl who slept in acres of tulle as her baby intelligence was distorted into the asphyxiating cage of her future. And yet she's drinking champagne, and wearing red Dior, and her hair is decorated with bridal opulence.

I walk back to her, wrenching the comb from her hair so that it falls to its rightful place at her waist. Then I walk away in a moment I've been unwittingly pre-empting for months. Every letter, every phone call, every plea that I've ignored from her this term has steeled me against this day, after which she can never be mine again.

As the doors swing shut behind me, I wait for a moment as if she'll follow. And then I remember that she's adhering to a different rulebook now: *we don't chase.*

Chapter Twenty-seven

Caitlin

Edward's party wasn't exactly what I'd imagined. From the way everyone had raved about it, I'd expected some kind of upscale cocktail evening, but the reality was more like the frat mixer I'd attended when I shadowed a freshman at NYU.

'Nice house,' I said as we arrived at his mansion deep in the countryside.

'Thanks,' Edward said dismissively. 'It's falling down and no one can be bothered to pay the heating bills, but, on the upside, no one ever notices a bit of extra damage.'

I looked more closely to see that the house *was* dilapidated. Paint peeled off the window frames and the stone front was discoloured and dirty. Slates were missing from the roof and the pillars at the front door were starting to crumble. For all its grandeur, it looked sad and neglected.

Luke and I followed Edward onto a path overgrown with thistles that led around the back. The garden was also abandoned, the grass too long and the pond in the centre covered in algae and choked with reeds. No one seemed to mind, because, although it was still afternoon, all the kids looked wasted. I recognized almost the entire Sixth Form, transplanted from their usual habitat but still hanging out in exactly the same cliques.

'Caitlin!' Penny squealed as she practically knocked me over. 'You're here!'

I hugged her, feeling underdressed as I took in her silver party dress and teetering stilettos that kept getting stuck in the dirt. Obviously she'd been responsible for that day's outfit, as Lila was unsteady in her identical heels and whispered that she wanted to put her flats back on. The other Stars were similarly dressed and similarly drunk, and I joined them as they danced occasionally to music pumping out from a wooden gazebo hidden behind trees at the edge of a paddock.

Katrina handed me a cup of something that made my eyes water. She was wearing a metallic bandage dress so tight that she could barely walk.

'Edward, go and find Caitlin a new outfit,' she ordered him. 'How could you let her turn up in jeans?'

Edward shrugged easily and led me inside the house as Luke headed off to phone Stella once again. It was dark, and he held my hand as we wove our way through messy but ornately decorated rooms to a hidden stairwell.

'These rooms were servants' quarters,' he explained. 'My dad had them renovated into an apartment for me and Jack.'

It didn't surprise me that he had his own place,

complete with kitchen, den and two bathrooms.

'Where am I supposed to find something to wear?' I asked dubiously. 'Or was this just a ploy to get me up here?'

'Kind of,' he admitted as he pulled me into the room at the end of the hallway.

'This is your bedroom?' I asked, staring around at the bare walls, the minimal décor and the severely right-angled furniture.

Edward gestured at the bed as if I were an idiot.

'I see it,' I defended myself, 'but usually bedrooms are more than literally that.'

'All my stuff's at school,' he said as he lifted me onto the bed, throwing a stack of cushions to the floor and raising a cloud of dust.

'Do you even sleep in here when you're home?' I asked.

He shrugged. 'There's another room I use.'

He pinned me to the bed by my wrists. I let him kiss me for a few minutes, but he pulled back just as I was about to remind him of my relationship rules.

'Have you considered running for Head Girl?' he said.

I was blindsided, not to mention a little offended by the speed with which he'd changed gears. 'Head Girl? As in, *Stella Hamilton, Head Girl of Temperley High*?'

He looked nonplussed. 'Why are you so convinced she's going to win?'

'Who else could possibly win?' I stammered. '*Lucy?*'

'No.' He kissed me on the cheek. 'You.'

'That's crazy. I haven't even been here a semester yet! Who'd vote for *me*?'

He smiled. 'Being new could be an advantage. You don't have all the long-running feuds the other girls have. You're a blank canvas ...'

'Thanks a lot,' I said huffily.

'... because no one knows much about you. You can be whoever you want.'

'Why do you care if I run or not?' I asked.

'Do I have to spell it out? You're pretty – even dressed as a rabbit – clever *and* popular. You could change everything!'

He kissed me again, making me forget Luke altogether and struggle to keep on topic.

'I'm flattered, but there's no way I'd compete against Stella after all she's done for me. And why would I run against you?'

'What if I wanted you on my team?' he said lightly, pausing to let his words sink in.

'You want to put together your own team?' I asked. 'Are you for real?'

Since kick-off I'd heard a lot of speculation about Edward and Stella's campaign strategy now they were no longer dating, but no one had seriously suggested anything like this.

'You can see why I don't want to run alongside Stella and Luke, can't you?' he asked. 'It's awkward. Besides, what's the point if the outcome's already decided? With you on board and someone to compete against, it'll be way more exciting.'

I didn't believe him. 'I'm not sure, Edward. I'd never dare stand up and give a speech in front of all those people. I'd die of fright!'

'You don't know what you're capable of,' he said. 'I have complete faith in you.'

A fantasy I'd never before dared to entertain vividly entered my mind; of me and Edward being crowned Head Girl and Boy at Elevation. I was wearing a beautiful dress that set off my golden hair (my hair often turned gold in my daydreams these days). Stella and Luke stood at the back of the hall, civilians in a sea of equals. Luke's expression showed he knew he'd made the wrong choice, and Stella was glaring at the Star who suddenly held all the cards. The two cutest boys in school were now fighting over me.

I snapped back to brunette reality.

'No one would vote for me,' I said quickly. 'They all want Stella.'

'Not everyone likes being bossed around.'

I wondered if this were true. Stella was never short of servants, but that was their choice. None of us were friends with her against our will, were we? I pushed from my mind the image of us sitting around the Star table, no one daring to take her space even when she wasn't there. Five obedient girls, cowed by the name she'd carved into wood.

'I can tell you this because I know Stella better than anyone,' he said thoughtfully. 'If she didn't think you

211

had a shot at winning, she wouldn't have let you be a Star. She wanted to keep a close eye on you.'

'Why are you saying this?' I asked, wondering whether to be pleased that Stella's friendship with me was so strategic. 'You and she go way back!'

'Stella thrives on challenges,' he said. 'And wouldn't you like to make your mark?'

I considered being able to prove once and for all – to my dad as well as my fellow students – that I was no wallflower. Maybe he'd been right when he'd suggested I should be less boring. Then I shook my head.

'Katrina is Stella's manager. Competing with them both would be too much pressure.'

He seemed to give up. 'I think you're wrong, but if you're sure, I'll find someone else.'

He started to kiss me again, stopping only when we heard voices. Cocking his head to one side, he rolled his eyes dramatically. 'How did they get up here?'

I listened to the scuffling outside, laughing as Edward opened the door to Penny, Lila and Katrina.

'What do you want?' he asked with mock-annoyance.

Katrina unfolded her arms to reveal a large green stain across her dress. 'Cocktail shakers should only be given to people with opposable thumbs,' she said. 'Quentin is going to wake up to a very big bill.'

Edward led us into yet another room, which appeared to be a walk-in closet. The Stars were lost to the world as they took tentative steps towards the clothes.

'It's like heaven,' Penny gasped as she held her hand

out to touch the racks of dresses. 'What *is* this place, Edward?'

Edward looked bored. 'It's my mum's dumping ground. God knows what's in here.'

He held out his empty cup. 'As much as I'd like to watch this, I'm going for a refill. Take anything you want.'

He kissed me again before leaving. 'Think about what I said,' he murmured into my ear.

Penny looked after him. 'He's so perfect,' she cooed. 'Handsome, romantic and with the best wardrobe I've ever seen. *Ever.*'

They set to work with clinical precision, trying on and discarding and complimenting each other as fabric flew around the room like feathers.

'This is going to be the best night of our lives,' said Penny as she zipped Katrina into filmy yellow gauze.

Chapter Twenty-eight

Stella

Edward likes his parties to be called *soirées*, but orgies might be a more apposite description. By the time I arrive, Quentin is unconscious on a lilo in the pond, wearing only floral hot pants and flippers but still clutching a martini glass – I presume one of the other Stripes will make sure he doesn't actually drown – and rumours are loudly circulating that Henry and Delia have been caught doing something entirely non-aspirational behind the gazebo. It says much that they didn't even bother going inside.

Edward's father works for most of the year in Singapore and his mother is usually on a retreat in Geneva. Edward says this is rehab for people with plenty of time to hone new ailments. I assume the latest of these is excessive cocktail-making, because the table in the gazebo is obscured by an odd array of spirits that I presume weren't Edward's choice. I pour myself an apricot schnapps with a mixer of Campari and then set off to find the Stars.

The party has spilled over from garden to house, and, bracing myself, I step inside. It's mercifully dark enough that I don't have to see which of the rugby team is sweating on me, but the Stars are always identifiable by the fact that this event heralds the start of bikini season. I squint, looking for acres of bare flesh, but am surprised to see them wearing couture gowns instead. Penny and Lila are together in matching white Grecian dresses – I wonder if Lila mixed Quentin's soporific cocktail in order to get rid of him for the night – with Mary-Ann at their side. She was probably an unwilling participant, but she looks incredible in a black Valentino gown that I'm sure belongs to Edward's mother. Ruby, I'm glad to note, is nowhere to be seen.

I head towards them, hoping to find Katrina before she finds out about Edward's decision from someone else, but, just as I think I catch a glimpse of her, Luke steps into my way.

'Where have you been?' he asks.

I feign deafness, indicating the speaker system, but he takes my hand and leads me back into the garden, where there are no more excuses. We sit on the swing set that Edward's parents kept even after Edward launched himself around it in a complete circle in tribute to his favourite Thorpe Park ride. I remember the exact tree he cracked his head on, and the crunch of his shoulder – not to mention the screams he later denied – as the Lawrences' physician fused it back into its joint. It was Syrena's most-requested bedtime story for years.

I consider telling Luke where I've been, but can't face rehashing it. 'Are you drunk?' I ask him hopefully.

He shakes his head and holds up a bottle of water. 'I said I'd look after Quentin. I don't know where he's got to, though.'

I don't tell him about his failure as a chaperone, largely because I'm curious to see how long the buoyancy of Quentin's generously proportioned head will keep him afloat.

'I'm sorry I didn't tell you . . .' I begin, wondering how best to get out of this, but he holds up his hand.

'There's something I want to say.'

My heart accelerates as I consider all the things it could be. *Don't pull out of the election*, I think desperately. Anything but that.

'Edward told me you've decided not to be campaign partners,' he says. 'And I can't tell you how happy I am that you want to run with me instead.'

'I definitely want to run with you,' I say emphatically, in case he senses my doubt.

He smiles. 'I know how much the election means to you, and that it's a big deal for you to change your team now. But this is great. If you win, we'll win together.'

Luke's happiness seems odd until I consider that perhaps he now expects Edward to win. Perhaps he's only willing to take part because he's sure he'll never have to be Head Boy.

'And if he wins?' I ask carefully.

'Then I'm sure Caitlin will be a great Head Girl, once Edward manages to convince her of it.'

I choke on my drink, but Luke is too caught up to notice. 'It's really generous of you to free him up to run alongside her. And we're all friends, so it won't be like we're competing against each other.'

My mind is racing as I try to take this in. Edward ditched me so he could run with Caitlin, after *I* set them up? It's inconceivable that he can be serious enough about her to trust her with this, let alone that she'd dare betray me. I was convinced that her apparent commitment to that purity ring would prevent any significant attachments forming between them. And yet, how could I have been so reckless as to risk it?

Luke is still talking. 'I've wanted to say this to you for such a long time – five years, actually – but you and Edward were together for so long and then I didn't want to rush you.'

'Don't say it,' I blurt out.

'Stella . . .' He looks baffled. 'It's nothing bad! I want to tell you that I love you.'

He's holding my hand, but suddenly we're looking at each other across an abyss rather than a dented swing set. Silence grows between us.

'Did you hear what I said?' His voice is uncertain. 'I . . .'

I shake my head and stand. 'I have to go,' I say indistinctly. 'I'm sorry.'

The hurt that crosses his face is almost unbearable. 'I'm sorry,' I mutter again, uselessly.

*

I run back into the dark house and up the stairs into Edward's empty apartment, slamming myself into the first room I pass. My stomach hurts; my whole body hurts, as if I'm physically filled with the abhorrent force that has made Luke fall in love with me. I crumple into a ball and rock back and forth, almost convulsing in pain as I try to hold in sobs that wrack my whole body.

After a while I count down from ten and haul myself upright to face the mirror. It's only as I look past my reflection that I see I'm in Jack's room, to which he's apparently never returned since moving to Singapore to work for his dad, straight after Siena's funeral. I take in the untidy piles of notes on semi-arid environments and vectors and the failure of absolutism; the school uniform still hanging pressed against his door; the bedside table photograph I've never even seen of Siena and Jack looking insanely happy at some prizegiving. I turn the frame to the wall, noticing as I do that the bed has been recently slept in, Edward's favourite WWE mug abandoned on the floor, and his shirt folded roughly by the pillow.

The sink below Jack's mirror is cluttered with toiletries, and I smell something caramel and forgotten. Before I can register that it's Siena's perfume I tumble into banalities like the bikini strap tan line at the base of her neck; the freckles she hated on her shoulders; the tiny white scar on her finger where she was bitten by Syrena's pet mouse. The night she told me all the details of her *protracted* first kiss with Jack; her hysterics as Syrena tidily emptied a bucketful of slugs into her aromatherapy bath; the number of times I called her mobile phone to hear her tell me that she checked her messages *periodically*, tried my hardest to finish her summer coursework so she wouldn't get into trouble on her return to school, and roamed the house in endless loops and circles and a desperate, frenzied certainty that if I just opened the right door at the right moment, she'd be waiting for me.

The door swings open, making me jump, and I begin to reapply my make-up.

'Oh, it's you,' Katrina says as she joins me in the mirror. 'What have you been up to? You look terrible.'

'Thanks,' I mutter as I stare at myself. I consider telling her that she looks terrible too, but she actually looks stunning and I don't think she'd believe me.

She applies layers of lip gloss. 'So when were you planning to tell me that Edward had left us? Don't you think that, as campaign manager, I should be informed of details like this?'

'I was going to tell you tonight,' I say.

She rolls her eyes. '*So* good of you to fit me in. How did you drive him away?'

Indignation sweeps through me. 'If anything, he's worried about where *your* loyalties lie. No wonder he doesn't think we can be a team anymore.'

She laughs. 'Yes, of course you think it's my fault.

Of course you didn't see that playing games with two boys could only have ended this way.'

'What games?'

'You screwed Edward over last summer and he *still* agreed to run with you. It was only a matter of time before he moved on, despite all your efforts to keep him hanging. But don't worry; I'm sure playing with Luke will keep you busy for a while yet.'

'I'm not playing with Luke,' I say. 'And I didn't play with Edward either. I broke up with him because I didn't love him; because I . . .'

'Yes, what *is* your excuse, Stella? I don't blame Edward for jumping ship, because our campaign is shaping up to be a complete disaster.'

'I'm sure running with me has lost its appeal now Edward won't be involved anyway,' I snap. 'And I hardly see you these days. All you've done this term is hang around Caitlin.'

'Can you blame me?' She raises her voice. 'You've been a complete nightmare since kick-off. I thought you were my best friend, but this isn't friendship; it's control. You try to control all of us into doing just what you want.'

'I'm trying to keep us together,' I defend myself. 'The Stars need to be united to win this election, and sometimes that means making difficult decisions.'

'And sometimes it involves lying,' she says. 'Doesn't it?'

We're still talking to each other's reflections, and

she holds my gaze through the mirror as if wondering how to continue. 'I know that you and Edward never slept together,' she says finally.

I start to comb my hair. 'You shouldn't believe everything Caitlin tells you.'

'I believe this,' she says. 'You told us that sex wasn't a big deal so we'd feel bad if we hadn't done it. You let all of us think we had to copy you. But you know that it's a big deal, don't you? You've never done it, but you treated our first times like experiments and then used them against us. I know you did everything you could to keep me and Edward apart.'

'Everyone lies about sex,' I say. 'Surely you know that.'

She's upset. 'No they don't, Stella. You lie, because our feelings don't matter to you. But we're not pieces in a game. We're *people*. Doesn't it matter to you that you're a megalomaniac? You should care what people think of you.'

'But, you see, I *don't* care,' I say as vehemently as if this is true. 'And you should take responsibility for your own mistakes.'

'You can't have it both ways,' she says. 'You can't control us and then blame us when we don't know our own minds. Not any longer.'

I'm so caught up in our argument that I haven't looked at her properly until she steps back from the mirror and I turn from our reflections. *It can't be.*

'Where did you get that?'

It is. I know it is.

She looks down at her floaty butterfly dress. 'Edward gave it to me. Not that it's any of your business.'

It's Siena's dress. It's the dress she's wearing in the photograph that Jack cared about enough to keep beside his bed as the first and last thing he saw of the world every day.

'Take it off,' I say. '*Now.*'

She looks disbelieving. 'Are you serious?'

'Deadly,' I say. 'Get it off.'

'It's not yours!' she shouts. 'Edward gave it to *me*!'

I can't think of anything but the dress; of how Siena must have looked in it; that she might care that I didn't save it for her; that it might still have smelled of her body lotion, or her hairspray, or just *her*, until Katrina put it on and eradicated those things forever.

And so I pick up her pint of claret and throw it right over her, shaking uncontrollably as red liquid spatters and spreads across the gossamer.

She's unnaturally calm. 'You stop Edward sleeping with other girls because you don't want to lose your hold on him. You pushed him and Caitlin together because of that purity ring, didn't you? And it's backfired. You think you're so untouchable, but without Edward you're nothing in this election. And maybe Caitlin should win, because any other option – *anyone* – would be preferable to you.'

She unzips the dress so roughly that it rips as it falls

to the floor. She leaves the room in her underwear, but somehow her dignity is intact.

Mary-Ann finds me later on the swings. I ball up the remains of Siena's dress and hold it close to my chest where she can't see it. Avoiding her eyes, I watch Lila carry an armful of rocks towards the pond.

'I've been looking for you everywhere,' she says. 'Edward told me about the new election plan. But it's not a problem, is it? I mean, you'd rather run with Luke instead?'

'Of course,' I say. 'It's all worked out perfectly.'

It's obvious that I'm crying, but I still turn away before continuing. 'We should never have left school today. No good ever comes of it.'

She sits on the swing beside me, her spidery legs outstretched. 'We have to leave eventually, Stella. Isn't there anywhere else you'd rather be?'

We lean back and swing in synchronicity, our hair sweeping the ground. I'm looking for my favourite star, but the sky is cloudy and I can't make it out. Without its marker I'm rootless and lost.

'You can go to university, or art school,' Mary-Ann considers. 'You and Luke can go travelling – maybe not backpacking, but you know he'd go anywhere you wanted. And one day you'll get married and have children. We've a lot to look forward to when this is over, Stella.'

The election occupies me so fully that I've never

looked beyond it; never looked beyond Temperley High or to a life that Siena didn't experience. It occurs to me that I don't know how to grow older than her, or how to want for things that she was never able to consider. I try to imagine a future in which I walk the Inca Trail, and graduate from university; in which I walk up the aisle towards someone as yet faceless, and produce little fair-haired babies; and it's as foreign a concept as if it's happening to a stranger. It's purposeless and empty, a life I must learn to endure as Siena's memory grows fainter and less relevant until it's as if she was never here.

Mary-Ann is clutching something toxic-looking, and I drink it as fast as I can until the pain in my chest starts to dull.

'Where's Katrina?' I ask as it occurs to me how strange it is that she hasn't tried to find me. No matter who's to blame for our fights, she's always the one to chase.

Mary-Ann pauses. 'Caitlin's cleaning her up. They're with Luke.'

Anger towards Katrina, tiring and unfair, surges through me. 'Mary-Ann, I'd like you to be my campaign manager,' I hear myself say.

Her eyes bulge. 'Are you high?'

'No,' I say. 'How could I be? You know we all get low on medication during bank holidays.'

She shakes her head. 'We can't do that to her.'

'It's not working out,' I say stubbornly. 'We're not

224

a good team anymore, and it's time for a fresh start.'

'She'll be devastated,' she says. 'You've been planning this for years.'

'Edward and I had been planning for years too,' I say. 'Why did he promise to run with me if he was going to do this?'

'He promised because you asked him to,' she sighs. 'Everyone does what you ask them to, Stella. He did the best he could.'

I dismiss this. 'Mary-Ann, I have to win.'

'Why do you *have* to win?' she says. 'Don't you mean, you *want* to win?'

'I have to,' I insist.

She lapses into silence, and when she speaks again her voice is timid. 'Stella, you do *want* to run with me, don't you? I mean . . . you're not getting back at Katrina for something?'

'Of course not,' I say feebly. 'I want to run with you.'

She nods miserably after another long silence. 'I'll do it.'

I can't muster a smile, let alone a *thank you*, but she doesn't seem to notice. I wonder why my influence over her, even when she's aware of it, always blinds her to the truth. For the second time tonight, my power strikes me as loathsome. And yet who would I be without it?

Chapter Twenty-nine

Caitlin

'Have you heard?'

It was the first full day of the summer semester and so far no one had talked about anything but the election. If it had been a hot topic before, that was nothing compared to the buzz it was generating now. It made sense that the Stars were all intent on getting the scoops first.

This time it was Lila who threw herself on the couch between me and Penny and tried to catch her breath. Her purple wedges were not designed for physical activity, and, having failed to unknot the ribbons tying them around her legs, Penny cut them with her nail scissors. They fell on the floor as Lila winced before continuing.

'The list of candidates is on the noticeboard. Guess who Stella's campaign manager is?'

'Katrina, of course!' Penny looked at Lila as if she were mad.

Lila wiggled her liberated toes. 'No. Mary-Ann.'

Penny's jaw dropped. Even I was a little shocked.

'It can't be!' gasped Penny. 'What would this *mean*? Surely Stella knows that being campaign manager is about *so* much more than admin. No one can orchestrate an internet strategy like Katrina. And what about the merchandise? Katrina was getting bunting, T-shirts, shot glasses . . .'

Lila nodded. 'Stella's got this one really wrong.'

'She doesn't even have Twitter,' Penny said. 'Or Facebook, or anything else. She's socially barren without Katrina.'

I tried to process this. Although I'd only recently gotten into social networking, I already couldn't imagine life without it. It was the only sure-fire way of keeping up-to-date with essential school business. 'She doesn't have *Twitter*?'

'Katrina tweets for her,' Lila said. 'Stella prefers her opinions not to be traceable. But Mary-Ann's not exactly drowning in fans. She's got the fewest followers of us all, including you, and you're only just getting started.'

I was pleased that Lila had noticed the progress I was making. The successful Easter egg hunt had gained me most of the Shells and Removes, and logging onto my account recently was like receiving fan mail.

'How could she do this without consultation?' Penny added. 'Stella's team was a joint decision, decided by committee, because it seriously affects us all.'

'She didn't ask us because she knew we'd never agree,' said Lila grimly. 'Mary-Ann would have been last in line for this position. And that's not the only bad news.'

Penny cracked her bubblegum. 'What else?'

'Stella and Edward aren't running together. She's

running with Luke, and Edward's got an opening for running partner. Can you believe it?'

'What's going to happen now?' Penny asked tremulously. The words *Stella might not win* would have been tantamount to blasphemy, but it was obvious what she was thinking.

Lila was trying to be strong for her. 'Stella and Luke are still popular without Edward, but his chances completely depend on his choice of partner. No one outside the Stars can compete with Stella, and it's not as if any of *us* is going to run.'

I sat back, thinking aloud. 'The competition is wide open now the vote is split between Stella and Edward. Any number of candidates might decide to stand.'

'Do you think Katrina knows?' asked Penny.

'Come in,' said Katrina cheerfully as I knocked on the door.

I went in tentatively with a cup of tea, having learnt how important it was in England in times of distress (remarkable, as it tasted like pond water).

'What's that for?' She eyed it dubiously. 'I wanted a strawberry frappuccino with non-fat cream, like always.'

'I've got some bad news,' I said carefully. 'You should probably sit down.'

She continued with her exercise DVD. 'Stretch and shake . . . stretch and shake . . .' she was muttering as she attempted some kind of flamenco move.

'This might be a big shock,' I continued.

'I already know about Stella,' she said, her eyes on the television. 'She made her plans pretty obvious at Edward's party.'

'You know?' I asked in surprise. 'Why aren't you more upset?'

She laid down her pom-poms. 'I'm upset about the way she's behaved,' she said frankly. 'But I don't want to be on her team. She can run with Mary-Ann, or anyone she likes. I don't care *what* she does.'

Katrina had never told me exactly what had gone down at Edward's party, but I was sure it was Stella's fault that she'd ended up crying and covered in red wine. Just as I was sure it was her fault that Luke had been left jettisoned and pale and silent. It was probably even her fault that Quentin's lilo had sunk under the weight of an unexplained rock fall and he'd spent the rest of his vacation in hospital with Weil's disease.

I sat on her bed and looked at the huge pile of election paraphernalia heaped in the garbage. I could see patterns for Elevation dresses, *Vote Stella* buttons and rosettes, streamers and even fireworks.

She smiled ruefully as she pulled down the *Vote Stella* poster she slept under. 'What can I do about it anyway?' she asked as she ripped it and tossed the pieces. 'Run for Head Girl myself? Because with my disciplinary record, I don't think I'd be allowed.'

It was impossible to contest this, because she always seemed to be in trouble for something.

'You know, I take responsibility for a lot of things,' she said as if she knew what I was thinking.

'I'm sure you do,' I said. 'But my idea might change that.'

I expected her to reject Edward's proposition outright, but she listened without speaking.

'Do you really want to put yourself through the campaign?' she asked finally, looking scared but excited.

'Maybe.' I frowned. 'I don't see what we have to lose. I think we have a great chance with Edward on our side. And what's the worst that can happen?'

I left Katrina to join Penny and Lila at the lunch table. Penny, who had been engrossed in her laptop, pushed it towards me as I sat down.

'Have you seen the election feed?' she said.

The online election pages had only been up for a few hours, but the students were doing a good job of sharing gossip about candidates. There was already a YouTube channel, a Facebook page and a Twitter account, not to mention numerous fashion forums, fan sites and about twenty pages devoted to Stella's hair.

Lila was looking at me. 'Everyone's very interested in you all of a sudden. Why are you trending everywhere?'

I scrolled down to find a series of photographs comparing my recent fashion choices favourably with Stella's. Edward obviously had good contacts.

'Wow,' I murmured. 'How did they get these? I've

never seen anyone taking pictures.'

I looked around, my unease at being secretly photographed mixed with a thrill at sharing the page with Stella as if we were actually comparable.

Lila looked suspicious. 'Do they know something we don't?'

I shook my head guiltily, wishing I knew how to tell them that Katrina and I were no longer on their team.

'Don't blame Caitlin,' said Penny miserably. 'It's supply and demand. Now she does so much sport it's inevitable that people want to see her in Lycra.'

After my quad run I'd been asked to join the cross-country team. Then Katrina had volunteered me for the netball spot Stella had forfeited after missing an important match. I'd turned out to be pretty good at both, so when Stella gave up swimming and hockey I started those too. This semester was tennis, and, to my amazement, I was actually looking forward to Sports Day.

Penny and Lila left as the bell rang, but then Ruby came and sat next to me, glancing furtively around the room. It was the first time I'd seen her this semester, and, although she appeared nervous, she was also happier than I'd seen her in months.

'Edward told me you're thinking about running for Head Girl,' she whispered. 'And guess what? I am too!'

'Edward told you to compete?' I asked.

'Not exactly, but he told me to have more confidence in myself, and I thought, why not? The row last term really made me think – after all those years, one mistake is all it took to be kicked out. You shouldn't be scared of your friends, Caitlin.'

In various ways Stella had sealed her own fate.

I suspected Edward's talk with Ruby had been designed to influence my decision, and it was the last nudge I needed. Katrina and I joined him at the tennis courts where he was finishing up a game with Tom.

'You know why we're here,' Katrina said. 'I think Caitlin should stand for Head Girl, and I want to be her manager.'

Edward suppressed laughter. 'That sounds dangerous. I take it you have your headstones picked out?'

Katrina held his gaze. 'It's not fair that Stella thinks she has a right to win. The school should be a democracy, not a dictatorship!'

She sounded self-conscious, as if she'd learned this phrase in General Studies and wasn't sure how to use it.

I giggled. 'It's not a dictatorship; it's a monarchy. Lila even said that the position is Stella's birth right. We should campaign for a republic, where people's lives aren't pre-determined and everyone is equal.'

Edward nodded. 'Why do you think I wanted you on board, Caitlin? The timing is perfect.'

'So you think we can win?' Katrina said.

He pursed his lips. 'Everyone loves an underdog, don't they?'

Chapter Thirty

Stella

We're doing group work in French, so Mary-Ann and I take ourselves off down the corridor to discuss the escalating levels of violence in Corsica. She stares blankly at the worksheet while I search for a pen, tipping my bag sideways to see to the bottom.

'What's wrong?' she asks.

'Nothing,' I say automatically.

She sighs in frustration and I force myself to elaborate. 'My belongings keep going missing. I thought I was being paranoid, but they *are*.'

She frowns. 'Do you think someone's stealing from you?'

We look around uneasily. Despite our hiding place under a table, I can see at least three camera phones pointing in our direction. Now the campaign has really begun, nowhere feels safe from eavesdroppers and even the most banal information is newsworthy.

'I don't know what to think,' I say.

'Is it Ruby?' she whispers.

I shake my head. 'Ruby only steals shoes and gold of eighteen carat or more.'

'And prescription medication,' she reminds me. 'And sometimes cutlery.'

I mentally list my losses. Clothes. Notebooks. Paintbrushes. Make-up. Perfume. 'Maybe she's branching out.'

'I'm sure you can get it all back when we clear our rooms at the end of term,' she says reassuringly as I finally locate a fluffy purple pencil that I can only assume belongs to Syrena. 'Lila's going to hire a cart.'

We look at our books again.

'Don't destroy your relationship with Luke,' she says suddenly.

I scan *Tricolore* for the statement before realizing she's deviated from the exercise. 'Luke and I are fine,' I say evenly.

'You've been avoiding him since Edward's party,' she points out. 'What on earth happened between you that night?'

'You know there's a rule that whatever happens at the party stays there,' I say. 'If only for Quentin's sake. And I've been very busy ever since. Luke understands my schedule.'

She looks uncomfortable. 'I'm not so sure. Luke might seem secure, but he probably doesn't feel that way inside. I know you're focused on the election, but you need to sort out how you feel, or both of you are going to get hurt.'

'You're hiding something,' I realize suddenly. 'What do you know?'

She scrolls through her phone and shows me the latest election feed. 'You really should keep an eye on this. It's your best way to gauge who people are supporting.'

'People are supporting me,' I say. 'I mean, they're supporting us.'

Mary-Ann sighs. 'Just look at it.'

I look reluctantly at a photograph of Edward's party. Of Caitlin at Edward's party, specifically, sitting very close to Luke in the gazebo. Her arm is around him and she's stroking his hair in a way that I'd never allow any girl to do.

I grip my pencil so hard that it snaps.

I find Luke doing homework in an empty classroom. At least, I assume he's doing homework until I see Caitlin with her hand on his arm.

'Can I speak to Luke alone, please, Caitlin?' I say.

She gets up, but she actually has the nerve to squeeze Luke's hand as she leaves.

'Where have you been?' he says wearily. 'I've been looking for you all day. All week, actually.'

I don't waste any time. 'I know you're spending the summer with Caitlin in New York. *And* I've seen the picture from Edward's party. She was all over you.'

'Was that picture taken after you rejected me and ran away?' he suggests. 'How *dare* you criticize me for anything I did that night?'

'It looks as if there's something going on between you two,' I say weakly. 'It makes me look stupid.'

'You know what?' He comes to stand in front of me.

'If you really think there's something between me and Caitlin, I'm not going to tell you otherwise. Because the truth is, and we *both* know it, that you've been looking for an excuse to finish with me for months. Now you've got one.'

My voice shakes. 'Do you have any idea what I gave up to be with you?'

He passes his hand over his face. 'What you *gave up*? Am I hearing things?'

'I'm committed to you,' I say hastily, worrying that I've gone too far. 'You know I am.'

'Everyone says you're only with me as a tactic,' he says. 'I never believed them, but maybe I should have listened.'

'Of course I'm not!' I say. 'If I were tactical, I'd have stayed with Edward and never gone out with you in the first place.'

His face is set. 'If you want to prove that, then pull out of the election.'

'*What?*'

He nods. 'Can't you see that it's ripping us apart? Walking away from it now is our only chance to have any kind of future.'

He's testing me. He already knows what my answer will be, but he needs to hear it.

'You know I can't withdraw,' I say. 'The election is all I have.'

He looks devastated. 'The *election* is all you have?'

I nod, but unexpectedly he holds my hands. 'I

236

know you're scared, and you're shutting me out with this act. You think you don't need anyone, but you can't do this alone.'

'The election means more to me than you do,' I say numbly. 'That's my choice.'

'So we're done?' he asks. 'That's really what you want?'

I know that if I look into his eyes I'll change my mind. So I stare at the floor until he lets me go.

'You've been drinking, haven't you?' he says as he steps back.

'No.' I blush with guilt.

'You have.' His voice is soft. 'You keep a bottle of vodka in your bag. I thought you were stronger than this. You were so adamant that you weren't going to turn out like your—'

I walk away, slamming the door behind me. But I've gone too far; I can't compete in the election without a running partner, and therefore hurting Luke will hurt me even more.

Chapter Thirty-one

Caitlin

'So Stella and Luke split up?' Caroline asked happily at dinner.

I'd been headed to the Star table, but, as Ruby and Caroline's corner looked so much more appealing than the prospect of Lila and Penny staring gloomily at a laptop, I'd joined them instead. Stella and Mary-Ann were also at the Star table, but the factions between the two groups were obvious.

'I can't believe they'd do it right before Speech Day,' Caroline continued. 'How can they coordinate their campaign now?'

'It's *really* bad timing,' I agreed, trying to ignore the goosebumps I got every time I thought about giving a speech to the entire school. Despite Edward's help, I had no idea how I was going to get through it.

'Is it true Luke's going to stay with you for the summer?' Caroline asked enviously.

I smiled, trying to convey a *yes* without lying. Actually Luke would be living in a dorm fifty blocks from my house and working the same hours as my mom, so he'd be lucky if he even got a glimpse of the skyline during daylight hours, but no one had to know that. It was enough of a coup that I'd been the one to tell him about the research opportunity, not to mention the fact that, as long as he was locked in an underground lab in Washington Heights, he couldn't be with Stella.

'Do you know what happened between them?' Ruby asked. 'Luke seems to talk to you more than anyone these days.'

'Not really.' I flicked my hair, trying to look mysterious, and moved some salad leaves around my plate. It was hard not to wonder when my photo was being taken. The previous week a terrible video posted online of me eating a sandwich had shown me why the other Stars only ate visually appealing food in public. If they ate anything at all, that was.

Ruby did a double-take. 'You took off your earrings?'

'Yes,' I said proudly. It had taken nerve, but I was determined that this had to be done. 'I think you should be a Star again, so I'm not going to wear them until they return yours. You've been punished for long enough.'

This didn't seem too radical, because the Stars as I'd first known them didn't exist. With Stella and Katrina fighting, and Lila and Penny surely wondering whose team to be on, numbers needed a boost. It was stupid to keep excluding Ruby when they were so unstable.

'I don't see that happening,' Ruby said. 'Especially not now I'm standing against Stella.'

I hoped I looked supportive rather than scared. 'You defended me last semester when Stella caught us in Lucy's room. Now I want to do the same for you.'

I glanced up as Katrina joined us. She removed

her own earrings, defiantly tying her hair back into a ponytail and looking so fierce that I burst into laughter.

Caroline spoke nervously. 'Penny and Lila look like they want to kill you.'

I looked over quickly to the Star table. Penny and Lila were irrelevant, because I only needed to know whether Stella had seen. But as usual her face gave nothing away.

Katrina grinned as she high-fived first me and then Ruby. 'We had no choice. We don't want to get walked over anymore.'

My phone rang and I tossed it aside as I saw who it was. 'Are you fighting with your dad?' Ruby asked, glancing at the display.

'It's nothing,' I said tightly. I hadn't spoken to him or my mom for a while, but I wasn't about to tell anyone that. There was no advantage to sharing family problems, and it was clear that Stella hadn't climbed the ladder by being a devoted daughter and sister.

My dad's call had ruined my mood, and I searched for a change of subject to distract myself. 'Did I tell you I've decided to apply to Oxford?' I asked, remembering the conversation I'd just had with Mr Trevelyan.

'I thought you wanted to go to Yale?' Katrina said.

'I was thinking about it . . .' I tried to sound casual, as if I hadn't worn a Yale pin since I was five, not to mention that I'd always planned to apply pre-med. 'But I'm going to apply to schools in England instead. After all, what better place to study English Literature?'

I hadn't spoken loudly, but Stella had a sixth sense for topics that involved her and she stopped beside me on her way out of the room. White had always been her favourite colour, but recently she seemed to wear nothing else, switching between dozens of ethereal dresses. Her complexion was clear as china against her lace collar, her cornflower eyes enormous, and she was particularly swan-like at that moment, her gilded surface serene and unfathomable.

'Why have you suddenly decided this?' she asked.

I considered backtracking, but she'd already seen the A* on the essay I'd laid on the table and the silver star Jamie had stuck beside the grade. Her expression didn't change, but I was sure I saw it flicker, just for a second, before her glacial veneer restored itself.

I took a deep breath. 'You're not afraid of a little competition, are you?' I said as boldly as I could. 'It must get boring to win every time.'

She smiled. 'Winning never gets boring. Not that you'd know.'

Katrina opened her mouth in outrage, but I didn't want her fighting my battles for me. I leaned back and looked Stella right in the eye. 'You know what? Neither of us has gotten in yet, but I have as much right to apply as you do.'

Ruby spoke back for the first time ever. 'Or is Oxford also your birth right?' she asked.

Katrina wasn't going to be left out, and she stood up as the whole room fell silent. 'The Head Girl always

241

goes to Oxford, Stella,' she said loudly. 'Hasn't anyone told you that Caitlin is a candidate this year?'

If Stella had known about me and Edward, she'd never let on, and Penny and Lila had continued to speculate about Edward's choice of partner as students amused themselves by writing their own suggestions in the space on the noticeboard. *Bella Swan . . . Primrose Everdeen . . . Carrie White . . .* had been scrawled and crossed out, but, judging by the stunned reaction to Katrina's words, none of these names was as unlikely as mine.

Mary-Ann, prim in Chanel tweed and a bow tie, grabbed her bag and followed Stella as she stalked out of the room without saying another word. Once they'd gone, Katrina reached for my hand and then Ruby's, and we sat like that for a moment as if understanding that something was about to change. Lila glared at us from the Star table, and then, after a moment's silent communication with Katrina, she shrugged in surrender.

'No one blames us for doing this,' Katrina murmured. 'They can see we had no choice.'

We broke apart as Edward joined us. 'I thought we were keeping you a secret until tomorrow?' he asked me.

'Sorry,' Katrina said contritely. 'It was my fault.'

Edward looked annoyed for a second and then grinned as he slung an arm around me. 'At least you did it theatrically,' he acknowledged. 'We should get a few virtual column inches out of it, which is the priority right now.'

Most of the students were still focused on our table so I kissed him hard, not pulling away until I heard the click of a camera.

'Nice work,' I heard Katrina murmur. 'I can see you're already getting the hang of this.'

'Can we go to your room?' I said into Edward's ear. 'I've hardly seen you recently.'

As we left the cafeteria, I knew without checking that everyone was watching.

'Did you want a last run-through before tomorrow?' he asked as he shut the door and picked up the speech we'd been practising.

'I guess so,' I said reluctantly. 'Unless . . .'

Sometimes I worried that our relationship felt more like business than anything else. Not to mention that we spent most of our time talking about Stella. Edward wasn't Luke, but that didn't mean that I didn't like being in a relationship with him. For now, at least.

'Unless what?' he asked, half-smiling.

Before I could think twice, I unbuttoned my top. I heard him inhale sharply as I tugged his shirt over his head and lay beside him, skin-on-skin for the first time.

Eventually he groaned and pulled away. 'You're killing me,' he said, running his hand through his hair.

'Don't stop,' I said impatiently. 'What's the matter?'

He looked exasperated. 'You have no *idea* how much

willpower it's taking not to rip your clothes off right now.'

'I want that too,' I said.

'You do?' It was the first time I hadn't reminded him of my unshakeable beliefs on the subject. 'Then what . . . ?'

'I don't know,' I said.

Why did sex have to be such a big deal, after all? People these days didn't get married until they were in their thirties. Was I supposed to wait until I was that old?

'I'll think about it,' I whispered, kissing his neck. He smelled like citrus.

'So will I,' he said hoarsely.

As he pulled me towards him, I considered the inescapable fact that sex would give me and Edward a bond that Stella could never compete with. Now she'd lost Luke, it might be my smartest move to stop her from clawing back Edward in her diminished state.

And if that wasn't worth a re-evaluation of my beliefs, then what was?

Chapter Thirty-two

Stella

Speech Day requires candidates to speak publicly about their suitability for the Head Girl or Boy role. Our manifestos detail the changes and improvements we'd make if elected (none of these ever comes to fruition, so you can write whatever you want) and are displayed in the library for wavering voters.

I sit beside Mary-Ann on the hall stage as the students file in. She's staring at her phone, a horrified expression on her face. I lean closer and feel myself turn red at a Twitter image of her wearing a short-sleeved shirt, the mosaic of scars on her arms clearly visible.

'Who posted that?' I ask.

She rolls her long sleeves further down so they cover her hands. 'Does it matter?' she says miserably. 'It's too late to do anything about it: everyone knows now.'

I try to sound strong, masking my guilt at having dragged her into this. 'Things will change today, as soon as we give our speech.'

'Maybe,' she says hesitantly, 'we should have written our own speech instead of . . .'

I have a horrible fear that she's right, but it's

too late to do anything about it.

'Siena won hands down with this exact speech,' I say firmly. 'There's no way we can fail.'

The whole school is here. Attendance isn't compulsory, but this is the nearest thing we have to reality television. I nod stiffly at Luke as he takes his seat beside Tom, his new campaign manager, but he doesn't even acknowledge me. We've had exactly one conversation since we split up, which clangs in my head as I watch him check his notes. *I won't withdraw, because I understand why you need to do this*, he said, looking exhausted and unhappy. *But you should know I don't want anything to do with this election and I never did.*

We've drawn lots to decide who should speak first. I drew second, so have to listen to Lucy drone on about scholarships for the most academically able, the opportunity for extended prep at exam times, and for PE for Sixth Formers to make way for extra – you've guessed it – study periods. Her voice is shaking and her tongue clicks against the roof of her mouth as if she desperately needs water. I recognize her polka-dot dress from Katrina's Scientology phase. Katrina could almost carry it off, but it makes Lucy look like a member of the WI. I scan the audience for their reactions, which are as you'd expect: expectancy. She draws to a halt just as Dr Tringle shakes her stopwatch, and squints at the dutiful applause. Hannah, her campaign manager, gives her a big thumbs up as she shuffles, pigeon-toed, back to her seat.

I stare at my shoes as Lucy's running partner, a squeaky-voiced boy I vaguely recall from the front row of our Fifth Form Maths class, gives a speech that is notable only for being more boring than hers. Then Mary-Ann squeezes my hand as she introduces me and I'm embarrassed because my palms are sweating. I put my papers on the podium and face the audience, wishing I were somewhere, or someone, else right now.

'Fellow students, staff and governors,' I begin. I flash a winning smile in the direction of Dr Tringle, who's listening intently. 'We're here to begin the process of electing the new Head Girl; I'm here to explain why I'm the best, and indeed the only, person to fulfil this role.'

I see a couple of Fifth Formers roll their eyes at each other. *Jealousy.*

'I've consistently proven myself capable of dealing with whatever life has thrown at me. I've been voted Student of the Year four times. I've won awards for my academic work, my extra-curricular activities –' someone interrupts me here with a loud whoop, which I ignore – 'and my contribution to school life. If you elect me to lead you next year, I'll offer the same dedication to the post of Head Girl as I've given to every other activity I've participated in.'

'Change the record, Hamilton,' shouts someone. It sounds like Ally, but the spotlight's in my eyes and I can't see beyond the first few rows.

I can hear sniggering, and I glance at Mary-Ann, who motions at my notes as if she's pointing out the emergency exits.

'I . . . if you elect me to lead you next year, I will—'

'You've read that bit,' she hisses.

I can't work out what's going on. How could I have misjudged this so badly? I stumble on, hardly aware of what I'm reading. I can hear people whispering and Dr Tringle telling them to be quiet. At the end she claps firmly and a few people join in. I stare at Mary-Ann, unable to react. We take our seats.

Chapter Thirty-three

Caitlin

I froze at the cat-calling that accompanied Stella's speech.

'Why are they being so mean?' I muttered to Edward. 'Will they do the same to me?'

He looked a little worried. 'Of course not,' he whispered staunchly. 'Stay calm.'

I breathed in, out, in, until Luke stepped forward for his own speech. He gave Stella a strange glance as he passed her and I felt horrible for him: she'd totally ruined his chances too. The speeches were supposed to be a joint effort, but he'd clearly had no clue what she was going to say.

Luke's speech was warm and funny, his smile enough to bring the house down, but the audience was buoyed up and wouldn't laugh in the right places. He was tense and I could tell he didn't get through everything he'd planned to say before he stopped talking and nodded awkwardly. The applause was half-hearted and Tom grimaced in disbelief as he took his seat.

That made me more nervous than ever. My heart hammered and my hands shook as my name was called. For a second I sat mute.

'You can do this,' Edward said as Katrina nodded in

support. 'I've already told you: I have complete faith in you.'

I looked around helplessly for an escape route. What had I been *thinking*? Public speaking was literally my worst nightmare, and I'd chosen *this* as my first attempt?

Then my eyes caught Stella's. Despite what had just happened, she looked pleased, and I understood why: she thought I'd lost my nerve. If I tanked, we'd be back on an equal footing. And the students yesterday had been so shocked by the news that their reaction to me was impossible to predict.

I got to my feet as Dr Tringle repeated my name. Walking to the podium felt like being sent to the gallows and I was sure I was going to pass out. I was too hot, and I took off my cardigan as Katrina adjusted the microphone and introduced me.

Dress to impress, Katrina had said as she lent me a beautiful blue Galaxy dress. Weirdly it did give me a sudden flash of confidence now, and I managed to smile as I stepped up to the podium.

'It doesn't matter if you're nervous,' Edward had told me as we practised. 'Your selling point is that you're normal and accessible.'

I took a deep breath. 'Classmates,' I began.

It came out a little croaky, but right then someone in the front row wolf-whistled. I knew it was probably a plant, but somehow it changed everything. I could do this, and I didn't need the speech Edward and I had prepared about policies and pledges. Katrina had arranged my cue cards in front of me, but I moved them aside before taking hold of the lectern with both hands.

'I'd like to start with a story about my first day at Temperley High,' I said, my voice growing steadier. Out of the corner of my eye I saw Edward raise his eyebrows, but he let me continue.

'Everyone can relate to starting a new school, right? It's scary. In fact, it's the scariest thing I've ever done. I was worried no one would talk to me; that I was wearing the wrong clothes; that I'd fall on my face in the hallway. I wasn't only starting a new school, I was starting a new *continent*. I was leaving my mom, my baby brother, my friends . . . you can imagine how I felt.'

There was a noticeable ripple of sympathy, and I saw some of the Shells and Removes waving *Vote Caitlin* flags. Katrina smiled and stepped backwards.

'Everything was different: the accents, the schoolwork . . . even the chocolate! I couldn't imagine how I'd ever find my place.'

Dr Tringle smiled encouragingly at me as I paused, and I grinned back at her.

'And that's why I, as your Head Girl, would work hard to make Temperley High feel like home. Because it *is* our home. It's *your* home.

'Your fellow students are your family, and should treat you as such. You shouldn't have to worry about which lunch table to sit on, or whether you fit in with the coolest kids, or if you can afford the right handbag or pair of *earrings*. If there's one thing I've learned since being here, it's that beauty and money and popularity don't make you better than anyone else.'

I couldn't resist glancing over my shoulder at Stella. She looked livid and I decided it was time to wind up.

'I'm not going to bore you with policies about what I will and won't do as Head Girl. What I *do* want to say is that I understand what it's like to feel insecure, and, as Head Girl, I'll make sure there's room enough for all of us to be ourselves, to fit in, and to be happy. Oh, and Edward and I will throw a huge party if we win. I promise.'

The applause was deafening and I stared in amazement as the audience got to their feet. The flags and rosettes that Katrina had handed out swelled like an ocean of validation. Pure adrenaline filled me as I took a second to appreciate this moment. I was pretty sure it was the best thing that had ever happened to me.

Edward, up next, had the good sense to introduce himself rather than let his manager Quentin near the microphone. Although he'd had no time to adjust his speech in light of my impromptu performance, he did a characteristically good job of getting the students onside with talk of his proposed victory party, and gaining the faculty's approval with plans for a new peer counselling programme specifically aimed at discouraging the friendship cliques that I'd just condemned. The reaction he got was almost as great as mine.

Mr Trevelyan stepped forward to quiet them as Edward took his bow, and we returned to our seats as Caroline introduced her candidate Ruby. Cowed by what she'd just witnessed, Ruby was barely coherent as she stammered her way through a near-replica of the pedestrian speech I'd planned to give, and no one listened to a single word. Her running partner Henry had attended the Summer Eights dinner the night before, and, too hungover to take off his Ray-Bans or speak above a whisper, he fared little better.

As the audience was dismissed, Edward looked at me like I was a stranger. 'I'm amazed!' he said.

'I'm sorry I changed our strategy,' I said worriedly. 'It wasn't planned, I promise.'

He laughed. 'Are you kidding me? You were incredible – it was exactly what everyone wanted to hear. It was a million times better than the speech we wrote.'

I relaxed in relief as we stood up.

'Shake everyone's hand,' he whispered, pushing me towards the other competitors. 'You're a politician now.'

I grinned happily as everyone congratulated me. 'You were brilliant,' said Mary-Ann, sounding awed.

'You really were,' agreed Ruby. 'You should be a professional politician. Would you consider competing in Miss World?'

'Nice work, Miss Popularity,' Tom muttered to Stella as he stormed past.

She seemed to wince as Edward gave me a giant bouquet of roses before twirling me around. 'To the girl of the moment,' he said. 'I'm so proud of you.'

As he put me down, I saw Luke shake his head at Stella before following Tom from the room. Outside the door was a group of Shells brandishing notebooks, and Edward pushed me towards them so I could begin signing my name.

Chapter Thirty-four

Stella

All I want to do after the speeches is drink away my humiliation, or, failing that, go to bed. I'm trying to choose between the two as I avoid my next lesson – English, which I was planning to cut anyway – and walk towards Woodlands.

I take a detour through the orchard, hoping not to see anyone, but Edward calls out to me from his seat in a wide branch of his favourite apple tree.

'Come and sit with me,' he says. 'I'm only three feet off the ground.'

The invitation is still unappealing, because I'm very fond of my Kurt Geiger wedges, and this must show on my face.

'Still as vain as ever?' he asks.

I hit him lightly as I remove my shoes and climb up to sit beside him. As he waits for me to clean my hands with sanitizer, I know he's thinking about all the times I made us late because I couldn't decide on an outfit or how to wear my hair. It seems like a lifetime ago.

'So how are you?' he asks. 'I'm sorry about what happened to you today.'

He takes my hand for a second, apparently unselfconsciously, and then lets it drop. It's at once strange to think of him being my boyfriend and strange that he's not.

Whatever our relationship, we understand each other as no one else can. For one, we're the only students never to have a familial presence on Parents' Day, and Sports Day, and prizegivings. Of course no one wants their parents hanging around, but if I'm truthful I wonder why I bother working so hard and winning all the prizes when no one takes any notice.

Edward's parents are almost as bad as Seraphina at keeping in touch. When we were Shells, we all received care boxes from home, and, not knowing better, I opened mine in front of the other girls. While they had teddy bears, jelly beans and pink hair slides, I had a ticket to a health spa with complimentary Botox and liposuction (you had to be eighteen to use it so I gave it to Mrs Denbigh, who was rendered unable to frown for six months), a cellulite-beating body scrub, a course of fibre-based appetite suppressants and battered copies of *Polo* and *Hollywood Wives* (Mrs Denbigh also took these). Instead of a letter with news from home was a signed portfolio photograph (*Much love, Sera!*).

I remember teasing Ruby about her My Little Pony stickers and then burning Seraphina's face out of the photograph with a cigarette lighter. I burned my fingers too, but I expect that was an accident. Edward, whose father sent an Action Man that he'd last played with aged six and a cheque to cover various damages to school property, set our boxes on fire; Mrs Denbigh, who extinguished the flames, never punished either of us.

'I'm not having a great week,' I acknowledge. 'You know Luke and I split up?'

I think I might cry, obviously as a delayed reaction to this morning's debacle, so I look away quickly. Edward usually gets embarrassed when I cry, but this time he smiles sympathetically and, after a second's pause, takes my hand again. 'I heard. I'm sorry it didn't work out.'

'Did he – did he tell you what happened?' I ask.

'No. We never talk about you like that. You're off-limits, you know?'

'Good.'

I hated hurting Edward when we broke up, but whilst Luke and I were together I could pretend that the end justified the means. Breaking up with him changes everything.

Instead of replying, he shakes a branch overhead so that apple blossom falls over us like confetti. I wonder what the other Stripes would make of this.

'It's good to see you,' I say. 'Maybe we could start having proper conversations again?'

I don't expect him to contest this – it's not as if I'm asking him to sign a contract – but he looks uncomfortable. I shift closer to him, trying to bring the situation back under control. I push my hand next to his, close enough that he can hook my little finger with his thumb. When he doesn't, I shift incrementally and graze against him.

He looks down, and I see him extend his fingers ready to enclose mine. He is deliberate as he holds still for a second. Then he takes his hand back.

'It's too difficult now we're officially campaigning against each other. And, besides, it's not respectful of Caitlin.'

The mention of Caitlin cuts across the atmosphere, and anything that was between us is lost. 'Of course,' I say, rallying enough to reply, 'If Caitlin's now that *important* to you.'

He fidgets. 'Stella, you chose Luke and I accept that. But please understand that it hasn't been easy for me. Please give me a chance to get over it.'

Edward has never spoken quite like this before and shame fills me, heavy and immobilizing, as I see that even now I'm treating him as a weapon to undermine Caitlin. Whatever my issues are with her, they don't involve him.

'I'm sorry,' I whisper. 'And I'm sorry about the election too. I promised to run with you, and I made it impossible.'

He flashes his familiar smirk. 'That's your loss; we had it in the bag. Today would have been a whole different story with me in your corner.'

'At least one of us is winning,' I say.

He jumps down from the tree and hugs me awkwardly, keeping a gap between us, and we stand for a moment underneath earnest names carved into a favourite tree: *Jack Lawrence + Siena Hamilton.* The worry that has crippled me since last summer threatens to surface now that the effects of our break-up are so undeniable. But as Edward kisses me on the head, once again the swaggering image of his brother, I let him go, and I wonder exactly what it was that I hoped he could give me.

Chapter Thirty-five

Caitlin

My high lasted the whole of Speech Day and intensified when Stella cut all her lessons and still hadn't reappeared by curfew. After celebrating with Katrina in the Common Room, I was en route to my bedroom when I passed her portrait.

Since she'd fainted in Art class, it had been moved into an alcove off the main quad where there was more space. She now worked on it there, standing on a platform the Stripes had made for her in Woodshop. I looked at it every chance I got, even though it felt like a deliberate reminder to everyone of her royal status. And it wasn't even finished yet.

I stopped short as I reached the spot where the painting had hung. It was no longer there. I doubled back in case I'd gotten confused, but there was no doubt this was the right place: the platform was there, and the outline of the frame was still visible in the paintwork.

'What's your damage, Heather?' said a voice behind me. It was a voice that had once thrilled me to my core, but now I wanted only to escape it.

'I didn't do anything,' I insisted as I turned reluctantly around, even though the denial just made me sound guilty. 'It was missing when I got here.'

Stella stared, trance-like, at the place where the painting had been. Then she came back to life. 'I hope no one gets a photograph of you at the crime scene. What *will* the Shells think of you?'

'Are you going to say I stole your painting?' I asked in horror. 'It was nothing to do with me!'

I was rooted to the spot as she walked away without responding. Before I recovered enough to move I heard a camera click and echoing, mocking laughter.

Chapter Thirty-six

Stella

I shift in my seat as Lila and Penny look at me accusingly. Their phones sit in front of them and I can see a stream of online updates. All are about me, and none are favourable.

'How can it be my fault?' I try again. 'I'm not posting these things.'

Lila raps her fingernails on the Star table. 'You think it wasn't your fault that Edward left you to form his own superpower? Or that you upset Luke so badly that he can't even look at you? Or—'

'Okay,' I interrupt. 'Some of it might be my fault. But it's just a temporary setback, Lila. We're still on the same team.'

'We *were* on the same team,' corrects Lila. 'Now I just don't know.'

Penny pats my hand hopefully. 'Do you have a masterplan?'

'Such as?' I say.

'Swapping Edward for Luke was such an *interesting* strategy,' she begins confidently. 'We were sure you knew what you were doing.'

'Luke was not a strategy!' I argue, still unable to admit to them that losing Edward was his choice and not mine. 'Why on earth would I have deliberately put myself between him and Edward?'

'The universal truth – there's no such thing as bad publicity.' Penny shreds her napkin. 'It's all about keeping in the public gaze, no matter how. My dad says that's only one of the reasons why Liz Hurley is so admirable.'

'I'm not sure I agree,' Lila says. 'It was all very well when Luke and Edward wanted Stella, but right now she's undesirable to them both. Who'll support *that*?'

'Caitlin's a Star too,' Penny says, her faith in me visibly receding. 'Our fans don't know which way to turn. All my Twitter followers are as confused as I am. If you *don't* have a masterplan, what can I tell them?'

'Caitlin's not a Star,' I manage, but our eyes fall onto her engraving at the place Ruby once sat.

'She has the earrings,' Lila says. 'Even if she's not wearing them.'

'Only because Ruby screwed up last term,' I say recklessly. 'Caitlin was never really supposed to have them – she was never part of the plan.'

Lila looks disgusted. 'You know there's more at stake here than just you. We *all* need a Star to win this election, and you're not delivering what you promised.'

Penny nods. 'Last summer you promised that splitting from Edward wouldn't affect the election. Otherwise we'd have vetoed your break-up or chosen another candidate. You said you were a dead cert.'

'I am a dead cert,' I say.

'Do you understand what's happening?' Lila persists. 'You got trounced at Speech Day and now the student body has turned on you. If you drop out, we can all back Caitlin, but if you both stand, something terrible could happen, like Lucy winning! Having a Star win is what's important. No one's bigger than the brand.'

I'm floundering too much to remind her of what should be obvious: that I *am* the brand. 'Caitlin's broken us up! Look at us fighting and divided! We were never like this before she came along.'

'We were.' Being a mathematician makes Lila annoyingly literal. 'You should accept that she's the right person for the job. All the younger kids love her. They follow her everywhere, and half of them are wearing purity rings and talking in American accents.'

'She's a novelty,' I say, more dismissively than I feel.

'It's been six months,' says Lila. 'You can't deny that she's got staying power.'

Ignoring her, I place my hand in the centre of the table. 'One,' I say as firmly as I can.

Lila almost laughs. 'You aren't serious? You can't *possibly* think we're aligned right now.'

We're interrupted as Caitlin rushes over, her eyes wide and upset. 'People are saying that I stole your portrait. This looks really bad, Stella.'

She holds out an iPad studded with crowns to show

me a photograph of herself beside the grubby canvas outline that stands out on the wall like a chalk body. She's wide-eyed and pure Disney in her pink Pucci dress: she couldn't look less like a burglar if she tried.

'I assume you're going to set the record straight?' she adds.

I sigh. 'Caitlin, rumours like that aren't worth my time.'

'Of course they are,' she stammers. 'You're just saying that because I've been trending all week – *everywhere* – and you've only trended once, and that was just because no one liked your nail varnish on Tuesday. It was heinous, by the way.'

She checks her iPad again. 'I suppose you're trending now, but that doesn't count because the portrait story is more about me than you. Rebellious behaviour won't appeal to my core demographic: it could alienate the Shells.'

I want her to know how it feels when your every move is stalked and criticized. 'I don't respond to gossip.'

She stares for a moment and then returns to her new table, while Lila scowls at me.

'We can't make you drop out, but we can withdraw our support,' she says. 'Quitting while you're behind is your best option, because, starting right now, the Stars are Team Caitlin.'

'You aren't serious?' I ask. I look around for help but none is forthcoming. Mary-Ann is at a violin lesson and across the room I see Caitlin and Ruby, not to mention the rest of their band of misfits, watching with open enjoyment. Only Katrina is avoiding my gaze and she's the last person I can turn to.

'We are,' Lila confirms. 'And there's something else too. I'm sorry it's come to this, but we've given you every opportunity to change your mind. As you won't, we have no choice but to no-confidence you.'

Everything seems to grind to a halt as she extends her hand. I feel myself go red, and as I glance around the room it seems that every single student is as shocked as I am.

I take off my earrings and give them to her without even trying to fight back. I'm pretty sure I feel every bit as bad as Ruby did when it happened to her, and I'm also pretty sure that I deserve to.

Chapter Thirty-seven

Caitlin

Ruby giggled. She'd been steadily recovering over the past few weeks until she was once more the spirited girl she'd been. The Shells and Removes, heeding my endorsement of her, had started talking to her again and I now counted her amongst my closest friends.

'This is incredible! I wish I knew who'd done it.'

'What's going on?' I asked as I sat down following my failed attempt to reason with Stella about her self-portrait.

'It was on Twitter this morning. Or Facebook. Or maybe there was an email . . .' Ruby frowned. 'There's so much news to keep track of. I forget who came up with the original idea, but it's really caught on.'

She pointed around the room. Every girl in the cafeteria had pulled back her hair to show off sparkly star earrings. As far as I could see, they were identical to ours.

'It's like a revolution,' I said.

'You're understating,' Ruby said. 'I don't think you know what this means. Those earrings are the Stars' identity. The others are going to be mad as hell.'

Katrina was staring at a group of Removes on the next table. 'You know Penny's dad had our earrings custom-made?' she asked in a low voice. 'I can't even tell the difference.'

'That's the best bit.' Ruby was smirking openly. 'I heard that Ally and her friends went out and bought a ton of the cheapest earrings they could find. It's a total insult.'

'We'll know whose are real when Ally's ears turn green,' Katrina suggested hopefully.

'Have you seen what's going on over there?' asked Ruby, nodding at the Star table.

We weren't close enough to hear what was being said, but there was no mistaking what was happening as Stella removed her earrings and handed them to Lila. Ruby smiled happily as if her old wounds had healed, while Lila and Penny stalked towards us.

I now headed up our table and everyone faced me with the same respect they'd once shown Stella. I knew everyone in the room would be ready with their phones, and I moved my chair so they would get my good side. It was amazing how ugly – and sometimes fat – one could look in candid pictures taken at the wrong angle.

'Stella won't back down,' Lila announced. 'We told her she can do what she likes, because we're joining your campaign. Although I don't see why she should keep hold of the Star table just for her and Mary-Ann.'

'I can't believe you took her earrings,' I said, trying to hide the delight I felt at this momentous event.

Lila opened her hand to show the evidence. 'We had to make a public statement to show we're on your team. Formally withdrawing support should make everyone see that they shouldn't even consider voting for her.'

I put on my (clear) glasses so photographic evidence of this conference would show it to be businesslike, but Lucy cut in before I could speak. 'You're welcome to join us on our table, of course.'

She and Hannah had been pushed out of their usual spots but were still listening eagerly.

Lila and Penny turned to Ruby. 'We're sorry, Ruby,' said Lila. 'Will you forgive us?'

Ruby did a good job of acting upset. 'You really hurt me,' she told them. 'You know I'd never treat you like that.'

'Stella had her own agenda,' I said, not wanting to spread the blame. 'Lila and Penny were helpless bystanders.'

Ruby frowned for a second, but then stood and hugged them both. 'I missed you,' she said tearfully. 'Let's never fight again. And *of course* you can sit here.'

As pleased as I was for Ruby – and not forgetting that I'd been the main campaigner for her reinstatement – it felt important that I was the one to extend the official invitation. 'Maybe it would be a good idea if you sat here,' I told them. 'Even if we have rights to the Star table, it's bringing nothing but bad luck and drama.'

'Thanks, Caitlin,' said Penny gratefully. 'We'd love to sit here instead. Although there isn't much *room*.'

She shoved her chair sideways, displacing Caroline.

I cast an eye over my new table, which seemed to take up half the cafeteria. Now so many Stars had joined, I felt a pang of regret about the inclusivity ethic my campaign had been built on. It had helped me gain followers, but it seemed I'd been too indiscriminate. There was no hierarchy and some very questionable people sat before me, as if the table were a dumping ground for the socially inadequate. The order created and maintained by the Star Salute was now abundantly clear: once I no longer had to fraternize with the general public, I'd implement something similar.

'Let's talk about something happier,' Penny suggested, interrupting Lucy, who was saying something dull about exams. 'Let's discuss the Elevation theme!'

She and Lila were the self-elected Presidents (and sole members) of the Elevation Committee, mainly because Penny's father was the director of a large PR company and was having his staff coordinate the event free of charge.

Lucy groaned, making me cringe with embarrassment for her. Why didn't she know how to behave when the Stars were around? 'Please tell me it's not ghostly cheerleaders. Or zombie pirates. Or slutty vampires. Or—'

'It's none of those things,' Penny said with dignity. 'Mrs Denbigh has vetoed the undead. You're going to love this! It's – wait for it . . .'

She and Lila had evidently been practising. They

paused before chorusing: 'It's *Stars and Stripes*.'

A stunned silence descended.

'You're kidding, right?' I asked.

We all looked around the room, where silver stars were conspicuously present. The Stripes' new soccer shirts were even emblazoned with a giant star front and back.

'Are you trying to make us a laughing stock?' I said. 'This whole Star thing is a disaster right now.'

Lila nodded. 'That's exactly why. Don't you see? It shows we don't take ourselves too seriously *and* keeps us in the public eye. Penny's dad says nine tenths of being a successful celebrity is—'

'But everyone already thinks they're a Star!' I protested. 'We should be losing the name, not becoming the butt of the joke.'

Lila was impatient. 'We shouldn't be losing the name; we should be reclaiming it.'

She scrabbled in her bag for a stack of black invitations. *Join us for a night with the Stars and Stripes*, it proclaimed in gold writing that was only visible when tilted sideways. Inside a six-point star were the words: *Dress code: silver stars.*

'What's this got to do with the Stripes?' I asked.

Penny shrugged. 'Nothing, really. It should just be *Stars*, but the boys complained that the theme always excludes them.'

'So it's nothing to do with America?' I asked.

Penny cocked her head. 'Oh, you mean like the flag?

I never thought of that. How funny!'

I started to smile. 'You could be onto something. This is clever – as if we're inviting everyone to *our* party.'

'Not only that,' Penny said. 'Everyone's so keen on silver stars that we have to evolve if we're going to stay ahead of the pack. So our dress code – just the *real* Stars – is going to be gold. When the venue is decorated gold too, it'll be crystal clear who the night belongs to.'

With a flourish she handed each of us a box containing earrings identical to the last pair, but in gold. 'They're only for *us*,' she said sniffily as Lucy held out her hand.

I smiled at Lucy, but secretly I could see Penny's point that a line needed to be drawn.

'Why have you only just announced a theme?' I asked, thinking of the pink prom dress hanging ready in my closet. 'Elevation is tomorrow and now we all have to buy new dresses.'

'You say that as if it's a bad thing,' said Penny. 'But the theme was always going to be gold. We just made it more exciting.'

She looked to Katrina for support, but Katrina was leafing through a magazine and appeared not to hear.

'Now we're all back together – well, almost all of us – we can play to our strengths, and we can match!'

Lucy was having a hard time saying something. 'You're Stars again,' she managed, looking at me. 'You said everyone should be equal, but this is the same as it was under Stella.'

'It's totally different,' I said smoothly. 'If I win tomorrow, it's for the good of us all. Not only will we be equal, but the earrings will show everyone that *we* levelled the field.'

Lucy wanted to argue, but I held her gaze until she looked away, wondering why she couldn't see how much she had to be grateful for. She was sitting with the Stars and the future Head Girl, wasn't she? I'd rescued her from obscurity and ensured she'd never be bullied again. Sometimes it felt as if helping out these people was more trouble than it was worth.

'I agree with Lucy,' Katrina said, proving my point. 'Starting this again will only cause trouble.'

'We're winning!' I said, irritated to have to include other people in my hard-won success. 'We're ahead in all the opinion polls and no one trusts Stella anymore. I'm surprised she dares show her face – she must be terrified about tomorrow.'

'We need to concentrate on *our* campaign,' Katrina said. 'If we win, I want it to be because we were the best, not because Stella got annihilated. That's no victory. She's already completely alone – what more do we want?'

Edward had drawn up a chair next to me. 'I think Katrina's right,' he said frankly. 'Stella's no angel, but does she deserve this?'

'How can you say that?' I raised my voice. 'I can't help it if everyone prefers me!'

Before I had to request privacy, everyone at the table

dwindled away. It was as if my mood could directly affect the group's dynamic.

Edward continued once we were left alone. He was flushed with annoyance, which was cute. It was rare that he showed this much emotion. 'They might prefer you right now, but if you carry on like this they might change their minds.'

'You put this campaign together,' I reminded him. 'You asked me to run with you because you knew we could beat her.'

He shook his head. 'I asked you to run with me because I thought you'd be a good Head Girl, not because I wanted my oldest friend destroyed. If you do win, I hope it's worth it.'

I spoke before remembering it was important never to reveal insecurities. 'You sound like you're still in love with her!'

He looked taken aback. 'You've changed since Speech Day, do you know that? You say you want to give ordinary students a voice; to show them they don't have to be perfect or in the right clique. But you don't want to stand against Stella; you want to replace her. You dress like her, you act like her: you say *I'm* in love with her, but *you're* the one who's obsessed with her. It's not working, and it's not you.'

I stood firm. 'This *is* me, and if you want us to be together you should get used to it.'

And it *is* working, I added silently as he shook his head in defeat and left.

I turned my attention to Stella, who was still alone at the Star table. The timing was perfect.

'Hey, Stella.' I unrolled a painting I'd stashed under the table. 'I think this is yours.'

'Give that to me,' she said through clenched teeth.

'Sure,' I shrugged. 'Just as soon as you tell the truth about what happened to your portrait.'

'I'm not going to do anything you tell me,' she said calmly. 'You don't threaten me.'

'Are you sure I don't?' I asked, reaching into my bag for the rolled-up canvas I'd stumbled on in the art room when I'd been looking for her portrait. I hadn't found that, but I had unearthed this painting of the Hamilton family on vacation, which I'd figured I could use as leverage to make her tell the truth.

I'd given her enough of a chance. If it were that important, she'd have stopped me.

But when I ripped it she looked as if she were in physical pain.

'There you go,' I said, tossing her the pieces. 'Now I'm finally living up to the *edgy* reputation everyone wants for me.'

Chapter Thirty-eight

Stella

After Caitlin leaves the cafeteria I sit alone for a long time. I contemplate the canvas pieces for a moment and then I slice them again.

'Vandalism isn't what I had in mind when I gave you that painting,' Mr Kidd says sternly as he approaches.

Seeing him makes me remember how much I like to paint, and the way it once helped me to shut out everything else. Mr Kidd has always been one of my favourite teachers, even though he's someone I'd never argue with. I never knew either of my grandfathers, but Siena told me that one of them reminded her of him.

I smile at him as brightly as I can. 'It was an accident, Sir.'

'Really?' he says sardonically. 'Are there any leads on the whereabouts of your self-portrait, by the way?'

'Not yet,' I say, thinking of my ever-increasing tally of missing possessions.

'Can I help?' he says more gently, gesturing to the mess in front of me.

I don't know why I care about this; I couldn't

even bring myself to look at the painting when it was whole. I gather up the fragments and hold them to my chest.

'No, thank you, Sir,' I say stiffly as I walk away.

Chapter Thirty-nine

Caitlin

I took off to the library, where Luke had a cup of coffee waiting for me. Even though things between us hadn't progressed beyond friendship, it was better than nothing. He wasn't the kind of guy to jump into a new relationship, especially when I was still dating his friend. I could live with that; we had plenty of time. It was just a pity that I'd be running the school with Edward rather than him next year.

He threw me a candy bar. 'I thought you might need chocolate. I hear you and Edward had a row tonight?'

I winced, dividing the chocolate and giving him half back. There was no need to tell him that I no longer ate junk food. 'Bad news travels fast, I see.'

He laughed. 'Tom told me. Apparently everything you do is newsworthy these days.'

My cheeks burned with embarrassment and I hoped he hadn't heard what had just happened between me and Stella in the cafeteria. 'Did he tell you what it was about?'

Luke shook his head. 'No, just that it was loud.'

I sighed in relief. I had the impression he might take Stella's side if he knew. 'I said some stuff I didn't mean.'

'I'm sure Edward did too.' Luke always saw the good in people. 'Everyone fights from time to time and it takes two people.'

'We haven't fought before. We're not really that kind of couple. Unlike ...'

'Unlike me and Stella?' He ruffled his hair and squinted at me in the fading light.

I laughed. 'I never said that.'

'It's okay. I never thought we'd end up fighting either. What an idiot I was.'

'You aren't the idiot,' I said sincerely. 'She's the one who let you go.'

He grinned. 'Ain't that the truth.'

'So what's going on with you two?' I asked. He usually shied away from questions about Stella, but as he'd brought up the subject I wanted to take advantage of it.

He was visibly upset. 'Stella needs to figure out what she wants.'

'What about what *you* want?'

He looked as though he'd never considered that before. 'What *I* want ...' he said quietly.

Then he changed the subject. 'So what about you?'

I sighed, not wanting to discuss Edward. 'Let him cool off? Then apologize?'

'Sounds good. Things were going well before this row, weren't they?' He leaned across and picked up my hand as I nodded. 'Purity ring still intact, though. Will you really wait until you're married?'

He'd let my hand drop, but was looking at me intently.

'Not necessarily,' I blushed. 'But how do you know if you're with the right person?'

He thought to himself. 'You just do. I can't explain it.'

This wasn't the response I'd hoped for. 'You still think Stella's the right person for you?'

'Of course!' He seemed surprised that I had to ask. 'She always will be. Even though the election has really run away with her. I don't know what she's trying to prove, because I loved her the way she was.'

'And how was that?' I asked, fascinated despite myself.

He twisted his pen between his fingers. 'She was funny, you know? She made me laugh. She took my side, no matter what. She knew how I was feeling, without me telling her. But it's more than that; it's more than I can ever explain. I knew the first time I saw her that there would never be anyone but her.'

We fell into silence. I struggled with my Biology exercise until, having destroyed the paper with my eraser, I looked up. 'Could you please help me? I don't understand this at all.'

'Of course.' He sat beside me, blowing the eraser dust away.

He held his pen funny because he was left-handed, and, although he was smart, his handwriting was spidery and messy. He had a little scar right under his nose and I wanted to reach out and touch the soft curls around his ears. I never noticed these things about Edward.

I hadn't thought of myself as competitive before I came to England, but somehow his words spurred me on. Why was he sure that Stella was the only one for him? He'd spent so long lusting after her that he'd never given anyone else a chance.

So suddenly that I was almost unaware of what I was doing, I kissed him full on the mouth. He froze for a second with a sharp intake of breath, and by the time I heard footsteps it was too late.

Chapter Forty

Stella

In my room I tip out the contents of a wicker sewing basket, finding the letters from Syrena that Mary-Ann keeps emptying from my pigeonhole and pushing under my door. They are unread and I think Syrena knows this as she's written on the envelopes of the last few. 'HELP!!!', 'I NEED TO TELL YOU SOMETHING' and 'STELLA I NEED YOU <u>NOW</u>' are accusingly visible. She's at a dramatic age.

I put the letters aside and leaf methodically through the pile of photographs beneath that chronicle the path I've followed like stepping stones from the moment Paula packed my belongings for my first term at Temperley High. I waited for her to go home before opening the cases and throwing armfuls of my own possessions back onto the floor.

I packed instead from the mausoleum of Siena's room, feverishly filling my cases with everything that could be used or altered, and many items that could not. Then I climbed inside the largest trunk, tucking my feet under me and closing my eyes until she was all around me. When Syrena clambered in and wrapped her arms tightly around my waist, I let her bend my legs in a way that gave me cramp. She kissed me and buried her face in my hair and whispered, so close to my ear that it tickled, that I shouldn't leave her.

I look at the images that exist like beacons to take me and keep me where Siena went; to build me into the success story she was; to make me sure of my decisions.

Tonight, for the first time, I'm sure that the path she would have chosen for me would not be this.

I close my eyes and try to imagine her. *Is this worth it?* she's asking me.

Yes, I try to say, but without conviction.

Without Luke, without the Stars, without Edward, what's left for me at Temperley High? This might have been Siena's victory but it's never going to be mine.

I want to withdraw from the election, I type into my phone. After a moment's hesitation, I send the message to Mary-Ann.

Chapter Forty-one

Caitlin

I'd never seen Edward so furious.

'What the *hell* is going on?' he shouted, throwing a pile of books against the wall with a crash.

Luke was waiting for me to own up and admit I'd instigated everything. My knees shook and my vision swam, but it wasn't for that reason I said nothing. It was because, in the instant before Edward appeared, I was sure Luke had been ready to kiss me back.

Luke got to his feet and started to stammer an apology. It had been a misunderstanding; Edward needed to calm down. Before he'd finished his first sentence Edward had punched him in the face. The force of it knocked Luke into the table, but I knew he wouldn't hit back even to defend himself.

I couldn't hold Edward on my own, but Mary-Ann and Lila appeared from the next workstation and stood in front of Luke to separate them.

Edward dropped his arm and turned to me. 'I was right, wasn't I?' he said softly. 'There's nothing you won't do to be like her.'

'I'm sorry,' I whispered as the enormity of what I'd done started to sink in. 'I'm sorry for hurting you.'

'*Hurting* me? Don't flatter yourself. You couldn't

hurt me if you tried. Surely you know why everyone wants to date you?'

He picked up my hand. 'Anyone who manages to get that ring off you would be a legend. We've been taking bets on you for months. *That's* why.'

He let go of me and walked away as Mary-Ann and Lila watched in shock.

'Whatever Stella's done,' Lila said, 'kissing Luke is never going to be okay.'

Luke gave me one last look and walked in the opposite direction.

Chapter Forty-two

Stella

I sit on the grass by the rose garden. I no longer fit easily inside the tunnel, but sometimes I still like to come here when no one's around, and tonight it's a good way to avoid the hall, where the voting booths are being set up for tomorrow and no one will talk about anything else. It's a warm evening, but it's drizzling steadily and no one else is out here.

Mary-Ann replies to my message. *Sleep on it and decide tomorrow. And you'll have to tell Luke yourself.*

I'm listening to my headphones when he comes around the corner. He draws to a halt when he sees me. I had no idea he still came here too: I guess we're both sentimental, or masochistic.

For a second I think he's going to leave again, but he strides towards me instead. 'What are you doing here?' he demands furiously.

Up close I see that his left eye is rapidly closing and his cheek is swelling up. He's always sustaining injuries on the football field so this isn't a big deal in itself, but something tells me I don't want details about this particular incident.

'It's a public space!' I protest, standing up. 'I have a right to be here too.'

'That's not the point,' he says. 'I don't want to see you. I don't want to be around you – I don't even know who you *are* anymore.'

'Then leave me alone.' He's making no sense and I wonder if he has concussion.

'I've left you alone for weeks and what good has it done? You owe me more than this.'

He forces me to look at him. His eyes are still angry, but they're hurt as well, and I realize now not only what I want, but what Siena would have wanted for me. It might be too late, but that doesn't change anything. I stare at his beautiful hair that kinks and curls in the rain, and my chest contracts.

'I came out here because it reminds me of you,' I say. 'I'm sorry I've invaded your space, but I didn't know you'd be here.'

He gives a short laugh. 'What a joke. Do you remember that you followed up our first meeting here by telling me to stay away from you, like I was some kind of stalker? God, I'm so *stupid*. You showed me exactly what you were like and I still fell for you.'

He hits the palm of his hand on a tree trunk and makes a noise that's somewhere between frustration and pain.

'Did you hurt yourself?' I ask, reaching for his hand.

'No.' I can see tears in his eyes as he shakes me off.

'I didn't hurt myself. *You* hurt me.'

There are tears in my eyes too. 'I'm sorry,' I say through the lump in my throat.

'You're sorry? What for? Rejecting me? Ignoring me? Casting me off like a – like a shoe you don't want? Do you have any idea how you've made me *feel*?'

His outburst amazes me. Is it possible that I've caused him this much pain?

Suddenly I can't think of anything but taking his pain away. I reach out for his hand again and hold onto it when he tries to shake me off.

'I'm going to withdraw from the election,' I say. 'It's over.'

I see something like hope in his eyes, but it dies away. 'It's too late,' he says dully.

I don't know what to say, but suddenly there's only one thing I want to do. Despair makes me reckless.

I have to stand on tiptoes to reach him because I'm not wearing heels, and I worry he'll push me away. He doesn't; he just looks at me, waiting. I put my arms around his neck and kiss him. He starts to jerk his head back, but then stops. For a moment we look at each other, our faces damp from the rain, and then slowly he starts to kiss me back.

At first I'm not sure what's happening, because kissing Luke has never felt like this. I wonder how it feels for him. My breathing is ragged and I think his is too, but I can't hear for sure because everything is mixed up and unclear. I'm getting a crick in my neck but I can't bear to stop.

At some point he pulls away and looks at me. 'Let's go inside,' he murmurs.

I'm lightheaded as I follow him.

Chapter Forty-three

Caitlin

Sure that no one would want to speak to me after what I'd done, I hurried back to Woodlands, cursing myself every step of the way for acting so recklessly at this late stage in the campaign. Although at least the drama helped me to shut out Edward's last words, which had stung more than they should have. Who cared what his reason was for being with me, after all? I'd had an ulterior motive too.

I stared at Stella's locked door. It was obvious that I needed something from her room; something that might redress the balance that had just tipped away from me.

Mrs Stone, a shrunken lady of indeterminate age, was vacuuming the far end of the hallway.

'Could you let me into Stella's room?' I asked her, gesturing to the enormous bunch of keys on her belt. 'She asked me to fetch something for her.'

She looked unconvinced. 'She never even lets *me* in her room, that one. Lord knows what skeletons she keeps in there.'

'It's fine.' I smiled broadly as she launched into a long story about the time she'd stumbled across the family of Dutch rabbits that Edward was breeding under his bed along with some unidentifiable leafy plants. 'Stella's my best friend. We're practically sisters.'

She was still talking as she jangled her keys in her liver-spotted hands.

'Come on,' I muttered under my breath as she finally unlocked the door.

'"*Rats!*" I shouted at the little buggers . . .' she wheezed as I shut myself in and looked around Stella's private domain for the first time.

I'd expected something more remarkable. The room was soulless and practically empty except for regulation furniture and a coffee table. Stella's bed looked like it had never been slept in, its white sheets tucked tightly into the corners. Her books were lined up in size order; the inscription in each said *Siena Hamilton* in loopy cursive. A bunch of essays heaped on her desk were marked with the same.

I'd modelled my own room on the other Stars', decorating the walls with huge photo montages of us, littering the dresser top with make-up and piling new clothes, still in their bags, against the door of a closet already full to bursting. I'd assumed that, in copying Katrina, I was copying Stella, because what could her room be but a more fabulous version of ours?

The walls were bare except for a mirror. In her closet, rows of her uniquely altered clothes hung before me, but, although I sifted through rack after rack of items marked with Siena's name, I didn't find anything that might be useful to me.

As I walked the length of the room, hoping preposterously for a loose floorboard or false panel, I ran my hand along the heavy curtains at the end of the room and nearly fell through. There was nothing behind them.

Holding my breath, I peeked through the gap in the curtains and jumped backwards at the sight of a figure standing there. Daring myself to look again, I relaxed to see that it was a dressmaker's mannequin. Of course it was. Stella's artwork – painted and otherwise – was famous on campus and it figured that she'd use her room as a studio. It also figured that she'd have a bay window, making her room way bigger than mine.

Students had speculated about Stella's Elevation dress for as long as I could remember, even taking bets on the colour and style she was going to wear. Having lost so much support, this was her only chance of getting votes, but I'd never really believed that a mere outfit could compete with months of canvassing.

The dress on the mannequin was ivory silk, with a fitted bodice and gauzy layers. The full-length skirt was covered in gold roses and crystals, and thin gold leaf ran through the fabric. The steel-boned corset, beaded with appliqué roses and more crystals, was so tiny that no one but Stella would ever fit into it without breaking a rib. It was completely, utterly Stella, and, if she wore it, it was debatable whether anyone would notice me at all.

I knelt on the floor and opened a wicker basket to reveal a pile of photographs. There was Stella as a Shell, dressed as Cinderella. As a Remove, her arm around Katrina as they held hockey sticks and an enormous trophy. In the Fourths, on a paintball team with a gang of Stripes. At first I couldn't figure out why two copies of each picture were taped together, and as I tried to make sense of it I could think only of elementary physics: *each force must have an equal and opposite force.*

Every photograph of Stella was mirrored in an earlier image of Siena. Stella was an angel at a Halloween party; so was Siena. Stella was on the netball court, hair pulled into a Stripes scarf; so was Siena. Stella was Éponine in *Les Mis*; so was Siena. Every single thing Stella had done at Temperley High was copied directly from her sister. I held up the images side by side in case they could be weird coincidences, but there was no way this was accidental. The poses; the outfits; even the expressions were the same, as if Stella had studied each picture before recreating it.

Weirder still were the images of Siena and Edward's brother Jack and the matching pictures of Stella and Edward. Then there were the shots of Siena and her clique. Three blondes, two brunettes, one redhead. *The Starlets*, she'd scrawled across the back. *The Stars*, Stella had written more carefully on her own. Katrina had told me, still dazed with pride, how Stella had made them all Stars – plucking them from homesick obscurity – in their first week at Temperley High, but apparently

Stella hadn't so much made friends as cast them.

Alongside the photographs were Siena's report cards, class projects, notes passed to friends: a life in miniature. Stella had chosen the same classes, generated the same gossip, played the same sports and written the same messages in identical handwriting as their lives unravelled in neat tandem.

Next was a photograph of Siena standing on a stool as two handmaids worked on her ivory dress. She was barefoot but regal as tendrils of hair escaped from the diamond-studded clips. I made out one of her attendants to be a younger Stella, and the other became clear as I flipped to the final image.

Stella and Siena looked uncannily similar to their mother as a radiant young bride. The bodice of her wedding dress – a replica of the dress that Siena wore and that hung before me now – had been let out. Her long hair was pale gold in clusters of sapphires that matched the ring finger she held protectively over the swell of her waist. Her expression was soft, as if she had nothing to fear from her future, and she was smiling at her new husband as if he were the centre of her world.

At the bottom of the workbasket was a large purse, which I opened and felt inside. The contents were ashy, and, when I drew out my hand, it was covered in black dust. I brushed it off, freaked out, and crammed everything back into the basket.

Meet me now, I texted quickly as I ran out of the room. *We've got a lot to do.*

Chapter Forty-four

Stella

Luke doesn't speak as he shuts his door behind us, which is unlike him, but then we aren't acting very much like ourselves. Perhaps we don't want to remember what being ourselves entails. Instead he takes my hand and leads me to his bed.

Relief floods over me that I've never done this before. I wonder why I've been kidding myself, chasing something that doesn't exist and cheating myself into believing I wanted more than this, because now it's clear that everything I need – and everything Siena has wanted for me since Luke and I first met in the rose garden – has been mine all along.

'I love you,' he says over and over again, kissing my fingernails, my nose, my ears, my eyelashes.

I kiss him too, again and again, because nothing will ever be better than being with him right now, in this second. It strikes me each time I do how beautiful he is; how strong; how reassuring; how perfect. My own shortcomings are swallowed up because he accepts me, and wants me, in spite of them.

He traces the outline of my face with his finger like a blind person. 'Don't cry,' he whispers, kissing my tears. 'Aren't you happy?'

I try to smile. 'Of course I am. This is the happiest moment I've ever had.'

This at least is true. The emotion is unprecedented, unexplainable; as if I'm literally falling in a way I should never have feared. He's all I can see and hear and feel: he's everything.

Afterwards I wonder how I could ever have thought of leaving him, and how I could have thought I had to hide from him what I am. He would love me whether I was fat, or thin, or happy, or sad, or rich, or poor. All the things I tried to change for him, and to hide from him, never mattered. But the way I changed and hid almost destroyed everything we could have had. Only now do I see that losing him would hurt me in unimaginable ways.

I'm not sure whether I sleep. I expect I do, but I don't remember any part of the night when I'm not conscious of lying in his arms; of trying not to move in case he wakes up and moves away from me. Finally I force myself to be stronger.

He rolls onto his back and pulls me on top of him. I tense for a second but then I surrender and fold, laying my head on his bare chest so I can feel his heart beating. His skin is cool and smooth. He gathers my hair in his hand and tugs it gently, twisting and combing it between his fingers. He kisses my neck and shoulders until I raise my head and then he wraps his arms tightly around me, enveloping me in warmth.

For a moment we look at each other, our faces close together, while I try to commit every detail of him to memory. Then I count down from ten and move away.

'What are you doing?' he mumbles.

I look at him through the gloom as I edge out of bed and pull on my clothes. His hair is standing on end.

'I'm just going to the hall to withdraw us,' I say. 'I'll come back.'

He doesn't argue, but I know he wants to keep me here with him, away from everyone, until the election has safely passed. But I have to make a clean break.

'There's something for you in the wardrobe,' he says. 'I got it for you to wear at Elevation, but maybe we could go out tonight instead and avoid the whole evening. We could actually leave school for once.'

I open the wardrobe to see a dress. It's made of black silk and covered with star-shaped gold sequins that cascade, waterfall-like, down the long skirt.

'I had it made for you,' he says. 'Katrina helped a lot. It should fit you perfectly.'

I hold the dress against myself as I look in the mirror, watching it shimmer.

'Katrina also convinced Penny and Lila to choose a gold theme,' he adds. 'She's pretty clever, actually: she made them think it was their idea.'

'Why would Katrina do this?' I wonder out loud.

'She found out why you got so upset at Edward's party,' he says softly. 'And I thought you should wear gold because—'

'Luke,' I say.

He ignores my interruption. 'Because you're like sunlight to me.'

I mentally sift through the things I could tell him if I knew where to start. How would it feel to shed the solitude I wear like corsetry; to lie beside him with no secrets to separate us? How would he feel if he knew that I chose Edward four years ago believing it was best for him, and that recent events have proven this to be correct? Would it be right or fair to tell him that I've spent the last six months wishing I'd stayed away from him and kept him from the pain?

There's no need to tell him this, because as I cross the room towards him – as I press my palm against his and know that no touch will ever mean more – I know I wouldn't, or couldn't, have changed a single thing.

I take a deep breath. 'I love you.'

It's all I can say; all that makes sense to me. *He*, at last, is all that makes sense to me, and his expression shows that he knows this.

Chapter Forty-five

Caitlin

A knock on the door woke me before the rising bell rang, and it opened before I could answer.

'I had to see how it looked this morning!' Katrina said excitedly as she rushed in and sat beside me on the bed. She was already fully dressed for Election Day.

For a second I wondered what she was talking about, and then I put my hands to my head as my memory came back.

I'd spent an hour the night before kneeling over the bathtub as Katrina dyed my hair. Under normal circumstances I'd never have stooped to something as low-rent as a home kit, but time was limited and I didn't want to give myself the chance to back out.

'Are you sure you know what you're doing?' I'd asked several times as my naturally cautious nature threatened to re-emerge.

'I'm a pro,' she'd reassured me. 'I might even make beauty therapy my career, if quantum physics doesn't pan out.'

Now I sat up, grabbing the mirror from my nightstand and staring into it. My fears had been unjustified.

'How do I look?' I asked, trying out my reflection from different angles.

299

Katrina's initial excitement seemed to fade. 'You look like . . .' she said confusedly. 'I didn't realize it would . . . I mean, why did you want to do it?'

'I needed a new look for Election Day, of course,' I said. 'My old hair was so boring and *brown*.'

She tried to smile as she walked to the door. 'It's definitely not boring and brown now.'

I heard her greet someone outside my bedroom. Recognizing the voice, I jumped up, pressing my ear against the keyhole.

'Where have you been?' Katrina asked. 'Didn't you sleep in your room last night?'

'I was with Luke,' Stella said, as if it didn't matter that I could hear. 'All night.'

'And?' Katrina asked. 'What was it like?'

Suddenly Stella's voice cracked, like she was crying. 'Like nothing will ever be the same again,' she said.

She lowered her voice after a moment's silence. 'Thank you for – you know. It means a lot to me.'

'I'm glad it does.' Katrina's voice was soft.

'And . . .' Stella took a breath. 'I'm sorry.'

'I know you are,' Katrina said.

Voting didn't open until midday but there were no classes. I checked my emails to pass the time and stared at a photograph of my mom and Charlie preparing their Central Park picnic – a July Fourth tradition that Mom had never made time for in living memory.

Have a great day, Charlie! I jabbed at the keyboard,

trying to feel happy that his relationship with her was shaping up so much better than mine had. If it had taken losing me to show her that her kids were important, at least I'd taken the hit for someone who truly deserved it. *Love you*, I added with a long row of kisses, hoping this would make up for the curious detachment I'd started to feel from them both.

Then I turned back to the mirror, adding lip gloss and practising my camera smile. I brushed my new blonde hair, tossing it back and forth so that light reflected off it and made it shine. With this spectacular new look, no one would be talking about what had happened last night. And I had no reason to worry about my election chances either. Edward was a pro; he'd be able to continue as if nothing was wrong. The speculation would probably count in our favour, not to mention the fact that we were the only candidates left in the running anyway.

I picked up my handbag – I was the first Star to have the new Petunia – and headed out.

Chapter Forty-six

Stella

Mary-Ann is waiting for me by the hall.

'I'm glad you made this decision,' she says. She smiles at me for the first time in weeks and laces her hand shyly with mine.

'Do you think I'm doing the right thing?' I ask.

'Yes,' she says firmly. 'It's a snake pit. You don't need this in your life.'

She stops me before we walk in. 'You should know that Ruby is a Star again,' she says nervously.

'I'm glad she is,' I say, meaning it.

Most of the Sixth Form is already inside, and I see Lila, Penny, Ruby and Katrina whispering by the voting booths. I make to avoid them, but Lila turns and nudges the others.

'Is this for real?' she asks as Mary-Ann steers me towards them. 'Are you here to withdraw?'

'Yes,' I say. 'Caitlin can be your candidate, just as you wanted. I don't want anything to do with the election. I don't even want to be a Prefect next year.'

They look blindsided.

'What do you mean?' Penny ventures. 'If you aren't a Prefect . . . what will you be?'

'I'll be *normal*,' I say.

'And so will I,' adds Mary-Ann. 'I don't want to be a Prefect without you.'

Penny looks to Lila for guidance, and I'm relieved not to be the person they consult anymore. 'We'll discuss this later,' Lila reassures her.

Unexpectedly, Katrina grabs my hand. 'One,' she whispers.

I take hers, putting it on top of mine. 'Two,' I say.

Mary-Ann takes Ruby's hand; three. Penny takes Mary-Ann's; four. Lila pauses for a moment and then takes Penny's, five, before adding her own; six.

Stars aligned, we whisper fiercely.

And then I look at the doorway, and thoughts of alignment evaporate.

Chapter Forty-seven

Caitlin

'What the hell do you think you're doing?' Stella asked as I walked over to her. She was as composed as ever, but I knew her better now and I could tell she was scared.

'I don't know what you mean,' I said nonchalantly.

'Your hair!' She sounded stunned.

I smiled. 'It's the biggest day of the year, right? I had to make a special effort.'

Stella didn't take her eyes off me as the other Stars looked from one of us to the other.

'What's going on?' Penny asked uncertainly.

'Nothing,' Stella and I said in unison.

Lila was losing interest. 'We need to get going, then. We've got lots to do. Party planning is *such* a high-pressure responsibility.'

'And I need to find a date,' Penny complained for the fiftieth time. She was still dating the stable hand, but the Stars' latest debate, proposed and won by Lila (*This house believes that no outsiders should attend official school functions with Stars*), had ensured that they wouldn't be going together.

'I should have let my dad hire me one of his clients. But it seemed so *desperate* to go with someone from *Holby City*,' she sighed.

'Especially if you had to pay them,' Ruby giggled.

'I heard you're here to withdraw,' I said to Stella, partly to restore some sanity to the conversation. 'I guess that means you can just kick back and enjoy Elevation without any pressure.'

In her heels she was as tall as me, and she stared with an intensity that made me uncomfortable, as if she knew more about me than I'd ever told anyone. 'I don't know where you heard that,' she said.

I took no notice of her. She was a spent force. If she were a celebrity, this would be the moment she joined a cockroach-eating reality show. But the others were as mesmerized by her as they'd ever been.

'What?' Lila asked. 'Stella, what are you talking about?'

Stella ignored her, as if she and I were the only people in the room. 'I'm still in,' she said firmly.

'You're *what*?' asked Luke.

Stella spun around, guilt written all over her face.

Chapter Forty-eight

Stella

'You're *what*?'

Luke looks as if someone's hit him. I suppose I might as well have done; a hammer blow would probably have hurt him less.

'You lied to me.' He stares at me as if desperate for a clue that I've changed my mind; as if he can remind me of everything that happened last night. 'You said you were coming back.'

'I'm sorry,' I say. 'I have to compete.'

'You have to,' he repeats. 'Why do you have to?'

I look to Caitlin, whose golden hair glows in the midday sun. She is Siena; more Siena than I will ever be, even after years of training.

'I don't understand what's changed in the last hour,' he says, trying to force my attention back to him. 'Is this because Caitlin has a new haircut?'

'It's nothing to do with Caitlin,' I say.

I still can't tear my eyes from her, but in a way this is true, because it's not Caitlin I'm seeing.

'Stella, listen to me,' he says quietly. 'There's a life waiting for you outside this. I know you think it's the election or nothing, but you're wrong. It's the election or *everything*.'

I try to listen to him, but Caitlin's blonde hair is my new centre of gravity. I think of withdrawing; of living for the next year under the rule of this profanity. And I can't let her do it without a fight.

'I hope Luke isn't too upset with you, Stella,' Caitlin says. 'Don't forget, you can't run without him. You need a partner.'

I look at Luke in despair.

'What are you asking me?' he says. 'To run in an election I don't believe in and can't win so you can play games with these silly girls?'

No one speaks, but I beg him silently with every fibre of my being.

'I'll do it,' he says finally. 'I'll do it as long as you understand I will *never* speak to you again after tonight.'

'I understand,' I whisper.

I remember how it felt to spend the night with him; to feel as if nothing mattered but him. But I must have known what was going to happen. The die was cast before we even met.

'I hope that one day you'll realize what you're forfeiting,' he says as he turns and walks away.

Chapter Forty-nine

Caitlin

After Luke stormed off, Ruby took the floor.

'Caitlin is a true friend,' she said grandly. 'And I'm going to repay her by withdrawing from the election. I want to stand alongside her, not against her.'

There was a short silence, during which I hoped no one would mention that they'd forgotten Ruby was still a Head Girl candidate.

'Wow, Ruby,' I said. 'That means so much to me.'

I smiled meaningfully at Lucy. 'Ruby will be a great Prefect next year.'

It didn't really matter if Lucy was standing or not – she was at worst an inconvenience – but it seemed a waste of her time. Not to mention that she was going to be humiliated when the results came in, and that she'd totally mess up the symmetry of the photographs.

I hoped she'd be smart about this. Being a Prefect would mean a lot to her: she was the only candidate who had actually bothered to write some policies, and she should really be considering her options. Without Mary-Ann and Stella, there would be a vacancy, and, if she didn't fill that sixth spot, someone else would.

Caroline, as Ruby's manager, was looking pissed. She evidently hadn't been consulted about Ruby's decision to withdraw and was a useful pawn.

'Thanks so much for your support, Caroline,' I said, still looking at Lucy. 'I won't forget it next year when I choose my Prefects.'

Caroline brightened up considerably. 'You're welcome, Caitlin. You know I've always supported you.'

'I'm withdrawing,' Lucy burst out. 'I don't want to stand against you either, Caitlin.'

I smiled. 'You're such a good friend, Lucy.'

'So there are just two candidates after all?' Lila said. 'You and Stella? Well, at least one of you is going to win.'

'It looks that way,' I said, although Lucy's decision had only served to make this official. There had always been only two candidates.

As the group disintegrated, I joined Luke on the stage. All the candidates were supposed to be here when voting opened, and it seemed a good idea to be on view, but Luke was visibly tense as the students gathered around us.

'Where's your partner, Richings?' someone shouted. 'Don't tell me she's dumped you *again*?'

'What about yours, Clarke?' added a different voice. 'Doesn't true love wait after all?'

Laughter broke out and I felt myself blush red.

'Just ignore them,' Luke said quietly. 'You're still going to win.'

'I know that, but we look lame without our partners,' I complained. 'Where the hell are they?'

A group of kids came in late, swinging open the double doors to show Edward and Stella huddled closely together outside. His arm was around her shoulders and it looked like they were kissing.

'Don't you get sick of always being second best?' Luke asked abruptly.

'What does that mean?' I asked, trying not to sound annoyed. Hadn't he noticed all the *Vote Caitlin* rosettes in the crowd?

He looked as if someone had broken him, but his voice was steady. 'Do you want to go to Elevation with me tonight?'

'Are you trying to make Stella jealous?' I felt I should ask this, even though I really didn't care.

He leaned in and it took all my willpower to stay still. Finally, slowly, he moved even closer. 'You're shaking,' he said.

I was pleased that we were on display to everyone. I tilted my head so he couldn't block me from any cameras.

He hesitated. 'I'm worried you've built this into something it's not.'

I haven't. I wasn't sure whether I spoke out loud. He kissed me softly and I shivered. 'You're so innocent,' he said.

'I'm not that innocent.'

The door swung open again as Edward entered, and I hesitated for a fraction of a second as I considered the effect on our election chances of me publicly kissing the opposition. But then I saw Stella watching from outside, and my lips were on Luke's.

Life as the new girl had been tough, but as Luke and I kissed we became the power couple that everyone envied. I headed the most popular clique in school. I had a hot guy. I was top of the class. People not only looked up to me; they wanted to be me. I was a success, and as a permanent fixture at Temperley High my opportunities were endless. As I stepped into the void Stella was about to create, no one could stop me from getting everything I deserved.

Chapter Fifty

Stella

Edward catches my arm as I pass him outside the hall.

'Where are you going?' he asks. 'Did you withdraw?'

'Edward,' I say. 'Tell me what's happening to me. What's happening to *us*? How did everything go so wrong?'

We both take a step back and then sit on the floor. I draw my knees up underneath my chin and turn towards him, hoping for an answer.

'Sometimes . . .' he says. 'Sometimes when I close my eyes, your face is all I see.'

I shift uncomfortably as a group of Fourths walks past. Just as they throw open the hall doors, Edward leans forward and kisses me. I freeze as his lips touch mine before gathering my senses enough to pull away.

'I have to go,' I stammer. 'Edward, this can never happen.'

'But isn't this supposed to happen?' he says. 'You and Luke are finished; Caitlin and I are finished. It's Elevation Day. You can see where this is headed.'

'No one knows where it's headed,' I say. 'Why can't we make our own futures?'

'You can't have it both ways,' he says, and for once he is just sad, with nothing to mask it. 'You knew what you were doing to me, even when you were twelve years old, and every year since.'

And Katrina's words chime with their truth.

You stop Edward sleeping with other girls because you don't want to lose your hold on him.

I've let him believe there was a way back for us because I wanted there to be; because I was determined to be with him as Siena was with Jack. I've kept him from other girls in case that meant the end for us; because even though I loved Luke in a way that couldn't be contested or ignored or changed, I couldn't set Edward free.

Edward stands and turns back to me as he opens the double doors. 'I understand it now,' he says. 'And if it could only have ended like this, at least it can end right here.'

Before he's swallowed up I see Caitlin and Luke kissing, right in the middle of the stage, underneath the portrait of Siena. From this distance, either Caitlin or Siena could be me.

Chapter Fifty-one

Caitlin

'Where have you been?' I asked Katrina when I tracked her down in her room later that afternoon. 'You're missing the fun.'

'Didn't you hear Penny screaming?' She was agitated. 'The crown is gone. She took all my Diazepam when she found out, so I had to help Lila look for it.'

'*What?*' I said in outrage. 'Someone stole my crown? Did no one hire security?'

'We don't know for sure that it was stolen,' she said. 'Penny swears it was in the hall this morning, but no one seems to know what's happened to it.'

'First the sash; now the crown,' I said. 'Does Stella really think stealing them is the same as winning them?'

She looked worried. 'I don't think she'd do that. The sash has been missing for years, ever since Siena died. Have you seen Stella this afternoon? I'm worried about her.'

Katrina's attitude had become so distorted that I didn't see how I was going to tell her about all the photographs I'd found in Stella's room. She might even blame me for snooping and let Stella off the hook for her own behaviour. That was a pity, because the Stars

314

deserved to know that Stella had never considered them friends at all.

'What do you think is the matter?' I asked, pretending I cared. 'Luke? Or Edward?'

'Maybe,' she said. 'Edward's known her for such a long time, but whatever exists between them is weird. Sometimes he seems really possessive.'

'Hardly,' I said derisively. '*She* controls all her relationships. Edward's just collateral damage.'

She looked miserable. 'Who knows? I'm not sure any of us should be Head Girl. This was supposed to be the best night of our lives, and now the crown's missing and everyone's fighting. I really don't feel like going to a party.'

'It's still going to be great!' I said, thinking about the replacement crown I could order from Harrods. It was better this way because the original crown was a little gaudy. If I were allowed style input this time around, I could ask for my name to be studded into it with sapphires. 'The crown doesn't make a Head Girl; the votes do. And we've worked too hard not to enjoy ourselves.'

She forced a smile. 'I haven't even decided what to wear yet. Can you help me?'

She was throwing dresses onto the bed when there was a timid knock at the door and Lucy and Hannah came in.

'Wow,' Lucy breathed, staring at all the discarded clothes that probably added up to more than most people's yearly salaries. 'You're going to look amazing.'

I was embarrassed that they were being so over-familiar. Sure, we'd hung out when I didn't know anyone else, and I'd allowed them to sit with me at lunch when there was strength in numbers. But I'd been Edward's girlfriend; I'd made out with Luke; I'd overthrown Stella and was about to be crowned Head Girl. Why would they think we still had anything to talk about?

Lucy was wearing her usual mom jeans and a shapeless tank top. Her face was shiny and her frizzy hair was unforgivably mousy. She wore glasses with little frames, even though everyone was wearing oversized frames right now. It was frightening to think that only a few months ago I wouldn't have known how much this mattered. And she was presentable compared to Hannah, who, in her off-duty sweats and tee, looked like a *before* picture in a Jenny Craig infomercial. She was even eating a candy bar. There was really no excuse.

'You have to choose the perfect outfit, Caitlin,' Lucy said. 'This is the only way Stella can claw back the advantage, so you mustn't give her the opportunity.'

What other criteria are there? Penny had asked months ago.

'But the hall was full when voting opened,' I said, my mind suddenly exploding with the memory of the white dress from Stella's room. 'Whatever Stella wears for Elevation, it'll be too late.'

'Hardly anyone's voted yet,' Lucy said in a timid don't-shoot-the-messenger voice. 'They all vote online during Elevation; no one uses the booths anymore. Didn't anyone tell you that Penny and Lila have pushed the announcement back? It used to be made at nine, but this year it won't be until nearly midnight. Penny said it wasn't ethical if the dresses weren't on view for at least three hours.'

I turned to Katrina in disbelief. 'People won't vote until they get a good look at her dress?'

Katrina looked embarrassed. 'You always knew this election wasn't about policies.'

'No, it's about *popularity*,' I said. 'Not dresses! I can't believe how shallow everyone's become.'

'You just have to make sure that everyone prefers your dress,' Lucy said. 'It's a shame we don't know what Stella's wearing.'

'How would that help?' Katrina asked.

'She likes to stand out from the crowd, doesn't she?' Lucy said, glancing at my blonde hair. 'She'd hate someone to wear the same colour.'

'The Stars' dress code is gold,' Katrina reminded everyone.

'Do you really think she'll take any notice of that?' I asked scornfully. 'Plus, she's not a Star anymore. She's not eligible to wear gold.'

Katrina shrugged and looked away.

'So what time are you going to Elevation, Lucy?' I asked casually, zipping myself into one of Katrina's dresses.

Lucy looked surprised. 'We're coming to pre-victory

drinks in Lila's room.' She looked at Katrina for affirmation.

Katrina was about to reply when I stepped in. 'See, I'm not sure there's space. We might have counted wrong when we invited you.'

'No, we didn't.' Katrina ignored my raised eyebrows. 'There's plenty of space.'

I wondered when she'd become such a bleeding heart. It wasn't long since she'd been spewing out insults at them herself.

'Really, there isn't,' I said through gritted teeth.

Lucy wasn't dumb, and for that I was grateful. 'I see,' she said slowly. 'Well, I suppose we'll just meet you over at the hall. Let's go, Hannah.'

I called to her as they reached the door: I didn't want to sound mean, but it needed saying. 'Lucy, are you at least going to wash your hair and put on some concealer?'

She swallowed hard. 'I'd hate to embarrass you,' she said in a brittle voice.

Katrina turned to me when they'd gone. 'What was that about?' she asked in amazement. 'I thought they were your friends.'

'*Were* is correct,' I sniffed. 'I've worked hard for this. I don't want them tagging along and ruining it. Plus, they've already voted! We don't need to be nice to them anymore.'

She looked upset. 'Have you forgotten that Lucy forfeited her own election place for you? You should think more carefully about how you treat people.'

Katrina was suddenly another obstacle. No wonder Stella hadn't wanted her as a campaign manager; she was even more boring than Mary-Ann.

She was trying out a dress that I hadn't seen before. It was short and form-fitting, its gold tassels showing off her tan as well as her slender legs. She must always have been pretty, but being close to Stella was like standing in shadow. Now I saw for the first time the distracting golden lights in her hair; her careless elegance; the determination so evident in her heart-shaped face. And I started to wonder if Stella had known more than she'd let on when she'd replaced her with Mary-Ann. The Katrina I thought I knew, defined by her giggling bitchy comments and professionally accessorized boho outfits, didn't exist any more than the Stella I thought I'd seen that day in the clock tower.

I unzipped the dress, which gaped, and put my own clothes back on. Katrina's closet was a total disappointment, and there was nothing here that resembled Stella's masterpiece.

'I'm going out,' I said. 'I'll see you later – *if* you aren't busy hanging out with total losers.'

She nodded slowly. 'It's probably best if you find your own dress – you've got so skinny that I doubt any of mine will fit you.'

I grinned to myself as I left the room. I got the feeling she'd been trying to insult me, but it didn't feel like anything other than a huge compliment.

Chapter Fifty-two

Stella

When it's time to get ready for Elevation, I pull back the curtains to fetch my dress. Then I close the curtains and open them again. I circle the room as if it's hiding from me. I check the wardrobe; under the bed; even in cupboards that are too small to house it. I touch the mannequin in case it's become invisible. And then I face the truth: my dress is gone.

I hear the Stars getting ready, clattering along the corridor in their high heels, screaming about waterproof mascara and rowing about music choices. I gather one of them – probably Lila – trapped her ear in her hair straighteners and injured herself. Rihanna pumps out of her room as their pre-victory party begins.

There are false starts as girls come back in search of keys, cigarette lighters and lip gloss, and then it's silent. I open the window and put my head outside, not so much for the fresh air as for the music I can now hear from the boys' rooms in Riverside. It gives me a link to the world, even if I can't be there. *The mirror crack'd from side to side*, I suddenly think, and duck back in. There's no need to freak myself out even more.

A knock at the door makes me jump, and I call out 'Come in' before I can think about what I'm doing. I don't know whether to be pleased or disappointed when Mrs Denbigh's head appears.

'What are you still doing here, Stella love?' she says. 'Why aren't you at Elevation with the others?'

Part of me wants to tell her that, for the last time, my surname isn't Love, but it doesn't seem to matter anymore. 'I'll go soon,' I say.

She sits awkwardly on the bed, ankles crossed in the way she taught us to sit when we were Shells in her Manners class. She doesn't mention the fact that I'm crying, or try to feed me a Garibaldi, and I'm grateful on both counts. 'It might not be as bad as you imagine.'

I nod stoically but ruin it by sniffing, exactly as she always instructed us not to. 'You're right. It might be *worse* than I imagine.'

'Maybe,' she concedes. 'But the chances are that nothing very dramatic will happen. And perhaps it will help to face everyone.'

'I doubt it.' I hope it's clear that she doesn't understand the situation.

'I know you girls all think I'm about a hundred years old, but I was your age once. I do remember what all this is like. And you're not yourself at the moment, Stella. Is there something you want to tell me?'

I look at her off-duty wardrobe: her brown skirt

and flat shoes, her green polo neck and wayward, bushy hair. She looks a bit like a tree, but a reliable one, offering shade. I've never thought of her in this way before, but now I remember having appendicitis when I was a Remove. Seraphina was unavailable so Mrs Denbigh stayed with me in hospital, even though it was unnecessary, and, when I couldn't sleep, she read to me from *Practical Horseman*. She held my hand as I had my anaesthetic, and when, to my everlasting shame, I called her *Mother* as it wore off, she didn't tell anyone.

For a split second I consider talking. Then the feeling passes. 'I don't want to go, thank you.' My tone offers no room for doubt.

She stands up and shakes out her skirt. 'Well, I can't force you. But I do think you should know that Luke looked very lonely tonight. Perhaps you'd consider going just to keep him company. These things are tough on boys too.'

'He's with Caitlin.'

'Maybe he's trying to protect himself,' she suggests. 'He has his pride, after all. Maybe Caitlin's not really the one he wants to be with.'

She ducks out of the door and returns a second later holding the gold dress I left in Luke's bedroom this morning. 'I'm under instructions to bring you this,' she says.

I nod mutely, wondering how many lifetimes could pass without me ever deserving Luke.

'I'll let you get on with your book,' she says. 'I'll be in my office if you need me.'

Damn her.

I sit for what feels like a long time with the dress laid out in front of me. I've never talked to anyone about my intended Elevation dress, so Luke couldn't possibly have known, but I see in his offering a different, freer future than the cage I constructed for myself. This flowing silk doesn't imprison me with steel that suffocates my idiosyncrasies; it accommodates them, encouraging me to be a better shape.

Gold fabric streams endlessly over my hands and I'm transfixed by shimmering sequins that reflect Siena's face in their stars like a million brilliant lights. And I'm fortunate to have experienced through Luke one thing that she never could. I may not have been able to keep him, but I'll never forget how it felt to love him.

I brush out my hair and apply my make-up as I learned when I was too young even to hold the brushes for myself, and I leave Woodlands. I glance up at the clock tower, half-expecting it to read something other than twenty to twelve, and then I throw open the hall doors.

Chapter Fifty-three

Caitlin

For once no one had exaggerated: Elevation was a *huge* deal. And it was going better than I could ever have imagined.

'How did they get it so wrong?' Penny had wailed when we'd arrived. Despite all the coffee Lila had forced down her, she was still baked and over-emotional. 'It's supposed to be Stars! It's supposed to be gold!'

'Penny, the theme is *Stars and Stripes*, and it's Independence Day,' said Katrina patiently. 'You can see how the party planners got confused, especially left unsupervised.'

Penny had described at length the venue that would be entirely decorated with gold stars, ensuring that the night belonged only to our comeback. Evidently something had been lost in translation. The room was decked out with American flags. The band was playing 'The Star-Spangled Banner'. The buffet was American-themed. Star-shaped decorations were plentiful but only in red, white and blue. Instead of being a party for the Stars, it was a party for me.

'You can't wear that!' Lila had said in horror when she'd seen my beautiful white dress. 'We're all in gold!'

'Gold doesn't suit me,' I'd complained. 'Anyway, we

can't all match! We don't want to look twelve, do we?'

'I clash with the walls!' said Penny. 'And there are carbs in the buffet! Someone is *so* getting fired for this.'

'I think it's great,' I said happily, taking a red Statue of Liberty cocktail and raising my glass. 'Cheers!'

Luke, who was acting distant, was the only thing making the evening less than perfect. 'Are you okay?' I tried to focus his attention on me.

He smiled guardedly. 'Of course. I just can't get used to you . . .'

I shook out my hair. 'Are you surprised?'

He nodded. 'It's . . . it's unexpected. What made you do it?'

I tried to keep my voice light. 'I wanted a change. Stella doesn't have the monopoly on being blonde, you know. Don't you like it?'

I could see my reflection in the window. My new sleek hair hung loose to my waist and the lights in the room made my golden highlights shine. I looked sensational.

He nodded. 'You're always beautiful. But you look very different.'

I thought back to kick-off when he'd told me not to copy the Stars. *You're a beautiful girl, just as you are,* he'd said. But what did he know anyway? It wasn't his opinion that mattered.

Edward and Katrina joined me when Luke went to fetch us more drinks. 'Don't you care that Luke's just trying to make Stella jealous?' Edward teased.

'Don't you care that Stella only dated you to copy her sister?' I shot back.

Edward thought for a moment before replying. 'No, I don't think I do.' He sounded surprised, as if he hadn't realized that he'd made his peace with it.

'You'll always love her,' I said. Although he'd been my boyfriend only hours before, it didn't hurt me to admit this.

'At least you two have one thing in common, then,' Katrina said. 'Now will you stop fighting?'

'Perhaps we should make a toast to winning,' I suggested after an awkward silence.

'Don't you think we should wait for the announcement?' Katrina sounded uneasy. 'It's bad luck to count your chickens.'

Ignoring her, I held up my glass. 'To beating Stella.'

Edward joined me, but Katrina stubbornly looked the other way. It was as if she'd totally lost sight of what was important. It wasn't even clear to me whose side she was on.

As always, Stella was preceded by her own hype; as always, I watched her arrival as intently as everyone else did. And, as always, she was way ahead of me.

'She's incredible,' Penny whispered. 'She looks like an angel.'

Penny might have been totalled, but she was right.

Stella had unexpectedly adhered to the dress code, but even in the same colour as the other Stars she looked entirely distinct. Her dress streamed like liquid gold. Her hair, in loose waves around her face and cascading down her back, was a glittering extension of the star-shaped sequins. And her face was restored like a remastered painting. Possibility and hope radiated from her like sunshine.

She walked slowly towards us through the centre of the room, her dress sparkling in the spotlights, and the crowds parted for her.

'What are we toasting?' she asked, taking a champagne flute from a passing waiter.

Edward smiled. 'Victory.'

She raised her glass as cameras flashed around us like lightning bolts. 'Perfect.'

'You're like a flame, Stella,' Penny said, swaying dreamily. 'And all the boys – and girls – are hypnotized by you, like creatures hovering around a lighted candle.'

Stella smiled at her. 'Can the candle help it?'

'No, but can't the Stella help it?' I said.

She gave me a contemptuous once-over and then spoke quietly so that no one else could hear. 'I know what you're doing, but you will *never* be me, and you'll be sorry you tried.'

Luke looked as though his sun rose and set with her face. She turned from me to him, and if I weren't wise to her powers of manipulation I might have believed that her sun rose and set with his face too.

Having been so strong until now, he was crumbling. As he took a tentative step towards her, I moved firmly into his path. He'd thank me later.

'Do you want to dance?' I asked him as a slow song began.

He and Stella locked eyes as if they were connected by something gossamer-thin but enduring. Then somewhere in the room a champagne flute shattered, and their eye contact was severed.

Luke shrugged as Stella's face fell in something like despair. 'Why not?'

We walked to the centre of the dance floor and I wrapped my arms around him, making sure we were right in the spotlight. He was a good dancer, but then again he was good at everything. We fit together, and soon he would see that.

I moved to kiss him, but he held back. 'I can't,' he said. 'I'm sorry, Caitlin.'

It figured that he wanted us to be alone before we kissed again. That was fine with me: we'd be spending the summer in the same city, with Stella thousands of miles away. Laying my head against his shoulder, I looked around, but she was nowhere to be seen.

Chapter Fifty-four

Stella

For a moment I watch Luke dance with Caitlin, and knowing how much I deserve this pain makes it even more acute. As it overwhelms me, I walk out of the hall and into the plush bathroom, which by some miracle is empty. My heavy heels echo as I check each of the stalls before standing in front of the giant mirror.

I've spent hours in front of mirrors over the years, wondering what it is that makes me beautiful. Tonight my features haven't changed and yet I'm ugly, because everything beneath this glossy surface is monstrous, and the surface is as brittle as porcelain.

I take off my shoes and hold one by its heel. They are silver, with heels that look like glass, and, even though they don't match my dress, I wore them because they were Siena's favourites. I wonder fleetingly how they fit us both, but it's not the size that's important; it's the weight. I hurl one at the mirror as hard as I can.

I don't expect it to break; at most, I hope to crack it into a spider's web that distorts and conceals my reflection. But the heel strikes a weak spot and the glass shatters like an explosion. The noise fills my ears and I see sparks as diamond shards fly everywhere, one stabbing my cheek as the others splinter on the floor.

Good, I think. *Now I'm as ugly as I feel.*

I'm addicted to my reflection and yet I hate it. I hate my face for making people look at me and judge me before I speak a single word. I hate my face for blinding people to the chaos beneath, and allowing me to lie and cheat while still they clamour to be my friend. I hate my face because it belongs to my mother, and to Siena; because it's not only destroyed each of us in turn but taken everyone around us with it.

I pace the room, noticing belatedly that I'm walking in broken glass so that bloody footprints follow me on white marble. In this instant I can't see a way out, and I don't want a way out. I feel like gouging the glass into myself, but I don't. Instead I pick up a razor-edged shard and use it to cut through my hair. It's made excuses for me for long enough. And, as I cut, I see that the glass belongs not to the mirror, but to the heel of Siena's shoe.

Cutting my hair frees me from my self-imposed plans for the future; by extension, it frees me from my sisters too. But forcibly separating myself from them seems suddenly nonsensical. How could I have thought I wanted to be free of Siena? How could I have believed that loving Syrena would damage or weaken us, when it's obvious – excruciatingly so – that the ties binding me to her are the only earthly things that matter?

As yards of my gilded prison slip away from me to the floor, I trace my hands over what remains. And, at the very instant I forfeit my best hope of seeing Siena again, I hear the chant begin outside.

Chapter Fifty-five

Caitlin

After a bell signalled the end of voting I waited patiently, trying not to bite my nails before the moment Penny and Lila took to the stage. As a reward for their work on the Elevation Committee they'd been allowed to announce the results, and they looked as if they were going to enjoy their moment. Never ones to ignore a trend, they had made Stars and Stripes minidresses out of flags, knotting them like togas. I estimated that they would fall down within ten minutes, which might have been their intention.

'Where's Stella?' I asked, looking around. 'Surely she won't miss the announcement, after all her drama?'

'Please can the teams join us on the stage!' Lila shouted as Katrina and I fought our way up the steps in front of Luke and Edward, Quentin and Tom. Mary-Ann waited on the floor, looking around anxiously.

'Stella Hamilton, where are you?' Penny said indistinctly, peering into the audience. 'Get on stage right now!'

'You can't announce the results without Stella here,' I objected. 'Go and find her!'

Penny and Lila conferred and then turned to me. 'We can't delay this, Caitlin,' Lila said. 'If we don't announce the winner now, the fireworks will be out of sync. It's bad enough that we never found the crown.'

I looked at Edward in frustration, but he only shrugged. Penny was crying again at the mention of the crown, and Lila took the microphone from her.

'This has been the most closely fought election Temperley High has ever seen,' she intoned seriously. 'But it's finally time for the results. Are you ready?'

Everyone had clustered around the stage and started to chant, although I couldn't hear who for. The band's reprise of 'The Star-Spangled Banner' drew to a close before a moment of tense silence.

But as the spotlights zoomed from me to the audience, I squinted in confusion. Instead of waiting intently for the announcement, the students were crowding around the windows at the back of the hall. The noise levels increased until I could hear nothing except the name they were whispering.

'What's going on?' Luke asked uneasily. 'Is this something to do with . . . ?'

Not pausing to tell anyone where I was going, I ran down from the stage and out of the room.

Out in the courtyard I could see that the door leading to the clock tower was open. There was no way I was going to let Stella get away with hiding out there any longer, and as new Head Girl I should be the one to bring this to an end. The punishment for being caught up there was so severe that, no matter what the vote count, she'd just disqualified herself from the whole event. All I needed to do was catch her in the act.

I was out of breath by the time I'd climbed the spiral stairwell, and I took a second as I reached a heavy door at the top. Using both hands, I turned the rusty metal latch and pushed against it.

The room I entered was empty but for a ladder up to an open trapdoor in the ceiling. I reluctantly took off my heels, wishing I'd had time to change before my dress got covered in dirt, and began to climb the rungs.

The floor I landed on was filthy, and I brushed dust from my hands and knees, blinking as my eyes adjusted. There was no electric light, but candles littered the wooden floor.

'I knew it,' I said.

This decrepit garret was the polar opposite of Stella's sterile bedroom, but the evidence I needed was right here. Essays, clothes, books and paintbrushes encapsulated her entire world in this tiny space. Wealth and decline were oddly juxtaposed in opulent, shroud-like evening dresses slung across the dusty floor; in brightly coloured, forgotten gemstones jammed into cracked floorboards; in exclusive, discarded beauty products covered in cobwebs. This attic, like Stella herself, was a memorial to unrealized expectations.

Light from the room below spread through gaps in the uneven floorboards that teetered with every movement. No wonder students were forbidden to set foot up here: too much weight and the whole tower would collapse into itself.

When I saw the portrait I wondered if my eyes were playing tricks on me, but, as I moved closer across the creaking floorboards and away from the safety of the trapdoor, it remained. It was changed from the last time I'd seen it, showing Stella now accessorized with the famous Head Girl crown and sash. Aside from the fact that her hair hung loose, the painting was a replica of the famous image of Siena. Her painted eyes stared at me in sad defiance of the coveted future she herself had shattered.

And then, hearing a noise, I picked up a candle to see better and walked towards the open window.

Chapter Fifty-six

Stella

Even as I look up at the clock tower I can believe it's not happening. Even as my eyes lock on the figure standing with nothing between her and the ground seventy feet below, I can believe that it's only my imagination.

Only when the students swarm from the hall and gather, as if this is entertainment, to watch the figure in the tower that they can see as clearly as I can, do I accept it. And then I can do nothing but watch the girl who wears my white dress, her feet bare and her hip-length hair shining like a river in the moonlight, until she blurs into my past.

Siena had left the dining room after her fight with Seraphina, and I followed her into the garden to see her drag off her beautiful white dress and throw it onto the ground. Before I could stop her, she had struck a match. Her dress was vaporized.

Even in the firelight she was deathly pale. She stood inches from the flames in her petticoat and bare feet as the remains of her ambition floated into the night like burning confetti.

I hurled myself at her. 'Where are you going?' I

asked as she pulled away from me.

'There's something I have to do,' she said. 'One day you'll understand.'

'No.' I reached for the sash that she was still wearing. 'Tell me what I did wrong and I can change. But don't leave.'

She prised my hands from the sash. 'Stay away from this,' she said gently.

She pulled the comb out of my hair so that waves crashed to my waist. 'This is what I want you to do for me,' she said, smoothing it with her fingers. 'I want you to wear your hair like this, and not listen to anyone who tells you differently.'

'Don't leave me,' I sobbed as I clung to her.

She was never demonstrative, but even less so now as she stepped away. 'I have to,' she said as she headed towards her car that final time and drove back to school.

Seraphina spent the next day as she would spend most of the ensuing years, at the head of the dining table amongst the remains of the celebration dinner, clad in some variation on the flimsy white georgette dress she'd worn that night. The room stood as it would stand forever, white streamers floating and falling, balloons deflating, decorative stars losing their sheen as the white tablecloth turned grey and dust obscured the unwashed plates. In the centre, candle wax had burned craters through the cake icing, and the figurines of Siena and Jack, unbalanced as the sponge began to subside, lay cracked on opposite sides of the plate.

After the funeral I returned to the cold embers of Siena's dress and swept everything that remained into her favourite Balenciaga bag. The bones of the corset were steel survivors, and I preserved them too. For years I did nothing more than stare at the ashes, but as Elevation drew closer I began to rebuild the dress from its skeleton. I draped dupion and organza, taffeta and lace. I sewed crystals and roses and leaves. I laced the corset with ribbons that tightened and tautened as if I might one day vanish into layers of tulle and crêpe. I worked until the dress was indistinguishable from its previous incarnation; until it was ready to fulfil the destiny for which it was intended.

Everyone on the ground gasps as the girl in the tower stands on tiptoe, reaching for something in the centre of the clock face. She works industriously, but someone shouts my name up at her and she's distracted. Her foot slips and her palms slap against the wall. The name-calling turns into a chant and finally, hideously, the courtyard echoes with an incantation of my name that rises on the air like confetti and fills every corner of the school.

The girl in the tower – the girl everyone believes is me – is unwinding something from the axis of the clock face. It's a gold sash; the Head Girl's sash, and I hear Siena telling me, *Stay away from this.*

And finally I understand that Siena never planned to leave me; that she climbed the tower that night in order to hide the symbol of the behaviours she despised in a place I'd never find it. She hid the sash to keep me from becoming as heartless as she believed she was; to give me a chance of loving someone the way she'd been incapable of loving Jack. When she died, she was trying to save me.

And now the clock is ticking, its rhythm filling my ears, and I see the girl's foot slip; see her fall to the ground where, soon afterwards, roses will grow.

'Siena!' I scream before I can stop myself.

My voice breaks as I feel Siena's loss again and again, shattering over me like glass. But, when I look up, the girl is still standing high on the ledge. This time she doesn't plummet to the ground. This time she recovers her balance and edges her way back, grabbing the window and swinging herself inside. This time she's safe.

Someone turns at the sound of my voice and nudges their neighbour in confusion. One by one they turn and stare, trying to connect the familiar girl on the ledge with the blood-streaked and hysterical vision I've become.

Then their attention turns back to the tower as something flames at the place where the girl just stood.

The tower is on fire.

*

339

I am running; I am fighting; I am screaming as I push my way through the crowds. Before I reach the door someone grabs hold of me, pulling me off my feet.

'You're not going up there,' says Edward fiercely. 'I won't lose you again.'

I twist around until I see Luke. He's running towards us and I struggle harder.

Tears are streaming down my face. 'Luke, please,' I say, my words hot and ragged.

Edward's face is set and he's hurting my wrists. He has his hand over my mouth and I can't breathe, but I kick as hard as I can against him, and suddenly I'm free, and Edward and Luke are behind me.

My chest burns as I claw my way through the once-locked doorway. I take the stairs two, three at a time; I become disconnected from myself as I climb higher and higher, pushing through another doorway and climbing a ladder into an attic filled with smoke.

Chapter Fifty-seven

Caitlin

It happened too fast for me even to be sure of the sequence of events. The curtain was old and threadbare, yet my candle was enough to set off a dull roar that dripped burning embers onto evening dresses in a blaze that spread to every corner of the room. I was surrounded by flames, too many to beat out, separating me from the trapdoor and the window and filling my head and lungs with disorientating, asphyxiating smoke that converged on me from all angles until the fire was a never-ending circle that spat and danced and laughed.

The doleful chime of the clock filled my head. *One.*

'Where is she?' yelled Luke as he and Katrina zoomed into vision. Edward was somewhere behind them.

I didn't know for sure who he was talking about, but I pointed into the thick black smoke beyond which nothing was visible.

Two, three.

Luke's reckless movements sent a piece of burning floor hurtling to the room below. Katrina pushed me out of the way and followed him into the blackness.

Four, five.

There was too much smoke; too much confusion.

I saw a girl trapped by the window as flames licked. I saw her reach for Luke's outstretched hand, using the rotten wood of the ledge to feel her way to safety.

Six, seven.

'Don't lean on that!' Luke shouted, but his voice was eclipsed by splintering wood and, beyond that, a shattering that filled my eardrums. There was nothing but glass; nothing but pain. An explosion like fireworks lit the world orange.

Eight, nine.

The force cleared a path, but the burning floor disintegrated as Luke stepped directly into the flames. I fell into nothing as wood and sparks rained down. I felt myself land; felt something hit me, and I saw black.

Ten, eleven.

They say that hearing is the last thing to go.

Stella.

Chapter Fifty-eight

Stella

The whole world is suspended as I fight and strain against steel bonds. I am trapped by throngs of students chanting my name; by a competition I despise; by a relationship that chokes me.

I am tipping; I am circling; I am swimming between light and dark, red and blue, weightlessness and deadening agony. I am giving myself over to it; I am gripping my diminishing senses. I am waiting to fall from a narrow ledge through time and space and infinity.

Something holds me there, in the heat and the pain and the past. But when it happens there is no choice to make. There is only her.

And I can push her away from danger, away from fire, away from me; until instead of falling, I soar.

I am a house of cards. I am the pieces of my sisters, jagged and dysfunctional and yet fitting me perfectly like wings made of feathers. I am a shooting star turning white in a galaxy of stars. And the light that surrounds me now is benign.

At the lakeside party of last summer, Edward holds my hand as I try to let him go.

'You'll change your mind,' he says. 'We're fate, Stella. It's inescapable.'

'Fate?' I ask, even though I understand. Sometimes we both wonder if we would exist without a legacy of identical siblings that sustains us like oxygen but suffocates us like failure.

He smiles slightly. He'll have no trouble spinning a version of our break-up that works to his advantage, but I know him better than that and I see a flash of the boy who also lost his pole star at the instant the clock stopped ticking.

Edward is gone, and I watch the smouldering vestiges of the campfire as I take in what's happened. Splitting with him is the first time I've ever veered off-course, but, as Luke arrives, my fear transforms into something else.

Even before he speaks, something seismic is happening. I've never let myself think about him this way, but now I can't seem to move. Luke is different to Edward because with him I can breathe.

This time I let him hold my hand. He tells me that, even though we've only been alone together once, almost four years ago, he's never stopped thinking about me. Now I can acknowledge that I feel the same. He tells me I'm the most beautiful girl in the world, and, because he thinks so, I believe that I am. He winds my hair around his fingers, tugging it like someone who has searched for me. His touch on my neck is electric and I stroke his arm, hoping to replicate this intensity in him. He kisses the inside of my elbow and I've never felt this before. I press my knee against his and there's nothing but him. He touches my chin and pulls me to face him and we don't wait any longer. We kiss until my jaw hurts and he has cramp in his leg and the sun is coming up and the party is over and not only am I forever his but I am found.

I once believed that I didn't exist except as a projection of Siena's past and Syrena's future; that I was merely an intersection of their characteristics, suspended in time. Now we merge and mesh into one sister until our duplications don't invalidate us, but bind us in an endless constellation. My sisters show me that beauty doesn't have to be our destruction; it can be our inspiration. And all the time I've been painting my inspiration, I haven't been painting myself.

I've been painting what we are to each other.

Memories flicker before me like flames and I blow them out one by one. I extinguish my struggle with Edward; the searing clock tower; Siena's bewildering loss.

And when there are no more flames, I see only the light of stars.

I see Luke, my one rebellion, who showed me that I could have something more than the rigid path I'd chosen. Luke, who shattered my careful plans into beautiful oblivion. Luke, who hardly saw the girl I could have been, but who never gave up on the girl I was.

I see Syrena, my future; the only second chance I'll ever need.

And I see Siena, the star I must await no longer and will never lose again. We are interwreathed as our future realigns itself into something glorious and unfolds before us in a blazing stream, with every golden sequin leading us into amaranthine avenues of hope.

Chapter Fifty-nine

Caitlin

I remember several things very clearly about July sixth. I remember fat summer raindrops on the window ledge after a week of damp humidity. I remember a rerun of *Friends*, where Ross gets stuck in his leather pants. I remember taking my first steps, clinging to a wall and a crutch and shuffling at a snail's pace.

I remember the sound of Stella's mother as she was led down the echoing hall and away. I remember the expression of the student nurse who sobbed uncontrollably as he took my blood. I remember the sensation of falling with nothing to tether me as my parents, battle-scarred by this experience of hospital, sat on each side of me and held my hands.

'She didn't suffer,' Dad said, his lips taut and pale.

Define suffering, I said in my head.

'Thank you for telling me,' I said out loud.

Then there are gaps. I don't remember how I came to sit alone outside the hospital in the dead of night, watching visitors leave the car park as if she might be amongst them. I don't remember what Luke said when he came to see me, although I knew he was a different Luke, who would never truly belong to the life ahead of him. I don't remember why I faked a relapse before the funeral even though being left behind was so much worse. I don't remember why the thought of leaving Temperley High was such a terrible one that I begged to return that September.

And I don't remember what happened to me between leaving hospital and returning to school, except that by then I'd uncovered the survival instinct to believe I deserved a different fate to Stella.

But I do remember why, in my need to understand how the terrifying symmetry of our existences had been rendered incomplete, I began to write my own account of events, to explain why sometimes the rightful winner is also the rightful recipient of a reader's sympathy.

Why is everyone so obsessed with the underdog anyway?

Epilogue

Caitlin

Welcome to my republic.

It's the first day after the summer vacation and I'm in the cafeteria at breakfast, working hard to ignore my best friend Katrina, who is in danger of boring me into a stupor.

'And Dr Tringle said, wouldn't it be great if this year the Prefects were elected democratically instead of the Head Girl choosing them?'

I snap back to attention. Democracy is a very bad idea, and Katrina should know that by now. An election will mean enduring a motley crew of the badly socialized in our new Prefects' house rather than the streamlined team I've already selected.

'Democracy is a great idea,' I say warmly. 'What a shame it's too late to change the process.'

'It's not too late,' she says. 'We can hold elections at the end of the week, as soon as Elevation is over. It would show we're committed to ending the apartheid.'

I really wish Katrina hadn't taken up Politics A level; she was much easier to cope with when she just talked about macrobiotic diets. I've run out of ways to tell her that the upcoming Elevation make-up ceremony is only a formality, and that my personalized, sapphire-studded crown will be delivered any day.

'I've been working on the list,' I say patiently. 'I have the paperwork right here.'

We're joined at this point by the others – Penny, Ruby, Lila and Mary-Ann – who have been out riding before breakfast. Usually the start of a semester would be a cause of excitement, but today the cafeteria is subdued and melancholy. The only constant is that we're the centre of attention.

'Congratulations, Prefects,' I say, passing them each a contract. Of course they all know they're Prefects, but this way I can put my stamp on it. 'I'm pleased to say you all made it.'

Lila looks dubious. 'Shouldn't we wait for Elevation before deciding any of this? Katrina said . . .'

My phone interrupts before I can tell her that this won't be necessary. It's my little brother Charlie, and I watch his face on the display until it stops.

'There's Luke,' whispers Penny as everyone spins around to look at the doorway.

Luke is as beautiful as ever and my heart skips at the sight of him. He nods grimly, while Katrina smiles as if it wasn't me he kissed onstage and slow-danced with at Elevation.

'It's good to see you, Luke,' she says.

Luke has agreed, at Dr Tringle's insistence, to stand for Head Boy again. Like me, he'll be unopposed. I haven't seen him since leaving hospital, but now we'll have plenty of time to work on policies and regain lost ground.

'I'm glad we're going to be working together this year,'

I say, turning his attention from Katrina to me.

He looks at me steadily. 'The only reason I agreed to be in another election is because things really need to change around here.'

He looks at the table, which is still engraved with a six-point star. 'No wonder everyone is so screwed up.'

'Totally,' I say, covering my name with my coffee. 'We're definitely the right people to introduce a new era.'

'What gives us the right to lead anybody?' Katrina says miserably. 'We loved being Stars so much that we thought everyone else loved us for it too. But *notorious* isn't the same as being well-liked.'

'You're splitting hairs,' I say. 'Are you saying you want to be like Lucy?'

We look over at Lucy, who's placidly testing Hannah with flashcards. She's completely unscathed and completely undistinguished.

'Lucy's alive, isn't she?' says Katrina.

'Nothing's changed,' I persist. 'Everyone's still looking at us.'

'They're looking at us because we have a dead friend,' she says flatly.

I wonder if it matters why we're the focal point, as long as we are. If no one looks at us, how will we know we matter? How will we even know we exist?

'Katrina, you're just stressed about today,' Lila says gently. 'We need each other now more than ever. Stella formed the Stars; she wouldn't want us to fall apart.'

'Have you finished eating?' Penny looks at my tray

during an awkward silence. 'We should get to the hall.'

I cover my untouched cereal, ignoring Luke's suspicious glance and wondering if he knows I've lost four pounds since the fire. 'I'm through.'

Ruby falls into step with me as we leave the cafeteria. In front of us, Katrina squeezes Luke's arm, while he responds by smoothing her hair behind her ear.

'Katrina and Luke have an amazing bond now,' Ruby whispers. 'Katrina says she'd never have got through the summer without him. Although I think it works both ways.'

I frown. 'What do you mean? When have they seen each other?'

'Didn't you know? They've been staying with Stella's family. I think it helped them to have something useful to do.'

There's no need to tell Ruby that Head Boy business will keep Luke far too busy from now on to fraternize with the Hamilton family.

'Is Edward coming back?' I ask instead.

Ruby shakes her head. 'Edward will probably disappear into that wreck of a house so he can think about Stella for the rest of his life.'

I avert my eyes from the bombsite that the courtyard has become. The area is cordoned off, but, by silent mutual consent, we avoiding walking anywhere near it.

Mary-Ann drifts along beside us, and I see bandages on her wrists. 'Doesn't that hurt?' I ask her.

She looks at me uncomprehendingly. 'Not like this,' she says. 'Nothing will ever hurt as much as this.'

When Lila and Penny had described their plans for decorating the hall, I'd imagined cardboard; sugar paper; Hallmark mourning. But this is Temperley High, where money is everywhere.

Stars drip from the ceiling, snake around the seats, and shine underfoot. They cover the windows, shaping images on the walls and floor. And wherever there aren't stars, there are flowers.

'Stella hates lilies,' Ruby whispers. 'So we got white roses.'

Beautiful and lethal, I decide, is appropriate. Her last class picture is projected onto a huge screen, and it seems bizarre to think that she lived with us as an equal. She can't have once been human, and played netball, and ironed her clothes with hair straighteners. It's more natural to see her as remote, and different, and gone.

One by one, the Stars drag themselves forward to share memories. I take in images rather than words, most of which don't even penetrate the white noise in my head.

Penny and Lila are last, although Lila is holding Penny upright.

'She was everything,' Penny sobs hopelessly. 'She's what we looked at, all the time. I don't even know what to *be* without her.'

Lila tugs her back as the lights dim and the projector whirs to life. One second I'm numbed by rose scent and starlight; the next I feel acute pain, like someone dragging blades across my skin. The sensation is so visceral, so brutal, that I instinctively put my hands to my face to check for shards of glass.

Stella is applying make-up in front of the camera as if it's a mirror. She pouts, her lips shiny with gloss, and lifts her hair over her shoulders so it falls around her face.

I see the amber flecks in her cornflower eyes; the tiny freckles on her nose; the crease of her dimples. She leans forward so her eyelashes touch the camera and then she kisses it.

'Stella, you're blurry,' Katrina's voice says off-screen.

Stella breathes hard, steaming up the lens. As the image fades to nothing, her laugh echoes and reverberates until it's obscured by sobbing from all around me. Shifting slightly, I see Luke hunch as if he's praying. His face is grey.

The next clip is jerky. Mrs Denbigh reveals herself as camerawoman by bellowing encouragement as each Star descends the stairs in a ball gown. This, I deduce, is the beginning of Winterval.

She keeps up a bracing list of instructions. 'Shoulders back . . . not *that* far back, Ruby . . . good toes, Katrina . . . Quentin, *not in the plant pot . . .*'

Then Stella hovers in the stairwell, slender in her long red dress and happy as I never saw her. The camera pans down unsteadily to show Luke in white tie, his hair pushed back so he can't tousle it. He watches Stella as I imagine him watching me.

He awkwardly puts a corsage on her wrist when she reaches him. He looks particularly tall and broad beside her, but treats her, as he always did, as if she's made of porcelain.

Mrs Denbigh tells them to *say something to the camera.*

'I'm with the most incredible girl in the world,' says Luke.

Stella looks up at him, but it's not an *I know how cute I am* expression. It's as if she can't believe how lucky she is. She doesn't speak, but as they turn she smiles with pure joy, and, squeezing his hand tightly, she wraps her other arm around his waist as if she can't bear to let him go. He kisses her.

I lean past Katrina to see the real Luke collapse in his seat as though he can't hold himself up.

The scenes flip rapidly. Stella is in pyjamas, eating cookie dough with a wooden spoon. She flicks some at Ruby, who screams, *'Carbs!'* She and Mary-Ann laugh as they make snow angels on the football field and then, in summer, turn cartwheels. She's winning the hurdles race at Sports Day even though all her competitors are far bigger than she is, and most are boys.

She's cheering at a soccer match in a Stripes shirt that reaches her knees; making out with Luke until Lila turns a garden hose on them; belting out 'River Deep – Mountain High' at a talent contest; charging across a field on her horse; eating Cheerios with Katrina, spoons held between their toes. Aged twelve, the Stars sit cross-legged in a candlelit circle, yelling, 'Stars aligned!' in childish, canary voices. They are caught by Mrs Denbigh, who threatens wearily to put them on clean-up duty. *I've just had a manicure,* Katrina tells her with temerity.

Then a huge Christmas tree is in shot, and Stella and

Katrina are covered in tinsel and wearing Santa hats. Their hair is waist length and shining, their skin translucent.

'Lessons are cancelled and Jamie's got champagne,' they tell the camera excitedly. 'Are you coming?'

'Of course!' Lila and Penny say behind the lens. 'We're just waiting for the others.'

Stella and Katrina grab each other, tossing away their hats and running like fauns. As Penny yells, 'Don't go!' Stella turns around and blows a kiss.

The heavy automatic door has swung open behind her and for a moment the winter sunlight surrounds her in a flaming halo. She is golden in the gloom of the hallway, laughing and unspeakably lovely and forever seventeen.

'Love you,' she calls. 'You haven't seen the last of me!'

She disappears as the screen fades to a shower of silver stars, and then black.

And even though the movie, like Stella herself, is nothing more than a chain mail of propaganda, I know why Luke's knuckles are white; why he grips the seat in front as if he's still in the tower and contemplating following her over the edge.

And as Katrina moves the projector screen from centre stage I see that the image of Siena has been shifted to the right, allowing another to share its prime spot. It's Stella's self-portrait, complete with sash and crown, and, as she looks down from the Head Girl's position, everyone in the audience gets to their feet.

*

When I hear whispering behind me, I shiver involuntarily at the echo of high heels on wood. I turn to see a petite figure with a mass of blonde hair cascading, waterfall-like, to her waist, and endlessly blue eyes.

Sunlight dances on her hair, casting star shapes on her cheek and bathing her in yellow light. *It's not Stella*, I tell myself. *It's not Stella.*

And now I remember this girl as the little figure who balanced on the edge of the tower that night and reanimated the clock before swinging herself nimbly back inside the attic to tell me, even as the fire smouldered and rumbled, that the white Elevation dress I'd bought that afternoon *off the rack* in an attempt to copy *her* older sister would never compete with her bespoke creation.

'I've seen you before,' I told her. 'What do you do up here? And why do you have all these clothes?'

'Stella doesn't want these things; she only wants Siena's,' the girl had said. 'She only thinks about Siena. She only wants to *be* Siena. I collect her so that I can keep her with me.'

'But you're only a child!' I was incredulous. 'Doesn't anyone miss you at home?'

She looked at me scornfully. 'I can do as I like.'

'You're wearing Stella's Elevation dress,' I said.

She smiled. 'It's my dress now. And I look *exactly* like Stella.'

I remember the girl who wasted precious seconds pushing a portrait through floorboards to safety and who screamed because her stolen white dress was caught and she couldn't leave it behind. I remember the girl Stella tore over burning floorboards to free; the girl she managed to push into the safety of Katrina's arms before the world turned on its side.

And I remember Syrena clawing like an alley cat against Katrina as an explosion knocked Stella backwards and upwards and away, her iridescent face lighting up the night sky like a flame.

Don't leave me.

I'll never leave you.

Stella's bedroom had held everything of Siena and nothing of herself, as if Siena's possessions could sustain her when everything else had slipped away. She had barely seemed to notice as Syrena stole her piece by piece and made the tower a treasure trove of her hijacked identity. While Stella had poured everything that was left of her into the recreation of Siena's dress, Syrena's attempt to imitate Stella through that final, devastating theft had forced them forever apart.

Standing before me in an ivory dress that is scorched and charred and childishly stitched back together, Syrena is an absurd replica of the sister it was meant for.

'Syrena was in the tower,' I say, trying to make sense of moments my therapist hadn't been able to. 'Stella and Syrena were both there.'

Katrina looks at me. 'Don't you remember what happened? Stella saved Syrena's life that night.'

'What's she doing here today?' I ask. 'And why is she wearing that dress?'

Syrena sits in front of us and smiles at Luke, her teeth denting her bottom lip.

'She's a Shell this term, and she's giving the eulogy,' Katrina says softly. 'As for the dress, do you think anyone wants to say *no* to her right now?'

I shake my head wordlessly as Syrena turns. She pulls up Katrina's sleeve and winces at the livid pink scar that runs the length of Katrina's arm. For a second I hear tearing wood and roaring flames; my throat screams with acrid smoke. I see Katrina shield Syrena, twisting her away from the impact as the sky is shattered and the universe burns around them.

Now Katrina smiles at Syrena's pained expression. *It's nothing.* They briefly touch hands as if they can communicate that way. Before Katrina can roll down her sleeve, Luke takes her bare arm in his as if the scar is a part of them all.

Syrena sashays down the aisle with a maturity she shouldn't possess to complete a grotesque, ruined triptych of family portraits. A phoenix risen from an annihilated family, she looks ready to find and reclaim the missing sapphire crown as if Stella isn't dead at all, but merely on hiatus, the underdog who will be forever a step ahead. She looks directly at me as she starts to speak, vengeance blazing like fire in her boundless cornflower eyes.

Acknowledgements

I would like to thank:

Venetia Gosling and everyone at Macmillan for their incredible expertise and enthusiasm, and for offering me and *Stella* such a warm welcome.

My colleagues Lucinda and Jenny for their fantastic support, and for their peerless knowledge of all things YA.

Alice, Anne, Ashley, Danielle, Helen, Jon, Lynn and Matt for offering, variously, generous support and suggestions, valuable feedback on the earliest drafts, and high-quality baked goods.

SCBWI, the Arvon Foundation, the Summertown Writers, and the students and staff on the Oxford Brookes MA Creative Writing course.

My mum and dad for their patience, reassurance and encouragement, and for my early introduction to *Great Expectations* and Estella.

Paul, who called me a writer before anyone else did, for his unwavering loyalty and faith in me.

My agent Claire Wilson, whose insights and imagination helped me to sculpt *Stella* into everything I had hoped it could be, and who has guided me through this process with exceptional knowledge, understanding and kindness.